"*The Book of Laughter and Forgetting* has something important to say, and it says it with stunning clarity and inventiveness."
—Anne Tyler, *Chicago Sun-Times*

"*The Book of Laughter and Forgetting* calls itself a novel, although it is part fairy tale, part literary criticism, part political tract, part musicology, and part autobiography. It can call itself whatever it wants to, because the whole is genius. . . . I ought to invoke Günter Grass and Garcia Marquez, because Mr. Kundera belongs in their demonic company." —John Leonard, *The New York Times*

"*The Book of Laughter and Forgetting* is at once an impassioned plea for the struggle of memory against the obliterating forces of modern life, an eloquent act of personal memory by a Czech writer living abroad who is forbidden to publish in his own country, and an absolutely dazzling entertainment . . . it is arousing on every level—political, erotic, intellectual, and above all, humorous. And it is proof once more that the strongest voices in world fiction today are those of writers in exile, whether they be political exiles like Solzhenitsyn and Gabriel Garcia Marquez or self-exiles like V. S. Naipaul."
—Charles Michener, *Newsweek*

"*The Book of Laughter and Forgetting* is a seven-part invention of immense wit, intelligence, and verve . . . a remarkable achievement."
—Robert M. Adams, *The New York Review of Books*

"This book, as it bluntly calls itself, is brilliant and original, written with a purity and wit that invite us directly in. . . . Kundera is able to merge personal and political significances with the ease of a Camus." —John Updike, *The New York Times Book Review*

PENGUIN BOOKS

WRITERS FROM THE OTHER EUROPE

General Editor: Philip Roth

THE BOOK OF LAUGHTER AND FORGETTING

Milan Kundera was born in Brno, Czechoslovakia, in 1929. He was enrolled in the Czech Communist Party right after World War II, then debarred from it after the incidents of February 1948 (the takeover of Prague), at which time he was a student. He worked as a laborer, then as a jazz musician, and finally ended up devoting himself to literature and film. He was a professor at the Prague Institute for Advanced Cinematographic Studies, where his students were the creators of the Czech New Wave in film. His collection of stories, *Laughable Loves*, appeared in print in Prague before 1968; the publication of his first novel, *The Joke*, was one of the events of the liberalization culminating in the Prague Spring of 1968. After the Russian invasion in August of that year he lost his post and his books were proscribed. In 1975 he and his wife settled in France, and in 1979, the Czech government, responding to the publication of the *The Book of Laughter and Forgetting*, revoked his Czech citizenship. Milan Kundera's other novels have not been allowed publication in his fatherland. *Life Is Elsewhere* won the Prix Médicis for the best foreign novel published in France in 1973, and *The Farewell Party* won a similar prize, the Premio Mondello, for the best foreign novel published in Italy in 1976. His works have been translated into twenty languages. Penguin Books also publishes Milan Kundera's *The Joke, The Farewell Party*, and *Laughable Loves*.

Also by Milan Kundera

The Book of Laughter and Forgetting

by MILAN KUNDERA

Translated from the Czech by
MICHAEL HENRY HEIM

Penguin Books

Penguin Books Ltd, Harmondsworth,
Middlesex, England
Penguin Books, 40 West 23rd Street,
New York, New York 10010, U.S.A.
Penguin Books Australia Ltd, Ringwood,
Victoria, Australia
Penguin Books Canada Limited, 2801 John Street,
Markham, Ontario, Canada L3R 1B4
Penguin Books (N.Z.) Ltd, 182–190 Wairau Road,
Auckland 10, New Zealand

Original title: *Kniha smíchu a zapomnění*
First published in France under the title
Le Livre du Rire et de l'Oubli by Éditions Gallimard 1979
This English translation first published in the United States of America by
Alfred A. Knopf, Inc., 1980
First published in Canada by
Random House of Canada Limited 1980
Published in Penguin Books 1981
Reprinted 1981, 1982 (three times), 1983, 1984 (twice), 1985 (twice)

LIBRARY OF CONGRESS CATALOGING IN PUBLICATION DATA
Kundera, Milan.
    The book of laughter and forgetting.
    (Writers from the other Europe)
    Translation of: Kniha smíchu a zapomnění.
    I. Title.   II. Series.
PG5039.21.U6K613   1981   891.8′635   81-8533
ISBN 0 14 00.5924 5   AACR2

Printed in the United States of America by
Offset Paperback Mfrs., Inc., Dallas, Pennsylvania
Set in Video Avanta

Grateful acknowledgment is made to the following for permission to
reprint from previously published material. Éditions Gallimard: excerpts
from *Rhinocéros* by Eugène Ionesco, copyright © Éditions Gallimard,
1959; excerpts from *"Le Visage de la Paix,"* taken from *Des Oeuvres
Complètes,* Volume 2, by Paul Éluard, copyright © Éditions Gallimard,
1968. Éditions Bernard Grasset: excerpts from *Parole de Femme* (1976) by
Annie Leclerc. Grove Press: Michael Henry Heim's translation of excerpts
from *Rhinocéros* by Eugène Ionesco authorized by Grove Press. *The New
York Times:* "Afterword: A Talk with the Author" by Philip Roth
originally appeared as an interview with Milan Kundera in *The New York
Times Book Review,* November 30, 1980; copyright © The New York
Times Company, 1980.

Several sections of this work were printed in *The New Yorker.*

WRITERS FROM THE OTHER EUROPE

The purpose of this paperback series is to bring together outstanding and influential works of fiction by Eastern European writers. In many instances they will be writers who, though recognized as powerful forces in their own cultures, are virtually unknown in the West. It is hoped that by reprinting selected Eastern European writers in this format and with introductions that place each work in its literary and historical context, the literature that has evolved in "the other Europe," particularly during the postwar decades, will be made more accessible to a new readership.

Philip Roth

OTHER TITLES IN THIS SERIES

Ashes and Diamonds
by Jerzy Andrzejewski
Introduction by Heinrich Böll

Closely Watched Trains
by Bohumil Hrabal
Introduction by Josef Škvorecký

The Farewell Party
by Milan Kundera
Introduction by Elizabeth Pochoda

Laughable Loves
by Milan Kundera
Introduction by Philip Roth

Sanatorium under the Sign of the Hourglass
by Bruno Schulz
Introduction by John Updike

The Street of Crocodiles
by Bruno Schulz
Introduction by Jerzy Ficowski

This Way for the Gas, Ladies and Gentlemen
by Tadeusz Borowski
Introduction by Jan Kott

A Tomb for Boris Davidovich
by Danilo Kiš
Introduction by Joseph Brodsky

CONTENTS

PART ONE
Lost Letters

1

In February 1948, Communist leader Klement Gottwald stepped out on the balcony of a Baroque palace in Prague to address the hundreds of thousands of his fellow citizens packed into Old Town Square. It was a crucial moment in Czech history—a fateful moment of the kind that occurs once or twice in a millennium.

Gottwald was flanked by his comrades, with Clementis standing next to him. There were snow flurries, it was cold, and Gottwald was bareheaded. The solicitous Clementis took off his own fur cap and set it on Gottwald's head.

The Party propaganda section put out hundreds of thousands of copies of a photograph of that balcony with Gottwald, a fur cap on his head and comrades at his side, speaking to the nation. On that balcony the history of Communist Czechoslovakia was born. Every child knew the photograph from posters, schoolbooks, and museums.

Four years later Clementis was charged with treason and hanged. The propaganda section immediately airbrushed him out of history and, obviously, out of all the photographs as well. Ever since, Gottwald has stood on that balcony alone. Where Clementis once stood, there is only bare palace wall. All that remains of Clementis is the cap on Gottwald's head.

2

It is 1971, and Mirek says that the struggle of man against power is the struggle of memory against forgetting.

That is his attempt to justify what his friends call carelessness: keeping a careful diary, preserving all correspondence, taking notes at meetings where there is discussion of the current situation

3

and debate of where to go from here. Nothing we do is in violation of the constitution, he tells them. Trying to hide, feeling guilty— that's the beginning of the end.

A week ago, while working with a crew on the roof of a new building, he looked down and had a sudden dizzy spell. He lost his balance and grabbed at a poorly fastened beam, but it came loose and he had to be pulled out from under it. At first the injury looked serious, but later, when he learned it was just a run-of-the-mill broken arm, he said to himself with satisfaction that now he'd get a week or two off and have time for some things he'd been meaning to take care of.

He had finally come around to the position of his more cautious friends. True, the constitution guaranteed freedom of speech; but the law punished any act that could be construed as undermining the state. Who could tell when the state would start screaming that this or that word was undermining it? He decided he'd better put the incriminating papers in a safe place after all.

First, though, he wanted to settle the Zdena problem. He called her long distance, but couldn't reach her. He wasted four whole days calling. Then yesterday he'd finally gotten through. She'd promised to wait for him this afternoon.

His seventeen-year-old son protested that he couldn't possibly drive with his arm in a cast. It really was pretty hard going. His injured arm swung helpless and useless in its sling on his chest. Whenever he changed gears, he had to let go of the steering wheel for a second.

3

Twenty-five years had gone by since his affair with Zdena, and all he had left of it was a few memories.

Once she showed up dabbing her eyes with a handkerchief and blowing her nose. He asked her what the matter was. A Russian statesman had died the day before, she told him. Some Zhdanov,

Arbuzov, or Masturbov. Judging by the number of teardrops, she was more disturbed by Masturbov's death than by the death of her own father.

Could that actually have happened? Or was her lament for Masturbov merely a figment of his present hatred? No, it *had* happened, though of course the immediate circumstances making the event credible and real escaped him now, and the memory had become implausible, a caricature.

All his memories of her were like that. They had taken a tram back from the apartment where they made love for the first time. (Mirek was particularly gratified to note that he had completely forgotten their copulations, couldn't conjure up a single second of them.) Bumping up and down in a corner seat, she looked gloomy, introspective, amazingly old. When he asked her why she was so withdrawn, she told him she hadn't been satisfied with their lovemaking. She said he'd made love to her like an intellectual.

In the political jargon of the day "intellectual" was an expletive. It designated a person who failed to understand life and was cut off from the people. All Communists hanged at the time by other Communists had that curse bestowed upon them. Unlike people with their feet planted firmly on the ground, they supposedly floated in air. In a sense, then, it was only fair they have the ground pulled out from under them once and for all and be left there hanging slightly above it.

But what did Zdena mean when she accused him of making love like an intellectual?

For one reason or another she hadn't been satisfied with him, and just as she was capable of imbuing an abstract relationship (her relationship to a stranger like Masturbov) with the most concrete of feelings (in the form of tears), she could give the most concrete of acts an abstract meaning and her dissatisfaction a political name.

4

Looking into the rearview mirror, he realized that a car had been tailing him all along. He had never had any doubt he was being followed, but so far they had acted with masterly discretion. Today a radical change had taken place: they wanted him to know about them.

In the middle of some fields about fifteen miles outside Prague there was a tall fence with a car-repair shop behind it. He had a good friend there and needed him to replace a faulty starter. He pulled up to the entrance. It was blocked by a red-and-white-striped gate. A heavy woman was standing beside it. Mirek waited for her to raise the gate, but she just stared at him, motionless. He honked his horn, but got no response. He looked out the window. "Not behind bars yet?" asked the woman.

"No, not yet," answered Mirek. "How about raising the gate?"

She looked at him impassively for a few more long seconds, then yawned, went over to the gatekeeper's cabin, dropped into a desk chair, and turned her back on him.

So he got up out of the car, walked around the gate, and went into the service area to look for his friend the mechanic. The mechanic came back with him. He raised the gate himself (the woman was still sitting impassively in the cabin), and Mirek drove his car in.

"That's what you get for showing off on television," said the mechanic. "Every broad in the country knows what you look like."

"Who is she?" Mirek asked.

He learned that the invasion of Czechoslovakia by Russian troops, which had made themselves felt everywhere, had changed her life as well. Seeing that people in higher places (and everyone was higher than she was) were being deprived of power, status, employment, and daily bread on the basis of the slightest allegation, she got all excited and started denouncing people herself.

"Then how come she's still working the gate? Haven't they even promoted her?"

The mechanic smiled. "They can't. She doesn't know how to count to five. All they can do is let her go on with her denunciations. That's her only reward." He raised the hood and peered inside at the engine.

Mirek was suddenly aware of someone a few steps away. He turned and saw a man in a gray jacket, white shirt and tie, and brown slacks. His strong neck and bloated face were topped by a shock of artificially waved gray hair. He stood there watching the mechanic leaning under the raised hood.

After a while the mechanic noticed him too. "Looking for somebody?" he asked, straightening up.

"No," answered the man with the strong neck and wavy hair. "I'm not looking for anybody."

The mechanic leaned down over the engine again and said, "Right in the middle of Prague, Wenceslaus Square, there's this guy throwing up. And this other guy comes along, takes a look at him, shakes his head, and says, 'I know just what you mean.'"

5

The bloody massacre in Bangladesh quickly covered over the memory of the Russian invasion of Czechoslovakia, the assassination of Allende drowned out the groans of Bangladesh, the war in the Sinai Desert made people forget Allende, the Cambodian massacre made people forget Sinai, and so on and so forth until ultimately everyone lets everything be forgotten.

In times when history still moved slowly, events were few and far between and easily committed to memory. They formed a commonly accepted *backdrop* for thrilling scenes of adventure in private life. Nowadays, history moves at a brisk clip. A historical event, though soon forgotten, sparkles the morning after with the dew of novelty. No longer a backdrop, it is now the *adventure* itself, an adventure enacted before the backdrop of the commonly accepted banality of private life.

Since we can no longer assume any single historical event, no matter how recent, to be common knowledge, I must treat events dating back only a few years as if they were a thousand years old. In 1939, German troops marched into Bohemia, and the Czech state ceased to exist. In 1945, Russian troops marched into Bohemia, and the country was once again declared an independent republic. The people showed great enthusiasm for Russia—which had driven the Germans from their country—and because they considered the Czech Communist Party its faithful representative, they shifted their sympathies to it. And so it happened that in February 1948 the Communists took power not in bloodshed and violence, but to the cheers of about half the population. And please note: the half that cheered was the more dynamic, the more intelligent, the better half.

Yes, say what you will—the Communists were more intelligent. They had a grandiose program, a plan for a brand-new world in which everyone would find his place. The Communists' opponents had no great dream; all they had was a few moral principles, stale and lifeless, to patch up the tattered trousers of the established order. So of course the grandiose enthusiasts won out over the cautious compromisers and lost no time turning their dream into reality: the creation of an idyll of justice for all.

Now let me repeat: *an idyll, for all.* People have always aspired to an idyll, a garden where nightingales sing, a realm of harmony where the world does not rise up as a stranger against man nor man against other men, where the world and all its people are molded from a single stock and the fire lighting up the heavens is the fire burning in the hearts of men, where every man is a note in a magnificent Bach fugue and anyone who refuses his note is a mere black dot, useless and meaningless, easily caught and squashed between the fingers like an insect.

From the start there were people who realized they lacked

the proper temperament for the idyll and wished to leave the country. But since by definition an idyll is one world for all, the people who wished to emigrate were implicitly denying its validity. Instead of going abroad, they went behind bars. They were soon joined by thousands and tens of thousands more, including many Communists, such as Foreign Minister Clementis, the man who lent Gottwald his cap. Timid lovers held hands on movie screens, marital infidelity received harsh penalties at citizens' courts of honor, nightingales sang, and the body of Clementis swung back and forth like a bell ringing in the new dawn for mankind.

And suddenly those young, intelligent radicals had the strange feeling of having sent something into the world, a deed of their own making, which had taken on a life of its own, lost all resemblance to the original idea, and totally ignored the originators of the idea. So those young, intelligent radicals started shouting to their deed, calling it back, scolding it, chasing it, hunting it down. If I were to write a novel about that generation of talented radical thinkers, I would call it *Stalking a Lost Deed*.

6

The mechanic shut the hood, and Mirek asked him how much he owed him.

"Zilch," said the mechanic.

Mirek got behind the wheel. He was touched. He had no desire whatsoever to go on with his trip. He would rather have stayed with the mechanic and swapped jokes. The mechanic leaned over into the car and slapped him on the shoulder. Then he went back to the gate and raised it.

As Mirek drove by, the mechanic made a motion with his head in the direction of a car parked in front of the repair-shop entrance.

The man with the thick neck and wavy hair was leaning up against the open car door, watching Mirek. So was the man behind the wheel. Both of them were brazen and shameless about it, and Mirek tried to return their expression driving past.

He kept an eye on them in the rearview mirror and saw the man jumping into the front seat and the car making a U-turn so they could continue to follow him.

It occurred to him that he should have done something about getting rid of those incriminating papers. If he'd gotten it out of the way the first day of his sick leave and not waited to talk to Zdena, he'd have had a better chance of pulling it off safely. But he couldn't keep his mind off Zdena. He'd been planning to go see her for several years now. But in recent weeks he had the feeling he couldn't put it off anymore, his time was running out, and he'd better do everything possible to make it perfect and beautiful.

7

Breaking up with Zdena in those far-removed days (their affair had lasted almost three years) filled him with a feeling of boundless freedom, and suddenly everything seemed to go right for him. Soon he married a woman whose beauty gave his self-esteem a big boost. Then she died, and he was left alone with his son in a kind of coquettish solitude that attracted the admiration, interest, and solicitude of many other women.

He had also been highly successful in his research, and that shielded him. Since the state needed him, he could afford to make cutting political remarks before anyone else dared to. As the faction trying to recall the deed gained in influence, he began appearing more and more often on television, and before long he had become a well-known personality. When, after the Russians came, he refused to disavow his opinions, they removed him from his job and surrounded him with undercover agents. He remained undaunted. He was in love with his fate and found pomp and beauty in the march to ruin.

Now don't misunderstand me. I said he was in love with his

fate, not with himself. Those are two very different things. His life assumed a separate identity and started pursuing interests of its own, quite apart from Mirek's. That is what I mean when I say his life became his fate. Fate had no intention of lifting a finger for Mirek (for his happiness, security, good spirits, or health), whereas Mirek was willing to do everything for his fate (for its grandeur, lucidity, beauty, style, and scrutability). He felt responsible for his fate, but his fate felt no responsibility for him.

He had the same attitude to his life as a sculptor to his statue or a novelist to his novel. One of a novelist's inalienable rights is to be able to rework his novel. If he takes a dislike to the beginning, he can rewrite it or cross it out entirely. But Zdena's existence deprived Mirek of his prerogative as an author. Zdena insisted on remaining part of the opening pages of the novel. She refused to be crossed out.

8

Why was he so ashamed of her, anyway?

The most obvious explanation was that very early in the game Mirek had joined forces with those who vowed to hunt down their own deed, while Zdena had always remained loyal to the garden where nightingales sing. More recently she had even joined the two percent of the population who welcomed the Russian tanks.

True, but I don't find it convincing enough. If the only problem was that she had welcomed the Russian tanks, he would simply have given her a good loud public talking-to; he would not have denied ever having known her. No, Zdena had done him a far greater wrong: she was ugly.

But that couldn't make any difference. He hadn't slept with her for more than twenty years.

It made a big difference. Even from so far away Zdena's big nose cast a shadow over his life.

A few years ago he had a beautiful mistress. Once she visited the town where Zdena lived, and came back upset. "How in the world could you have had anything to do with that awful woman?"

He claimed to have known her only casually and categorically denied ever being intimate with her.

Apparently, he was not totally ignorant of one of life's great secrets: women don't look for handsome men, they look for men with beautiful women. Having an ugly mistress is therefore a fatal error. Mirek did his best to do away with all traces of Zdena, and since the nightingale lovers hated him more and more, he hoped that Zdena, making her energetic way up the bureaucratic ladder, would be only too glad to forget him.

He was wrong. She would speak about him anywhere, everywhere, at the drop of a hat. Once by unfortunate coincidence they met at a social event, and she quickly made it clear by referring to past events that she had been intimate with him.

He was furious.

"If you hate her so much, why did you have an affair with her?" a mutual friend once asked him.

Mirek's explanation was that he'd been a twenty-year-old brat at the time, seven years younger than she. Besides, she was respected, admired, omnipotent! She knew practically everyone on the Central Committee! She helped him, pushed him, introduced him to influential people!

"I was a go-getter, man! Understand?" he shouted. "An aggressive, young go-getter. That's why I hung onto her. I didn't give a damn how ugly she was!"

9

Mirek was not telling the truth. Even though Zdena did cry over Masturbov's death, she had no influential contacts twenty-five years ago and was in no position to further her own career, to say nothing of anyone else's.

Then why did he make it all up? Why did he lie?

Mirek was steering with one hand. Looking up at the rear-view mirror, he saw the agents' car, and suddenly blushed. A completely unexpected memory had just surfaced.

After she reproached him for acting too much like an intellectual that first time they made love, he wanted to set things right and give her a demonstration of spontaneous, unbridled passion. So it wasn't true he'd forgotten all their copulations! This one he could picture quite plainly. He moved on her with feigned frenzy, making a long snarling noise—the kind a dog makes when at war with his master's slipper—and observing her (with mild surprise) stretched out there beneath him so calm, collected, almost indifferent.

The car resounded with that snarl from twenty-five years ago, the agonizing sound of his submissiveness and servile fervor, the sound of his willingness to conform and adapt, his laughable predicament, his misery.

Yes, it's true. Mirek was willing to proclaim himself an ambitious go-getter rather than admit the truth: he'd taken an ugly mistress because he didn't dare go after beautiful women. Zdena was as high as he rated himself then. A weak will and utter poverty—those were the secrets he had hoped to hide.

The car resounded with the furious snarl of passion, trying to convince him that Zdena was merely a phantom to be blotted out if he meant to obliterate his hated youth.

He pulled up in front of her house. The car on his tail pulled up behind him.

10

Historical events usually imitate one another without much talent, but in Czechoslovakia, as I see it, history staged an unprecedented experiment. Instead of the standard pattern of one group of people (a class, a nation) rising up against another, all the people (an entire generation) revolted against their own youth.

Their goal was to recapture and tame the deed they had

created, and they almost succeeded. All through the 1960s they gained in influence, and by the beginning of 1968 their influence was virtually complete. This is the period commonly referred to as the Prague Spring: the men guarding the idyll had to go around removing microphones from private dwellings, the borders were opened, and notes began abandoning the score of Bach's grand fugue and singing their own lines. The spirit was unbelievable. A real carnival!

Russia, composer of the master fugue for the globe, could not tolerate the thought of notes taking off on their own. On August 21, 1968, it sent an army of half a million men into Bohemia. Shortly thereafter, about a hundred and twenty thousand Czechs left their country, and of those who remained about five hundred thousand had to leave their jobs for manual labor in the country, at the conveyor belt of an out-of-the-way factory, behind the steering wheel of a truck—in other words, for places and jobs where no one would ever hear their voices.

And just to be sure not even the shadow of an unpleasant memory could come to disturb the newly revived idyll, both the Prague Spring and the Russian tanks, that stain on the nation's fair history, had to be nullified. As a result, no one in Czechoslovakia commemorates the 21st of August, and the names of the people who rose up against their own youth are carefully erased from the nation's memory, like a mistake from a homework assignment.

Mirek's was one of the names thus erased. The Mirek currently climbing the steps to Zdena's door is really only a white stain, a fragment of barely delineated void making its way up a spiral staircase.

11

He is sitting opposite Zdena, his arm swinging in its sling. Zdena is looking the other way, averting her eyes, and talking a blue streak.

"I don't know what you've come for, but I'm glad you're

here. I've been talking with some Party people. It would be crazy for you to spend the rest of your life working on a day-to-day construction crew. The Party hasn't closed its doors to you. I know it for a fact, an absolute fact. There's still time."

He asks her what to do.

"Request a hearing. You've got to take the initiative yourself."

He saw what she was getting at. It was their way of telling him he had one last five-minute grace period to come out and deny everything he had ever said or done. He knew their game: selling people futures for their pasts. They'd force him to go on TV and give the nation a contrite account of how wrong he'd been when he said those nasty things about Russia and the nightingales. They'd force him to repudiate his life; to become a shadow, a man without a past, an actor without a part; to turn even the life he'd repudiated into a shadow, a part abandoned by its actor. Only after transforming him into a shadow would they let him live.

He keeps his eyes on Zdena. Why is she talking so fast? Why is she so nervous? Why does she look away, avert her eyes?

It's only too clear: she's setting a trap for him. She's acting on Party or police orders. Her assignment is to bring him to his knees.

12

But Mirek is wrong! No one has given Zdena the authority to negotiate with him. Of course not. Nobody with any power would grant Mirek a hearing no matter how hard he begged. It was too late.

If Zdena goes ahead and urges him to do something to better his lot, if she claims her advice comes from highly placed Party officials, she does so only out of a confused, perplexed desire to help him. If she talks a blue streak and has trouble looking him in the eye, it is not because she has a trick up her sleeve, it is only because her hands are empty.

Has Mirek ever understood her?

He always thought Zdena was so fiercely faithful to the Party because she was a political fanatic.

He was wrong. She remained faithful to the Party because she loved him.

When he left her, her only desire was to prove that fidelity was the highest value of all. She wanted to prove that he had been unfaithful *in all respects* and she had been faithful *in all respects*. What seemed to be political fanaticism was only an excuse, a parable, a manifesto of fidelity, a coded plaint of unrequited love.

I can just picture her, waking one August morning to the terrible roar of airplanes. She runs out into the street, and people tell her in horror that Russian troops have occupied Bohemia. She breaks into hysterical laughter. Russian tanks have come to punish all the infidels! Finally she will witness Mirek's downfall! Finally she will see him on his knees! Finally she will be able to lean over him—knowing, as she does, the value of fidelity—and come to his aid.

Mirek has decided to put a brutal end to a conversation that has gone off in the wrong direction.

"Remember all those letters I used to send you? Well, I'd like them back."

"Letters?" she asks, looking up in surprise.

"Yes, my letters. I must have sent you a hundred at least."

"Oh, those letters," she says. "Now I remember." Suddenly she has found his eyes and is looking straight into them. Mirek has the unpleasant feeling she can see right into the bottom of his soul and knows exactly what he wants and why.

"Yes, of course. Your letters," she repeats. "I've just been rereading them. Who would have believed you capable of explosive emotions?"

She uses the words "explosive emotions" a few times more, and suddenly her speech is as slow and deliberate as it was quick and nervous before. She seems to be aiming at a target she is determined to hit, and she keeps her eyes pinned on him to make sure she hits it.

13

The arm in the cast swings back and forth on his chest, and his face is as red as if it had been slapped.

Yes, his letters must have been terribly sentimental. He had no choice. He absolutely had to prove to himself it was love that bound him to her, not weakness and poverty. And only a larger-than-life kind of passion could justify an affair with so ugly a girl.

"Remember how you called me your companion-in-arms in the struggle?"

If it is humanly possible, his blush deepens another shade. That infinitely ridiculous word "struggle." What did their struggle consist of? Endless meetings and callused backsides. But when they finally stood up to make a radical statement (the class enemy deserves harsher punishment, this or that idea must be formulated more forcefully), they felt like figures out of a heroic canvas: he is sinking to the ground, pistol in hand, and arm bleeding profusely, while she, smaller pistol in hand, marches on into a future he will never live to see.

At that time his skin still bore the marks of a post-adolescent case of acne, and the way he tried to hide it was to wear a mask of rebellion. He would tell everybody he had parted ways with his rich farmer father and had the utmost contempt for the centuries-old rural tradition based on land and property. He would describe the quarrel and his dramatic departure from home. There was not a shred of truth in it. Looking back now, he sees nothing but legends and lies.

"You were completely different then," says Zdena.

He pictures himself leaving her house with the packet of letters. He stops at the nearest trashcan, lifts the packet queasily with two fingers as if it were smeared with shit, and drops it in.

14

"What would you do with the letters, anyway?" she asked. "Why do you want them?"

He couldn't very well tell her he wanted to throw them in the trash, so he affected a melancholy tone of voice and started in on how he had reached the age when a man looks back over his life.

(The whole thing was making him very uncomfortable. He had the feeling his story sounded unconvincing, he was ashamed.)

Yes, he was looking back because he could no longer remember what he'd been like when he was young. He knew he'd gone astray. The reason he wanted to go back to his origins was to have a better idea of where he'd gone wrong. The reason he wanted to go back to his correspondence with Zdena was to find the secret of his youth, his beginnings, his point of departure.

She shook her head. "I'll never give them to you."

"I only want to borrow them," he lied.

She kept shaking her head.

He couldn't help thinking that the letters were right there in the apartment, within easy reach, and that she would let anybody read them at any time. He couldn't stand the idea that a piece of his life had stayed behind in her hands, and felt like smashing her over the head with the heavy glass ashtray on the coffee table between them and running off with the letters. Instead, he reiterated his story about looking back and needing to know more about his origins.

She looked up at him and silenced him with her eyes. "I'll never give them to you. Never."

15

When she saw him to the entrance of her apartment house, both cars were parked in front of the door, one behind the other. The secret agents were patrolling the other side of the street. They stopped when they saw Mirek and Zdena come out.

"Those two gentlemen," he said, pointing at them, "have been on my tail the whole way."

"Is that so?" she said dubiously. "Everybody's out to get you, right?" Her voice was dripping with overplayed irony.

How could she be so cynical as to tell him to his face that the two men staring at them with such conspicuous arrogance just happened to be out for a walk?

There was only one explanation: she was playing their game, a game calling for everyone to pretend the secret police didn't exist and no one was ever persecuted.

By now the agents had crossed the street, and Mirek and Zdena watched them get into their car.

"Bye," said Mirek, without so much as a glance at Zdena. He slipped in behind the wheel. In the mirror he could see the agents' car pulling out behind him. He could not see Zdena. He had no desire to see her ever again.

He did not realize she stood on the sidewalk looking after him for a long time. She had a frightened look on her face.

No, her refusal to accept the men across the street for what they were was not cynicism. It was panic. Things were starting to get too big for her. She wanted to hide the truth from him and from herself as well.

16

Out of nowhere a speed demon in a red sports car cut in between Mirek and the car of the secret agents. Mirek stepped on the gas. They were just entering a small town. There was a bend in the road. Mirek realized he was out of his pursuers' line of sight and ducked into a side street. His brakes let out a screech, and a little boy about to cross the street jumped back just in time. In the rearview mirror he saw the red car speed past on the main road. Before the agents' car appeared, he turned down another street. He'd shaken them for good.

The road he took out of town went off in an entirely different direction. No one was following him; the road was empty.

He pictured the poor agents looking all over for him, afraid their boss would bawl them out. He laughed out loud. Slowing down, he looked around at the countryside, something he had never actually done before. Always on his way to arrange or discuss something somewhere, he had come to think of space as a negative value, a waste of time, an obstacle to his progress.

Just ahead of him two red-and-white-striped crossing gates were slowly coming down. He stopped.

All at once he felt tremendously tired. Why had he even gone to see her? Why did he want the letters back?

He was struck by how silly, absurd, and childish the whole trip suddenly seemed. It wasn't the result of a plan or anything practical like that, it was just an uncontrollable urge, an urge to reach far back into the past and smash it with his fist, an urge to slash the canvas of his youth to shreds, a passionate urge he could not restrain and that would now remain unsatisfied.

He felt tremendously tired. He probably wouldn't be able to remove the incriminating documents from his apartment any longer. They had him where they wanted him, and they wouldn't let go. It was too late now. Yes, too late for everything.

In the distance he heard a train chugging along. A woman with a red kerchief on her head stood at the little house near the gate. The train pulled in, a slow local. An old man, pipe in hand, leaned out a window and spat. Then the station bell rang, and the woman in the red kerchief went up to the gates and turned the crank. The gates lifted, and Mirek started the car. He drove into a village, one long street ending at the station— a small, low, white building with a picket fence through which he could see the platform and tracks.

17

The station-house windows are decorated with pots of begonias. Mirek stops the car. Sitting at the wheel, he looks at the house and windows and red flowers. Another white house comes back to him from long-forgotten times, another white house with begonias blooming on the windowsills. It is a small hotel in a mountain village during summer vacation. A large nose peeks out from among the flowers at the window, and twenty-year-old Mirek looks up at that nose and feels unbounded love.

His first impulse is to step on the gas and break loose from that memory. But this time I won't let myself be cheated, I'll call the memory back and make it linger a while. So I repeat: Zdena's face and huge nose appear at the window among the begonias, and Mirek feels unbounded love.

Is it possible?

Yes, and why not? Can't a weak man feel true love for an ugly woman?

He tells her about rebelling against his reactionary father, she rails against intellectuals: they have calluses on their backsides and hold hands, they go to meetings, denounce their fellow Czechs, lie, and make love. She cries over Masturbov's death, he snarls on top of her like a mad dog, and they can't live without each other.

The reason he wanted to remove her picture from the album

of his life was not that he hadn't loved her, but that he had. By erasing her from his mind, he erased his love for her. He airbrushed her out of the picture in the same way the Party propaganda section airbrushed Clementis from the balcony where Gottwald gave his historic speech. Mirek is as much a rewriter of history as the Communist Party, all political parties, all nations, all men. People are always shouting they want to create a better future. It's not true. The future is an apathetic void of no interest to anyone. The past is full of life, eager to irritate us, provoke and insult us, tempt us to destroy or repaint it. The only reason people want to be masters of the future is to change the past. They are fighting for access to the laboratories where photographs are retouched and biographies and histories rewritten.

How long did he stop there at the station?

What did his stop there mean?

It meant nothing.

He immediately airbrushes it from his mind and forgets completely about the white house with the begonias. Once again he is speeding through the countryside without looking to either side. Once again space is merely an obstacle to his progress.

18

The car he had managed to shake was parked in front of his house. Both men were standing a few steps away from it.

He pulled up behind their car and got out. They flashed him an almost cheerful smile, as if Mirek's escape had been a little prank they'd all enjoyed together. As he walked past them, the man with the thick neck and wavy gray hair began laughing and nodded at him. Mirek felt a sudden anxiety at this show of intimacy. It implied more intimate ties to come.

He went into the house without flinching and opened the door to his apartment with his key. The first thing he saw was his son's face full of suppressed agitation. A stranger with glasses walked up to Mirek and identified himself. "Do you want to see the prosecutor's search warrant?"

"Yes," said Mirek.

There were two more men in the apartment. One was standing at the desk, which was piled high with stacks of papers, notebooks, and books. He picked the items up one by one, while the other man, seated at the desk, wrote down what he dictated.

The man with the glasses produced a folded piece of paper from his breast pocket and handed it to Mirek. "Here is the search warrant, and there," he pointed to the two men, "is a list of the items we are confiscating."

Papers and books were strewn all over the floor, cabinet doors were wide open, furniture had been moved away from the walls.

Mirek's son leaned over to him and said, "They got here five minutes after you left."

The men at the desk went on with their list: letters from Mirek's friends, documents from the early days of the Russian occupation, analyses of the political situation, minutes of meetings, and a few books.

"You don't seem to care much about your friends," said the man with the glasses, nodding in the direction of the confiscated items.

"You won't find a thing that goes against the constitution," said Mirek's son. Mirek recognized his own words.

The man with the glasses said it was up to the court to decide what did or did not go against the constitution.

19

The people who have emigrated (there are a hundred and twenty thousand of them) and the people who have been silenced and removed from their jobs (there are half a million of them) are fading like a procession moving off into the mist. They are invisible and forgotten.

But a prison, even though entirely surrounded by walls, is a splendidly illuminated theater of history.

Mirek has known this for a long time. He has been irresistibly attracted by the idea of prison all year, the way Flaubert was doubtless attracted by Madame Bovary's suicide. No, Mirek could not come up with a better ending for his life story.

They wanted to erase hundreds of thousands of lives from human memory and leave nothing but a single unblemished age of unblemished idyll. But Mirek is going to stretch out full length over their idyll, like a blemish. And stay there, like Clementis's cap on Gottwald's head.

They had Mirek sign the list of confiscated items and then asked him and his son to go along with them. After a year of investigatory custody he was put on trial. Mirek was sentenced to six years, his son to two years, and ten or so of their friends to terms of from one to six years.

PART TWO
Mother

There had been a time when Marketa disliked her mother-in-law. When she and Karel were living with his family (her father-in-law was still alive then), she had daily run-ins with her. The woman was so hostile and ready to take offense. They couldn't stand it very long and moved out. "As far from Mother as possible" was their slogan at the time. They found a place in a town at the other end of the country and didn't have to see Karel's parents any more than once a year, if that often.

Then one day her father-in-law died, and Mother was left all alone. They saw her at the funeral. She was meek and miserable and seemed smaller to them than before. Both had the same thought: you can't stay here alone now—come live with us.

Both had the same thought, but neither could quite come out and say it. Especially since the solemn walk she took with them the day after the funeral when, miserable and shrunken as she was, she gave them a lecture on every sin they had ever committed against her—and with a vehemence they found totally inappropriate. "Nothing will ever change her," said Karel to Marketa when they were alone in the train. "Sad as it may be, 'far from Mother' still holds."

But the years rolled on, and though Mother did not in fact change, Marketa must have changed, because she suddenly felt that all the things her mother-in-law had done to hurt her were actually harmless and silly and that *she* was the one at fault for attaching such importance to a few hard words. Until then she had looked at Mother the way a child looks at an adult, but now the roles were reversed: Marketa was the adult, and Mother, seen from a distance at least, was as small and defenseless as a child. She felt a surge of indulgence, tolerance, and even began corresponding with her. The old woman took to it very quickly, wrote back conscientiously, and demanded more and more letters from Marketa. They were the only thing that made living alone bearable, she claimed.

The thought that had taken shape at the funeral of Karel's father began running through their minds again. And again the son checked the daughter-in-law's kind instincts. Instead of saying, "Mother, come live with us," they invited her to stay for a week.

It was Easter, and their ten-year-old son had gone off on vacation. Eva was due the next weekend, on Sunday. They were willing to spend the whole week with Mother, except for that Sunday. You can come this Saturday, they told her, and stay until the next. We've got something on for Sunday, somewhere to go. They did not say anything more definite because they were not too anxious to talk about Eva. Karel said it twice more over the phone. From this Saturday to next. We've got something on for Sunday, somewhere to go. And Mother answered, Yes, children, that's very nice of you. You can be sure I'll leave whenever you want me to. All I ask is a bit of respite from my loneliness.

But when on Saturday evening Marketa tried to arrange a time for them to take her to the station the next morning, Mother announced clearly and simply that she would not be leaving until Monday. When Marketa looked surprised, she added, "Karel told me you had something on for Monday, somewhere to go, so I'd have to leave by Monday."

Now Marketa could certainly have said, "You've made a mistake, Mother, we're leaving tomorrow," but she didn't have the courage. She couldn't just make up a place to say they were visiting. She realized they'd been very careless about their alibi, so she didn't say anything at all and resigned herself to the fact that Mother would be staying with them all of Sunday too. Her only consolation was that the boy's room, the room they had put her in, was at the other end of the apartment and Mother would not bother them.

"Come on now, don't be mean," she said to Karel disapprovingly. "Just look at her, poor thing. She really breaks my heart."

2

Karel gave a resigned shrug. Marketa was right, Mother *had* changed. She was satisfied with everything, grateful for everything. Karel had expected a confrontation over some trifle. It never came.

Once when they were out walking, she gazed into the distance and asked, "What's the name of that pretty white village?" There was no village, just stone road markers. Karel felt an upsurge of pity when he realized how much his mother's sight had deteriorated.

But the defect in her sight seemed to explain something much more basic: what was large for them was small for her; what were stones for them were houses for her.

To tell the truth, this characteristic of hers was not entirely new, but at one time it had bothered them greatly. One night, for example, the tanks of a huge neighboring country came and occupied their country. The shock was so great, so terrible, that for a long time no one could think about anything else. It was August, and the pears in their garden were nearly ripe. The week before, Mother had invited the local pharmacist to come and pick them. He never came, never even apologized. The fact that Mother refused to forgive him drove Karel and Marketa crazy. Everybody's thinking about tanks, and all you can think about is pears, they yelled. And when shortly thereafter they moved away, they took the memory of her pettiness with them.

But are tanks really more important than pears? As time passed, Karel realized that the answer was not so obvious as he had once thought, and he began sympathizing secretly with Mother's perspective—a big pear in the foreground and somewhere off in the distance a tank, tiny as a ladybug, ready at any moment to take wing and disappear from sight. So Mother was right after all: tanks are mortal, pears eternal.

Mother used to insist on knowing everything about her son

and was angry when he tried to hide any of his life from her, so this time they decided to make her happy and tell her all about what they did, what went on in their lives, what they thought about things. They soon noticed, though, that Mother was only listening to them to be polite and would respond to their stories with a remark about her poodle, which she had left with a neighbor while she was away.

There was a time when he would have considered it egocentric or small-minded of her, but now he knew better. The years went by more quickly than they realized. Mother had laid down the field marshal's baton of her motherhood and moved on to a different world. On another one of their walks they had been caught in a storm. They put their arms under hers and propped her up on either side. If they had not literally carried her along, the wind would have blown her away like a feather. Karel was touched to feel how ridiculously little she weighed in his hands. He realized his mother belonged to a different order of creature: smaller, lighter, more easily blown away.

3

Eva arrived in the afternoon. Marketa went to pick her up at the station because she thought of her as *her* friend, not Karel's. She did not like Karel's female friends. Eva was different: she had met Eva first.

It was about six years ago. She and Karel had gone to a spa for a rest. Every other day Marketa took a sauna. Once she was sitting there sweating on the wooden bench with the other ladies when in came a tall, naked girl. They smiled even though they did not know each other, and after a few moments the girl began talking to Marketa. Because she was so straightforward and Marketa was so grateful for her show of affability, they quickly became friends.

Marketa was won over by her eccentricity. Coming up and talking to her like that! As if they'd made a date to meet there. She didn't waste time on polite clichés about how good the sauna is for your health and how hungry it makes you feel. No, she started right in about herself, the way people meeting through personal ads try to squeeze everything there is to say about themselves into the first letter they write to their future partners.

And who was Eva, in Eva's own words? Eva was a light-hearted man chaser. She didn't chase men to marry them, though; she chased them the way men chase women. She didn't believe in love. Only in friendship and sensuality. As a result, she had lots of friends. Men weren't afraid she wanted to marry them, women weren't afraid she wanted to steal their husbands. Besides, if she ever did get married, her husband would be her friend. She'd let him do whatever he wanted and wouldn't make any demands on him.

Next she remarked on Marketa's beautiful figure. It was quite unusual, in Eva's opinion. Very few women had really beautifully bodies. Her praise slipped out so spontaneously it gave Marketa greater pleasure than the usual run of male flattery. The girl had turned her head. Marketa felt she was entering a new realm of spontaneity, and made a date with Eva for two days from then—same time, same place. Later she introduced her to Karel, but he had always been odd man out in the relationship.

"Karel's mother is staying with us," Marketa told her apologetically on the way back from the station. "I'll introduce you as my cousin. You don't mind, do you?"

"Not in the least. In fact, I like the idea," said Eva, and asked Marketa for a few basic facts about her family.

4

Mother had never been particularly interested in her daughter-in-law's relatives, but the words "cousin," "niece," "aunt," and "granddaughter" made her feel warm inside. They formed a comfortable sphere of intimate concepts.

And here she had another confirmation of something she had long known: her son was an incurable eccentric. How could Mother ever be in the way with a relative visiting? She could understand their wanting to talk by themselves, but it made no sense at all to send her away a day early just for that. Fortunately, she'd figured out a way to handle them. She simply made believe she'd mixed up the schedule they'd agreed on. She almost enjoyed the look on that poor girl's face as she tried to tell her to leave on Sunday.

Yes, she had to admit they were nicer than before. A few years ago Karel would have shooed her away without mercy. That little ruse of hers yesterday had actually been for their own good. One day it would spare them pangs of conscience for having needlessly packed their mother off to her loneliness a day early.

Besides, she was very happy to have met the new relative. She was a very sweet girl (and looked just like somebody—but who?). For two whole hours she'd had to sit there answering her questions. How did Mother wear her hair when she was a girl? In a braid, of course. It was still the Austro-Hungarian Monarchy. Vienna was still the capital. Mother went to a Czech school, Mother was a patriot. She would be glad to sing them a patriotic song or two, the kind they sang back then. Or recite a few poems! She was sure she could still remember a lot of them. Right after the war (after World War I, in 1918, the year the Czechoslovak Republic was founded—goodness, Marketa's cousin didn't even know when the First Republic was founded!) Mother had recited a poem at a special school assembly. It was to celebrate the end of the Austrian Empire. To celebrate their independence! And suddenly, just think, at the last stanza she drew a complete blank and couldn't for the life of her go on. There she stood, silent, the sweat dripping down her forehead. She thought she would die of shame. But then—who would ever have expected it—the audience broke out into thunderous applause. Everyone thought the poem was over, no one realized the last stanza was missing! But Mother still felt mortified. She was so ashamed she ran and locked herself in the girls' room, and the principal himself ran after her and pounded and pounded on the door and begged her not to cry, begged her to come out, told her what a success she'd been.

Marketa's cousin laughed, and Mother stared at her for a long time. "You remind me of somebody, but heavens, who can it be?"

"You were out of school by the time the war was over," interjected Karel.

"Don't you think I know when I went to school?" said Mother.

"You graduated in the last year of the war. We were still part of Austria-Hungary."

"Don't you think I know what year I graduated?" said Mother, getting angry. But even as she said it, she knew Karel was right. She *had* graduated during the war. Then where did that memory of the school assembly come from? Suddenly all her self-confidence was gone, and she stopped talking.

Marketa's voice broke the brief silence. She was saying something to Eva, something with no connection at all with Mother's recitation or 1918.

Mother felt abandoned in her reminiscences and betrayed by the sudden lack of interest and the tricks her memory was playing on her.

"Well, you have a good time together, children," she said to them. "You're young. You have a lot to talk about." And filled with a sudden uneasiness, she left them for her grandson's room.

5

Karel was very touched at seeing Eva ask Mother so many questions. He had known her ten years now, and she had always been like that. Forthright and fearless. He had made friends with her (he and Marketa were still living with his parents at the time) almost as quickly as Marketa did several years later. One day he received a letter at work from a girl he did not know. She claimed to know him by sight and had decided to write him because social conventions meant nothing to her when she found a man she liked. She liked Karel and thought of herself as a hunter. A hunter of unforgettable experiences. She didn't believe in love. Only in friendship and sensuality. She enclosed a snapshot of a naked girl in a provocative pose.

At first Karel was afraid to answer. The whole thing might be a practical joke. But finally he gave in. He wrote to the girl at the address she had given him and invited her to meet him at a friend's apartment. It was Eva—tall, skinny, and poorly dressed. She looked like an overgrown teenage boy wearing his grandmother's old clothes. She sat down across from him and told him that social conventions meant nothing to her when she found a man she liked. She believed only in friendship and sensuality. Her face showed clear signs of uncertainty and effort, and Karel felt more of a brotherly sympathy for her than desire. But then he said to himself, Why miss an opportunity? and to her, by way of encouragement, "Perfect. A meeting of two hunters."

These words, the first to check the flow of her confession, gave Eva new strength. For nearly a quarter of an hour she had heroically held the fort by herself.

He told her she was beautiful in the picture she had sent him and asked (in the provocative voice of a hunter) if it excited her to show herself naked.

"I'm an exhibitionist," she said, the way she might have said she played women's basketball.

He told her he'd like to have a look.

She perked up and asked him if there was a record player in the apartment.

Yes, there was, but all his friend had was classical music: Bach, Vivaldi, and some Wagnerian operas. Somehow Karel couldn't see her stripping to the *Liebestod*. Eva was not any happier with the records than he was. "Isn't there any rock?" No, there wasn't any rock. He had no other choice: in the end he had to put on a Bach suite. Then he settled down in a chair in the corner, the one with the best view. Eva tried to move to the rhythm, but after a while she gave up. It just wouldn't work with that kind of music.

"Shut up and strip," he barked out at her.

With Bach's celestial music still wafting through the room, Eva went back to her bumping and grinding. The fact that the music had never been intended for dancing made her performance especially grueling, and Karel suspected that from the sweater she pulled

34

off first to the panties she pulled off last, time seemed never ending to her. While the music filled the room, Eva twisted her body into various dance movements, discarding clothing piece by piece as she went. Never once the whole time did she so much as look up at Karel. She concentrated as completely on herself and her movements as a violinist executing a difficult piece by heart and afraid of being distracted by looking up at the audience. When she was finally stark naked, she turned around, leaned her forehead against the wall, and grabbed herself between her legs. Karel threw his clothes off, never letting the quivering back of the masturbating girl out of his sight. He was in ecstasy. It was fantastic. No wonder from that day on he kept watch over Eva.

Besides, she was the only one of his women who wasn't the least bit fazed by his love for Marketa. "Your wife has got to understand that no matter how much you love her, you're a hunter, and your hunting is no threat to her. But no wife will ever understand that. No," she added, "no woman will ever understand her man," as if she were the misunderstood husband in question.

Then she offered to do everything in her power to help.

6

The room Mother went to, her grandson's, was no more than twenty feet and two thin walls away. Mother's shadow was still with them, and Marketa felt uncomfortable.

Fortunately, Eva was in a talkative mood. A lot of things had happened since they'd last gotten together: she'd moved to another town and, more important, married an older man there, a wise man who thought of her as an irreplaceable friend. And as we know, Eva had a great gift for good company, but didn't believe in love, with its ego trips and hysteria.

She'd also started a new job. She was earning a pretty good salary, but she had to work for it. She had to be back on the job tomorrow morning.

"Really?" said Marketa, horrified. "When do you have to leave?"

"There's an express at five A.M."

"That means getting up at four! God, that's awful!" And suddenly she felt—well, if not angry, then at least annoyed that Karel's mother had stayed. Eva lived far away and was very busy, and here she'd set aside this Sunday for Marketa, and now they couldn't even spend it together the way they'd planned because the ghost of Karel's mother was still haunting them.

Marketa was in a bad mood, and since it never rains but it pours, the phone began to ring. Karel picked up the receiver. His voice was hesitant, his responses suspiciously laconic and suggestive. Marketa had the feeling he was choosing his words very carefully, trying to hide the real sense of what he was saying. She was certain he was making a date with another woman.

"Who was that?" she asked. Karel said it was a woman colleague who lived in the neighboring town and was supposed to come and have a meeting with him that week. From then on Marketa did not say a word.

Was she really that jealous?

Once upon a time she had been. Yes, when they had first fallen in love. But that was years ago. Now what she felt as jealousy was really only habit.

To put it another way, every love relationship is based on unwritten conventions rashly agreed upon by the lovers during the first weeks of their love. On the one hand, they are living a sort of dream; on the other, without realizing it, they are drawing up the fine print of their contracts like the most hard-nosed of lawyers. O lovers! Be wary during those perilous first days! If you serve the other party breakfast in bed, you will be obliged to continue same in perpetuity or face charges of animosity and treason!

In those first weeks it was decided between Karel and Marketa that Karel would be unfaithful and Marketa would submit, but that Marketa would have the privilege of being the better one in the couple and Karel would always feel guilty. No one knew better than

Marketa how depressing it was to be better. The only reason she was better was for want of anything better.

Down deep, of course, Marketa knew that the telephone call didn't mean a thing in itself. But what it *was* did not count nearly so much as what it *represented:* an eloquent condensation of her whole life situation. Everything she did she did for Karel. She took care of his mother. She introduced him to her best friend; in fact, she gave her to him. For his very own, for his pleasure. And why did she do so much? Why did she try so hard? Why like Sisyphus did she roll her boulder up the hill? No matter what she did, Karel was spiritually elsewhere. He made dates with other women and constantly eluded her.

While she was still in school, she was indomitable, rebellious, almost too spirited. "Nobody's ever going to lead you by the nose," her old math teacher liked to say to her in jest. "I pity your husband in advance." She would laugh proudly. She thought the words boded well. But then suddenly, with no warning, against her will and better judgment, she found herself in a completely different role. And all because she hadn't been on her toes the week she unknowingly wrote the contract.

Being better all the time wasn't any fun. All her years of marriage suddenly fell on her like a ton of bricks.

7

Marketa was acting more and more upset, and Karel's face had begun to show signs of anger. Eva panicked. She felt responsible for their happiness as a couple and tried her best to disperse the clouds filling the room by talking a mile a minute.

But it was too much for her. Karel, provoked by the injustice of it all—this time it was absolutely plain, refused to open his mouth. Marketa, unable to overcome her bitterness or deal with her husband's anger, stood up and went into the kitchen.

Eva meanwhile tried to persuade Karel not to spoil the evening they'd all looked forward to for so long. But Karel would not be moved. "There comes a time when you just can't take it anymore. I'm fed up. Always being charged with something. It's no joke, this constant guilt trip she's got me on. And for trivialities, trivialities! No, I can't stand the sight of her anymore. I can't stand the sight of her!" Once started, he couldn't seem to stop. Eva begged him to listen to her defense of Marketa, but he refused.

So she let him be and went in to see Marketa, who was cowering in the kitchen. Marketa knew something had happened that shouldn't have happened. Eva tried to convince her that the telephone call in no way justified her suspicions. "Well, I can't take it anymore," said Marketa, though deep down she knew that this time she was in the wrong. "It's always the same. Year after year. Month after month. The same women and the same lies. Well, I'm sick and tired of it. Sick and tired! I've had enough!"

Eva realized she wouldn't get very far with either of them, so although uncertain of whether her vague plan was entirely honest, she finally decided it was worth trying. If she was going to help them, she had to go ahead and act on her own initiative. Karel and Marketa loved each other, but they needed someone to lift the burden they were both struggling under. Someone to set them free. So the plan she'd come with wasn't only in her interest (though there wasn't any doubt it was first and foremost in her interest, and that bothered her a little because she never wanted to act selfishly with her friends), it was in their interest too.

"What do I do?" asked Marketa.

"Go to him. Tell him not to be upset."

"But I can't stand the sight of him. I can't stand the sight of him!"

"Then lower your eyes. That will make it all the more touching."

8

The evening was saved. Marketa made a big show of taking out a bottle. She handed it to Karel, implying he should open it as if opening the final race at the Olympics. While the wine flowed into their three glasses, Eva danced over to the record player, picked out a record, and went spinning around the room to the music (Ellington this time instead of Bach).

"Do you think Mother's asleep by now?" asked Marketa.

"The sensible thing to do would be to go in and say goodnight to her," Karel advised.

"If we go in and say goodnight, she'll start in on one of those stories of hers and we'll waste another hour. Remember, Eva's got to get up early tomorrow."

Marketa felt they'd wasted enough time for one day. She took her friend by the hand and, instead of going in to Mother, led her in the direction of the bathroom.

Karel stayed behind with his Ellington. He was glad the clouds had dispersed, but was not looking forward to the evening's adventure. The business with the telephone call had turned into a sudden revelation of something he had refused to admit to himself: he was tired and not particularly in the mood.

A number of years ago Marketa had gotten him to make three-way love to her and his mistress, whom she was jealous of. When she first suggested it, he went dizzy with excitement! But it hadn't been a very pleasurable evening. In fact, it had been downright grueling—two women kissing and hugging in his presence, but never for a minute forgetting they were rivals and constantly checking up on which one he paid more attention to, which one he was more tender with. He was careful to weigh his every word, his every touch, and felt more like a diplomat than a lover—scrupulously attentive, considerate, courteous, and fair. And even so he'd failed.

First his mistress burst into tears right in the middle of everything; then Marketa clammed up completely.

If he could have believed that Marketa requested their little orgies out of pure sensuality—she was, after all, the worse one in the couple—he would certainly have enjoyed them. But since it had been established early in the game that *he* was worse, all he could see in her debauchery was a painful denial of self and a noble attempt at meeting his polygamous lapses halfway, turning them into an integral part of marital bliss. He was marked forever by the sight of her jealousy, a wound which he himself had opened during the first stage of their relationship. When he saw her in the arms of another woman, he felt like falling to his knees and begging her forgiveness.

Could those wanton games actually be an exercise in penitence?

Somewhere along the line it occurred to him that if three-way sex was ever going to be any fun, Marketa had better not have the feeling she was in bed with a rival. She'd have to find somebody on her own, somebody Karel didn't know and had no interest in. That's why Karel engineered the clever little encounter between Marketa and Eva in the sauna. It worked, too. The two of them had become friends, allies, and conspirators—raping him, playing with him, making merry at his expense, and lusting after him together. Karel hoped Eva would succeed in ridding Marketa of the anxiety she associated with love, so he could finally be free of her accusations. Free, period.

But now he began to realize that changing what had been Law for all those years was out of the question. Marketa was still the same, he was still the accused.

Then why had he introduced Marketa to Eva in the first place? Why had he made love to them? Anyone else would have made Marketa into a lighthearted, sensual, happy woman long since. Anyone but Karel. He felt like Sisyphus.

Sisyphus? But hadn't Marketa just compared herself to Sisyphus?

Yes, during their years together husband and wife had become twins. They had the same vocabulary, the same ideas, the same destiny. Each had made a present of Eva to the other, each to make the other happy. Each was rolling a boulder up a hill. Both were tired.

Hearing the gurgle of splashing water in the bathroom and the laughter of the two women, he realized he could never live the way he wanted or have the women he wanted the way he wanted them. He felt like running away to a place where he could put together a story of his own, in his own way, with no loving eyes looking on.

In fact, he didn't much care about putting together that story of his. All he wanted was to be alone.

9

It made no sense for Marketa to assume Mother was asleep and avoid saying goodnight to her. Impatience had led to imprudence. During Mother's stay with her son all kinds of thoughts had begun stirring in her head, and this evening they had become particularly unruly. It was all due to that nice cousin of Marketa's who kept reminding her of someone from her youth. Now who could it be?

Finally it came to her: Nora! Of course. Exactly the same build, the same way of carrying herself, the same beautiful long legs.

Nora had never been particularly kindhearted or modest, and Mother had often been hurt by the things she did. But that was not what she was thinking about now. What was more important now was that she'd suddenly stumbled on a piece of her youth, a greeting from across half a century. It made her feel good to think that everything she'd lived through was still there with her, all around her, talking to her. Even though she'd never really liked Nora, she was glad to meet her here in a completely tame version and in the person of someone who showed her the proper respect.

The minute it came to her, she wanted to run in and tell them. But she held herself back. She knew very well that it was only thanks to her little ruse she was still there and that those two sillies wanted to be alone with their cousin. Well, *let* them go on with their secrets. She wasn't at all bored in her grandson's room. She had her knitting, she had her reading, and most of all she had things to think about. Karel had really set her thinking. He was absolutely right, of course: she had graduated during the war. She'd gotten mixed up. That story about reciting the poem and forgetting the last stanza had taken place at least five years earlier. The principal really had pounded on the door of the girls' room where she'd locked herself up to weep. But she couldn't have been more than thirteen at the time, and it was nothing but a Christmas assembly. There was a decorated Christmas tree on the stage, and after the children sang their carols, she recited her poem. And just before the last stanza she drew a blank and couldn't go on.

Mother was ashamed of her memory. What should she tell Karel? Should she admit she'd mixed things up? As it was, he thought of her as an old woman. Oh, they were nice to her, all right, but Mother couldn't help noticing they treated her like a child, with a kind of condescension she found distasteful. If she owned up and told Karel he'd been right and she'd confused a Christmas assembly with a political rally, they'd grow a few inches taller and she'd shrink even more. No, no, she wouldn't give them the satisfaction.

She'd tell them she actually had recited the poem after the war. True, she was out of school then, but the principal remembered her because she'd been the best in elocution and he invited her to come and represent the graduates by reciting a poem. It was a great honor! But Mother deserved it! She was a patriot! They had no idea what it was like when Austria-Hungary fell apart after the war. The elation! The songs! The flags! And again she felt very much like running out and telling her son and daughter-in-law about the world of her youth.

In fact, she almost felt it her *duty* to go and talk to them. True, she'd promised not to bother them, but that was only half the truth. The other half was that Karel refused to see how she could have recited a poem at a school assembly after the war. Mother was getting on in years, and her memory wasn't what it once was, so she couldn't explain it to him right away, but now that she'd finally remembered exactly how it had been, she couldn't simply make believe she'd forgotten her son's question. That wouldn't be nice of her. So she'd go in to see them (whatever they had to say to one another, it couldn't be that important) and apologize by telling them she didn't mean to interrupt and wouldn't ever have come out again if Karel hadn't asked how she could have recited a poem at a school assembly after she'd graduated.

At that point she heard a door opening and closing. She put her ear up to the wall. She heard two women's voices and the door opening again. Then laughter and some water running. The two girls must be getting ready for bed, she said to herself. She'd better hurry up if she wanted a chance to have her say.

10

Mother's entrance was a hand held out to Karel by a playful, grinning god. It was so badly timed it was perfect. She did not have to apologize at all. Karel immediately showered her with questions about what she'd done all afternoon and whether she wasn't a little depressed and why she hadn't come out and said hello.

Mother pointed out that young people always had lots to talk about and an older person had to understand and keep out of the way.

By then he could hear the two squealing girls rushing toward the door. The first to enter was Eva in a dark blue nightie that ended exactly where the black fleece of her private parts began. The sight of Mother gave her a terrible fright, but since she couldn't very well retreat, she flashed her a smile and crossed quickly to the armchair, which she hoped would hide her poorly masked nudity.

Karel knew Marketa could not be far behind, and suspected she would be in her evening clothes, which in their private language meant that all she would have on was a string of beads around her neck and a red velvet sash around her waist. He knew he ought to be doing something to keep her from coming in and Mother from turning pale. But what could he do? Could he yell, "Don't come in!"? Or, "Quick, put your clothes on. Mother's here!"? Maybe there was a shrewder way of holding Marketa back, but Karel had no more than a second or two to think things through and couldn't come up with anything. In fact, he was infused with a sort of euphoric apathy that deprived him of all presence of mind. So he didn't do a thing, and Marketa appeared on the threshold of the room stark naked except for her necklace and red velvet sash.

At that very moment Mother turned to Eva and said with an amiable smile, "You must be on your way in to bed, and here I am, keeping you up." Eva, who had caught sight of Marketa out of the corner of her eye, said no, or, rather, screamed it, as if trying to use her voice to cover her friend's nakedness. Meanwhile, Marketa had come to and retreated into the hall.

When she reentered the room a few moments later wearing a long housecoat, Mother repeated what she had just said to Eva. "I don't want to keep you up now. You must be ready for bed."

Marketa was all set to nod yes when Karel shook his head a gleeful no. "Not in the least, Mother. We're so happy to have you here with us." So Mother finally had a chance to set the record straight about her recitation at the assembly celebrating the end of World War I, when Austria-Hungary fell apart and the principal invited an alumna of the school to come and give her rendition of a patriotic poem.

Neither of the young women had any idea of what Mother was talking about, but Karel listened with great interest. Let me make it absolutely clear: the story about the forgotten stanza was of no particular interest to him. He had heard it many times and forgotten it many times. What he found interesting was not so much the story told by Mother as Mother telling the story—Mother and her giant-pear world with a Russian tank perching on it like a ladybug. The girls' room door with the principal's benevolent fist pounding on it had totally upstaged the eager impatience of the two young women.

Karel was very pleased with the way things were going. He looked over at Eva and Marketa with great relish. Their nakedness quivered impatiently under nightie and housecoat. With renewed vigor he launched into a further round of questions concerning the principal, the school, and the First World War, and crowned it all by asking her to recite the patriotic poem whose last stanza she had forgotten.

Mother concentrated for a moment. Then, utterly engrossed, she began reciting the poem she had recited at the school assembly when she was thirteen: not a patriotic poem at all, but some lines about a Christmas tree and the star of Bethlehem. No one noticed the difference, not even Mother. All she could think of was whether she would remember the lines of the last stanza. And she did. The star of Bethlehem burned bright and guided the Three Kings all the way to the manger. She was excited by her success, and laughed and tossed her head proudly.

Eva started clapping. When Mother turned to look at her, she remembered the main thing she'd come out to tell them. "You know who your cousin reminds me of, Karel? Nora!"

11

Karel looked over at Eva, unable to believe his ears. "Nora? Your friend Nora?"

He remembered Mother's friend well from his childhood. She was a strikingly beautiful woman—tall and stately, with the magnificent face of an empress. Karel had never liked her—she was proud and standoffish—but he had never been able to take his eyes off her. How could there possibly be any similarity between her and happy-go-lucky Eva?

"That's right," answered Mother. "Nora! Just take a look at her. That stately build. That way of walking. That face."

"Stand up, Eva," said Karel.

Eva was afraid to stand up. She wasn't sure the short nightie would cover her private parts. But Karel was so insistent she finally had to obey. Standing there, her arms pressed against her side, she tried to pull the nightie down in front as unobtrusively as possible. Karel, meanwhile, was straining to see the resemblance. Suddenly there it was—distant and difficult to pin down, but there. It appeared only in brief flashes, over almost before they began, but Karel tried to hold onto them. He longed to revive in Eva a lasting, durable picture of beautiful Nora.

"Turn around," he ordered.

Eva did not want to turn around: all she could think of was how naked she was under her nightie. Even Mother began to protest. "You can't put that girl through her paces as if she were a soldier!" But Karel would not give in.

"No, no, I just want her to turn around," he insisted, and Eva finally obeyed.

Let's not forget that Mother's sight was very bad. She mistook stones for a village, saw Nora in Eva. All Karel had to do was squint a little and he would see huts instead of stones too. Hadn't he envied Mother her perspective all week? So he squinted, and sure enough, there instead of Eva he saw that beauty out of his past.

He had an unforgettable secret memory of her. Once when he was about four, he and Mother and Nora had gone to a spa together (he didn't have the slightest idea where it was). They told him to wait for them in an empty changing room and abandoned him among the piles of women's clothes. He'd been standing around for some time when in walked a tall, magnificent, naked woman— her back to the child—and reached over to the hook on the wall where her bathrobe was hanging. It was Nora.

The image of that taut, naked body seen from behind had never left him. A small boy at the time, he had looked up at her from below. For that kind of distortion, given his present height, he would have to look up at a fifteen-foot statue. He was so near the body and yet so remote. Doubly remote. Remote in space and in time. It towered over him far into the heights and was cut off from him by a countless number of years. That double distance had brought on a dizzy spell in the four-year-old. He was having another one now, an extremely intense one.

Looking at Eva (who was still standing with her back to him), he saw Nora. The distance between them was five feet and one or two minutes.

"Mother," he said, "it was awfully nice of you to come out and chat with us. But now the girls want to go to bed."

Mother went off to her room, humble and obedient, and Karel immediately began telling the two women about his Nora memory. He crouched down in front of Eva and turned her around so her back was facing him again and his eyes could retrace the path they had taken when he was a child so long before.

All at once his lethargy was gone. He pulled her down to the floor. While she lay on her stomach, he crouched again at her heels and ran his eyes up along her legs and on to her behind. Then he threw himself on top of her and began making love.

He had the feeling that the leap he had just taken was a leap across endless time, the leap of a little boy hurtling his way from childhood to manhood. And as he moved on her, each time he went back and forth, he felt he was describing the movement from childhood to maturity and back, the movement from a boy staring powerless at an enormous female body to a man gripping that body and taming it. That movement, usually measuring six inches at most, was as long as three decades.

Both women were soon caught up in his frenzy. From Nora he went over to Marketa, then back to Nora, then back again to Marketa. They had been at it for quite some time when he felt he needed a little time out. He was in top form and felt strong as never before. He sank into an armchair and looked over at the two women lying before him on the wide couch. It wasn't Nora he saw during this short break, it was his two old friends, Marketa and Eva, bearing witness to his life. They made him feel like a grandmaster who has just finished off two opponents on adjoining chessboards. He was so delighted with the analogy he couldn't help saying, "I'm Bobby Fischer." Then he burst out laughing and shouted it. "I'm Bobby Fischer! I'm Bobby Fischer!"

12

While Karel was shouting that he felt like Bobby Fischer (who at just about this time had won the world championship in Iceland), Eva and Marketa were lying on the couch in one another's arms. "Okay?" whispered Eva in her friend's ear.

Marketa answered, "Okay," and pressed her lips firmly against Eva's.

An hour earlier, in the bathroom, Eva had asked her to come and pay a return visit some time. She would have liked to invite Karel along, but both Eva's husband and Karel were jealous and would never put up with having the other man around.

At first Marketa didn't see how she could possibly say yes, so she just laughed and didn't say anything. But a few minutes later, while they were sitting in the living room with her mother-in-law's idle chatter sailing past her ears, Eva's offer seemed as impossible to refuse as originally it had seemed impossible to accept. The specter of Eva's husband was among them.

And later, when Karel shouted out he was a four-year-old and squatted to peer up at Eva, she had the feeling he was in fact turning into a four-year-old and retreating from her into his childhood, leaving the two of them alone with an unusually active male body, a body so efficient and well tuned it seemed impersonal, empty, ready to receive any soul they might come up with—the soul of Eva's husband, say, a total stranger to her, faceless and formless.

Marketa let that mechanical male body make love to her and then watched it throw itself between Eva's legs, but she tried not to look at its face. She wanted to think of it as the body of a stranger. It was a masquerade party. Karel had put a Nora mask on Eva and a little-boy mask on himself; Marketa had severed his head from his body. He was a headless male body, Karel had disappeared, and a miracle had come to pass: Marketa was footloose and fancy-free!

Am I trying to confirm Karel's suspicion that their little

homespun orgies were nothing but exercises in suffering and self-denial for Marketa?

No, that would be an oversimplification. Marketa really did desire the women she thought were Karel's mistresses, she desired them with both her body and her senses. But she desired them with her head as well. True to the prediction of her old math teacher, she wanted to take the initiative, keep things going, catch Karel offguard —all within the bounds of that damned contract, of course.

The only trouble was, as soon as she lay down on the wide couch with them, all erotic fantasies flew out of her head. Just looking at her husband brought her back to her role, the role of the better one in the couple, the one who gets hurt. Even though she was with Eva—whom she liked a lot and wasn't at all jealous of— the presence of the man she loved too much weighed heavy on her and dampened the pleasures of the senses.

The minute she severed his head from his body, she felt the new and intoxicating touch of freedom. The anonymity of their bodies was sudden paradise, paradise regained. With an eerie pleasure she blotted out her wounded, overvigilant soul and became all body, a body without past or memory and, as such, all the more willing and receptive. She stroked Eva's face tenderly while Karel's headless body went through its vigorous movements on top of her.

But all of a sudden the headless body stopped short, and a voice that reminded her unpleasantly of Karel's shouted out the incredibly ridiculous "I'm Bobby Fischer! I'm Bobby Fischer!"

It was like being waked out of a dream by an alarm clock. And just when she'd pressed up to Eva (the way people press up to their pillows in the morning to keep out the gloomy light of day), Eva had asked, *"Okay?"* and she had answered "Yes," and pressed her lips to Eva's. She'd always liked her, but today for the first time she appreciated her with all her senses—for herself, for her body, for her skin—and she was drunk with this sudden revelation of physical love.

While they lay there on their stomachs, side by side, their backsides slightly raised, Marketa could feel the eyes of that unusually active body on her skin. Soon it would be making love to them again. She tried to ignore the voice going on about seeing beautiful Nora; she tried to be all body, a body pressing against a dear friend and a headless man.

When it was all over, her friend went right to sleep. Marketa envied her that animal sleep; she wanted to inhale it from her lips, fall asleep herself to its rhythm. She snuggled up close to her and closed her eyes to fool Karel into thinking they'd both fallen asleep. Before long he went in to bed next door.

At four-thirty in the morning she opened the door to his room. He gave her a sleepy look.

"Go back to sleep. I'll take care of Eva," she said, giving him a tender kiss. Before he could roll over, he was asleep again.

"So it's okay?" Eva asked her again in the car.

Marketa was not quite so determined as she had been the night before. Yes, she wanted to do away with those old unwritten agreements. Yes, she wanted to stop being the better one in the couple. But how could she do it without destroying their love? How could she do it loving Karel the way she did?

"Don't worry," said Eva. "He'll never find out. The way you have things set up between you, you're the one who gets to be suspicious, not him. There's nothing to be afraid of. It'll never enter his mind."

13

While Eva was dozing in her bumpy compartment, Marketa returned home from the station and went back to sleep (she would have to be up again in an hour to get to work on time). Now it was Karel's turn. His job was to take Mother to her train. It was their morning for trains. In another few hours (by which time both husband and wife would be at work) their son would alight on the platform and put a definitive end to the events.

Karel was still full of the beautiful night. He was well aware that of the two or three thousand times he had made love (how many times *had* he made love in his life?) only two or three were really essential and unforgettable. The rest were mere echoes, imitations, repetitions, or reminiscences. And well aware that yesterday's session was one of the two or three really great ones, Karel was full of boundless gratitude.

During the drive to the station Mother never stopped talking.

What did she say?

First, she thanked him. She'd had a wonderful time with her son and daughter-in-law.

Second, she lectured him. They had done her a great injustice. When he and Marketa were living with her, he had been impatient with her—coarse, even—and inconsiderate. Mother had suffered a great deal. Yes, she admitted, they'd been very nice this time, different from before. They'd changed. Yes. But why had they waited so long?

Sitting through the long litany of charges (he knew it by heart), he was not the least upset. He had been watching her from the corner of his eye and was again amazed at how tiny she was. It was as though her whole life had been a long gradual shrinking process.

But what did that shrinking process entail?

Was it the actual shrinking of a person as he abandons his adult proportions and starts down the long path through old age and death to that far-off place where all is void and without proportions?

Or was it just an optical illusion caused by the fact that Mother was moving into the distance, that she was in another place, that she looked like a lamp, a doll, a butterfly to him?

"By the way, what's become of Nora?" he asked during one of the breaks in her litany.

"She's an old woman now, of course. Almost completely blind."

"Do you ever see her?"

"Didn't you know?" asked Mother, quite annoyed. The two women had long since parted ways. They'd quarreled bitterly and would never be reconciled. Karel should have remembered that.

"Do you have any idea where we went on vacation with her when I was a little boy?"

"Of course I do," said Mother, naming a Czech spa. Karel knew it well, but he'd never dreamed it was the spa where he'd seen Nora naked.

He pictured its gently rolling countryside, its wooden colonnade and carved columns, the surrounding hills and meadows ringing with the bells of sheep set out to pasture. Then he took Nora's body and (like a collage artist, cutting out part of one engraving and pasting it over another) planted it down squarely in the idyllic landscape. And the thought went through his mind that beauty is a spark which flares up when two ages meet across the distance of time, that beauty is a clean sweep of chronology, a rebellion against time.

And he was filled to the brim with that beauty and a feeling of gratitude for it. "Mother," he said out of the blue, "Marketa and I were wondering whether you wouldn't like to come live with us after all. It won't be any trouble to find a slightly larger apartment."

"That's very kind of you, Karel," she said to him, stroking his hand, "very kind. I'm happy to hear you say that. But my poodle is accustomed to things at home, you know. And I'm friendly with the women in the neighborhood."

By this time they are aboard the train, and Karel is trying to find her a compartment. They all seem too crowded and uncomfortable. Finally he puts her in a first-class compartment and runs off to settle the extra fare with the conductor. And since he has his wallet ready, he takes out a hundred-crown note and puts it in Mother's hand as if Mother were a little girl going on a long, long journey, and Mother accepts the money matter-of-factly, without any show of surprise, like a schoolgirl accustomed to receiving occasional gifts of money from adults.

And then the train starts moving—Mother is at the window, Karel on the platform—and he waves for a long, long time, until the last possible moment.

PART THREE
The Angels

1

Rhinoceros is a play by Eugène Ionesco during which people obsessed by a desire to be identical to one another gradually turn into rhinoceroses. Gabrielle and Michelle, two American girls, were doing an analysis of the play as part of a summer-school course for foreigners in a small town on the Riviera. They were the pets of Madame Raphael, their teacher, because they always kept their eyes on her and carefully wrote down her every word. She had given the two of them a special assignment today: an oral report on the play for the next class meeting.

"I'm not so sure I understand what all those people turning into rhinoceroses is supposed to mean," said Gabrielle.

"Think of it as a symbol," Michelle told her.

"True," said Gabrielle. "Literature is a system of signs."

"And the rhinoceros is first and foremost a sign," said Michelle.

"Yes, but even if we accept the fact they turn into signs instead of rhinoceroses, how do they choose what signs to turn into?"

"Yes, well, that's a problem," said Michelle sadly. They were on their way back to the dormitory and walked awhile in silence.

Finally Gabrielle spoke up. "Do you think it could be a phallic symbol?"

"What?" asked Michelle.

"The horn," answered Gabrielle.

"True," said Gabrielle, but then she hesitated. "Only why do they *all* turn into phallic symbols—men *and* women?"

Again they trotted along in silence for a while.

"Something just occurred to me," Michelle said suddenly.

"What?" asked Gabrielle, curious.

"Madame Raphael even hinted at it," said Michelle to pique Gabrielle's curiosity even further.

"Well, what is it?" asked Gabrielle impatiently.

"The author meant to create a comic effect!"

Gabrielle was so taken by her friend's idea, so involved in what was going on in her head, that without realizing it she began walking more and more slowly. The two girls had nearly come to a halt.

"You mean the symbol of the rhinoceros is meant to create a comic effect?" she asked.

"Yes," answered Michelle, smiling the proud smile of revelation.

The two girls looked at each other, enthralled by their own daring, and the corners of their mouths started twitching with pride. Then suddenly they let out short, shrill, breathy sounds very difficult to describe in words.

2

"Laughter? Does anyone ever care about laughter? I mean real laughter—beyond joking, jeering, ridicule. Laughter—delight unbounded, delight delectable, delight of delights . . .

"I said to my sister or she said to me, come let's play laughter together. We stretched out side by side on the bed and started in. At first we just made believe, of course. Forced laughs. Laughable laughs. Laughs so laughable they made us laugh. Then it came—real laughter, total laughter—sweeping us off in unbounded effusion. Bursts of laughter, laughter rehashed, jostled laughter, laughter defleshed, magnificent laughter, sumptuous and wild. . . . And we laughed to the infinity of the laughter of our laughs. . . . O laughter! Laughter of delight, delight of laughter. Laughing deeply is living deeply."

I quote this text from a book called "Woman's Word." It was written in 1974 by one of those passionate feminists who have made their mark on our times. It is a mystical manifesto of joy. After denigrating sexual desire in the male, which, dependent on the transitory nature of the erection, is fatally betrothed to violence, annihilation, and doom, the author extols its positive antipode—female joy, pleasure, delight—as expressed by the French word *jouissance,* which is soothing, ubiquitous, and uninterrupted. A woman who has managed to remain true to her inner self takes pleasure in everything: "eating, drinking, urinating, defecating, touching, hearing, or just plain being." This enumeration of sensual delights runs through the book like a litany. "Living is happiness. Seeing, hearing, touching, drinking, eating, urinating, defecating, diving into water and watching the sky, laughing and crying." And if intercourse is beautiful, it is beautiful because it is the sum of all the individual sensual delights: "touch, sight, hearing, speech, and smell, as well as drinking, eating, defecating, meeting, and dancing." Suckling is a delight, giving birth a delight, menstruating a delight, that "mild, almost sweet flow of blood, that tepid saliva of the stomach, that mysterious milk, that pain with the burning taste of happiness."

Only an imbecile could make fun of this manifesto of delight. Mysticism and exaggeration go together. A mystic must not fear ridicule if he is to push all the way to the limits of humility or the limits of delight. St. Theresa smiled through her agony, and St. Annie Leclerc (for that is the name of the author whose book I have been quoting) claims that death is an integral part of joy that only men are afraid of, miserably dependent as they are on "their petty egos and petty power."

The sound of laughter is like the vaulted dome of a temple of happiness, "that delectable trance of happiness, that ultimate peak of delight. Laughter of delight, delight of laughter." There is no doubt: this laughter goes "far beyond joking, jeering, and ridicule." The two sisters stretched out on their bed are not laughing at anything concrete, their laughter has no object; it is an expression of being rejoicing at being. When moaning a person chains himself to the immediate present of his suffering body (and lies completely outside past and future), and in this ecstatic laughter he loses all memory, all desire, cries out to the immediate present of the world, and needs no other knowledge.

You are no doubt familiar with the scene in B movies in which a boy and a girl are running through a spring (or summer) landscape holding hands. Running, running, running, and laughing. By laughing the lovers are telling the whole world, all movie audiences everywhere, "See how happy we are, how glad to be alive, how perfectly attuned to the great chain of being!" It is a silly scene, a kitschy scene, but it does contain one of the most basic human situations: "serious laughter, laughter beyond joking."

All churches, all underwear manufacturers, all generals, all political parties have that laughter in common; they all use the image of those two laughing lovers in the publicity for their religion, their product, their ideology, their nation, their sex, their dishwashing detergent.

And that is the laugh Michelle and Gabrielle are laughing as they emerge from a stationery store holding hands and swinging little packages of colored paper, glue, and rubber bands in their free hands.

"Madame Raphael will love it," says Gabrielle. "Just you wait." And she lets out a shrill, breathy sound. Michelle expresses agreement and responds with same.

3

Soon after the Russians occupied my country in 1968, I (like thousands and thousands of other Czechs) lost the privilege of working. No one was allowed to hire me. At about that time some young friends started paying me regular visits. They were so young that the Russians did not have them on their lists yet and they could remain in editorial offices, schools, and film studios. These fine young friends, whom I will never betray, suggested I use their names as a cover for writing radio and television scripts, plays, articles, columns, film treatments—anything to earn a living. I accepted a few of their offers, but most I turned down. I couldn't have gotten to them all, for one thing, and then too, it was dangerous. Not for me, for them. The secret police wanted to starve us out, cut off all means of support, force us to capitulate and make public confessions. They kept their eyes out for all the pitiful little escape routes we used to avoid encirclement, and they meted out severe punishments to the friends who gave me their names.

One of those generous donors was a girl by the name of R. (Everything has since come out into the open, so I have nothing to hide in her case.) Shy, delicate, and intelligent, she was an editor of an illustrated weekly for young people with a huge circulation. Since at the time the magazine was obliged to print an incredible amount of undigested political claptrap glorifying our brothers the Russians, the editors were constantly looking for something to attract the attention of the crowd. Finally they decided to make an exception and violate the purity of Marxist ideology with an astrology column.

During those years of excommunication I wrote several thousand horoscopes. If the great Jaroslav Hasek could be a dog merchant (he sold many stolen dogs and charged top pedigree prices for many mutts), I might as well be an astrologer. Parisian friends had once given me a whole series of books by the French astrologer André Barbault, whose name on the front page was adorned by the proud title of Vice-Président du Centre International d'Astrologie. Right underneath, disguising my handwriting, I wrote, "*À Milan Kundera avec admiration, André Barbault,*" and leaving the books thus dedicated lying around unobtrusively on my desk, I would tell my wide-eyed Prague clientele by way of explanation that I had once served as Barbault's assistant for several months in Paris.

When R. asked me to do an astrology column for her magazine under a pseudonym, I was delighted, of course, and I instructed her to explain to the editorial board that the texts would be written by an important nuclear physicist who had requested her not to divulge his name for fear his colleagues would laugh at him. That seemed to give our undertaking a double cover: a nonexistent scientist and his pseudonym.

Which is how, under an assumed name, I came to write a fine, long introductory article on astrology and short, rather silly monthly texts for individual signs, accompanying the latter with my own drawings of Taurus, Aries, Virgo, Pisces. The pay was miserable, the job itself not particularly amusing or remarkable. The only amusing part of it was my existence, the existence of a man erased from history, literary reference books, even the telephone book, a corpse brought back to life in the amazing reincarnation of a preacher sermonizing hundreds of thousands of young socialists on the great truths of astrology.

One day R. announced to me that the editor-in-chief was all excited about his astrologer and wanted a personal horoscope from him. That fascinated me. The editor-in-chief owed his job at the magazine entirely to the Russians. He had spent half his life taking Marxism-Leninism courses in Prague and Moscow both!

"He was a little ashamed to tell me," laughed R. "He certainly wouldn't want it to get around he believed in medieval superstitions or anything. He just can't help himself."

"Fine, fine," I said. I was happy. I knew the man well. Besides being R.'s boss, he was a member of the highest Party committee dealing with hiring and firing, and he had ruined the lives of many of my friends.

"He wants complete anonymity. All I'm supposed to give you is his date of birth. You have no idea who he is."

"Even better." That was just what I wanted to hear.

"He says he'll give you a hundred crowns."

"A hundred crowns?" I laughed. "Who does he take me for, the cheapskate!"

He sent me a thousand crowns. I filled ten pages with a description of his character and a chronicle of his past (about which I was quite well informed) and future. I spent a whole week on the opus and consulted regularly with R. After all, a horoscope can greatly influence, even dictate, the way people act. It can recommend they do certain things, warn them against doing others, and bring them to their knees by hinting at future disasters.

R. and I had a good laugh over it later. She claimed he had improved. He yelled less. He had begun to have qualms about his hardheadedness—his horoscope warned against it. He made as much as he could of the speck of kindness left in him, and staring out into nothingness, his eyes would show signs of sadness, the sadness of a man who has come to realize that the stars hold nothing but suffering in store for him.

4

(On Two Kinds of Laughter)

Those who consider the Devil to be a partisan of Evil and angels to be warriors for Good accept the demagogy of the angels. Things are clearly more complicated.

Angels are partisans not of Good, but of divine creation. The Devil, on the other hand, denies all rational meaning to God's world.

World domination, as everyone knows, is divided between demons and angels. But the good of the world does not require the latter to gain precedence over the former (as I thought when I was young); all it needs is a certain equilibrium of power. If there is too much uncontested meaning on earth (the reign of the angels), man collapses under the burden; if the world loses all its meaning (the reign of the demons), life is every bit as impossible.

Things deprived suddenly of their putative meaning, the place assigned them in the ostensible order of things (a Moscow-trained Marxist who believes in horoscopes), make us laugh. Initially, therefore, laughter is the province of the Devil. It has a certain malice to it (things have turned out differently from the way they tried to seem), but a certain beneficent relief as well (things are looser than they seemed, we have greater latitude in living with them, their gravity does not oppress us).

The first time an angel heard the Devil's laughter, he was horrified. It was in the middle of a feast with a lot of people around, and one after the other they joined in the Devil's laughter. It was terribly contagious. The angel was all too aware the laughter was aimed against God and the wonder of His works. He knew he had to act fast, but felt weak and defenseless. And unable to fabricate anything of his own, he simply turned his enemy's tactics against him. He opened his mouth and let out a wobbly, breathy sound in the upper reaches of his vocal register (much like the sound Gabrielle and Michelle produced in the streets of the little town on the Riviera) and endowed it with the opposite meaning. Whereas the Devil's laughter pointed up the meaninglessness of things, the angel's shout rejoiced in how rationally organized, well conceived, beautiful, good, and sensible everything on earth was.

There they stood, Devil and angel, face to face, mouths open, both making more or less the same sound, but each expressing himself in a unique timbre—absolute opposites. And seeing the laughing angel, the Devil laughed all the harder, all the louder, all the more openly, because the laughing angel was infinitely laughable.

Laughable laughter is cataclysmic. And even so, the angels have gained something by it. They have tricked us all with their semantic hoax. Their imitation laughter and its original (the Devil's) have the same name. People nowadays do not even realize that one and the same external phenomenon embraces two completely contradictory internal attitudes. There are two kinds of laughter, and we lack the words to distinguish them.

5

A weekly news magazine once ran a picture of a row of uniformed men shouldering guns and sporting helmets with Plexiglas visors. They are looking in the direction of a group of young people wearing T-shirts and jeans and holding hands and dancing in a circle before their eyes.

It is obviously the period immediately preceding a clash

with the police, who are guarding a nuclear power plant, a military training camp, the headquarters of a political party, or the windows of an embassy. The young people have taken advantage of this dead time to make a circle and take two steps in place, one step forward, lift first one leg and then the other—all to a simple folk melody.

I think I understand them. They feel that the circle they describe on the ground is a magic circle bonding them into a ring. Their hearts are overflowing with an intense feeling of innocence: they are not united by a *march*, like soldiers or fascist commandos; they are united by a *dance*, like children. And they can't wait to spit their innocence in the cops' faces.

That is the way the photographer saw them too, and he highlighted his view with eloquent contrasts: on the one side the police in the false (imposed, decreed) unity of their ranks, on the other side the young people in the real (sincere and organic) unity of their circle; on the one side the police in the *gloom* of their ambush, on the other the young people in the *joy* of their play.

Circle dancing is magic. It speaks to us through the millennia from the depths of human memory. Madame Raphael had cut the picture out of the magazine and would stare at it and dream. She too longed to dance in a ring. All her life she had looked for a group of people she could hold hands with and dance with in a ring. First she looked for them in the Methodist Church (her father was a religious fanatic), then in the Communist Party, then among the Trotskyites, then in the anti-abortion movement (A child has a right to life!), then in the pro-abortion movement (A woman has a right to her body!); she looked for them among the Marxists, the psychoanalysts, and the structuralists; she looked for them in Lenin, Zen Buddhism, Mao Tse-tung, yogis, the *nouveau roman*, Brechtian theater, the theater of panic; and finally she hoped she could at least become one with her students, which meant she always forced them to think and say exactly what she thought and said, and together they formed a single body and a single soul, a single ring and a single dance.

Her two American students were in their dormitory room poring over the text of Ionesco's *Rhinoceros*. Michelle was reading aloud:

"LOGICIAN *(to the Old Man):* Take a sheet of paper and do the following problem. If we take two paws from two cats, how many paws does each cat have left?

"OLD MAN *(to the Logician):* There are several possible solutions. . . . One cat may have four paws, the other two. . . . There may be one cat with five paws . . . and another with one. . . . If we take two paws away from eight, . . . we may have one cat with six paws . . . and one without any paws at all."

"I don't see how anybody could cut off a cat's paws," said Michelle, interrupting her own reading. "Do you think *he* could?"

"Michelle!" Gabrielle said loudly.

"And how could one cat have six paws?"

"Michelle!" Gabrielle said again.

"What?" asked Michelle.

"Have you forgotten so soon? You're the one who said it!"

"What?" asked Michelle again.

"The dialogue is meant to create a comic effect."

"Oh, that's right," said Michelle, giving Gabrielle a happy look. The two girls looked into each other's eyes, then the corners of their mouths began twitching with pride, and finally they let out a short, breathy sound in the upper reaches of their vocal registers. And then another one of those sounds and still another. "Forced laughs. Laughable laughs. Laughs so laughable they made them laugh. Then it came—real laughter, total laughter —sweeping them off in its unbounded effusion. Bursts of laughter, laughter rehashed, jostled laughter, laughter defleshed, magnificent laughter, sumptuous and wild. . . . And they laughed to the infinity of the laughter of their laughs. . . . O laughter! Laughter of delight, delight of laughter . . ."

Meanwhile, Madame Raphael roamed the streets of that little town on the Riviera, utterly alone. Suddenly she raised her head as if sensing a sliver of melody on the wings of a breeze, a fragrance from far-off lands. She stopped and in the depths of her soul heard the rebellious scream of a void yearning to be filled. She felt that somewhere nearby a flame of great laughter was flickering and perhaps somewhere not far off a group of people was holding hands and dancing in a ring. . . .

She stood there for a while, looking around nervously. Then the secret music suddenly disappeared (Michelle and Gabrielle had suddenly stopped laughing; all at once their faces fell at the thought of an empty night without love), and Madame Raphael, strangely restless and on edge, made her way home through the warm streets of the small town on the Riviera.

6

I too once danced in a ring. It was in the spring of 1948. The Communists had just taken power in my country, the Socialist and Christian Democrat ministers had fled abroad, and I took other Communist students by the hand, I put my arms around their shoulders, and we took two steps in place, one step forward, lifted first one leg and then the other, and we did it just about every month, there being always something to celebrate, an anniversary here, a special event there, old wrongs were righted, new wrongs perpetrated, factories were nationalized, thousands of people went to jail, medical care became free of charge, small shopkeepers lost their shops, aged workers took their first vacations ever in confiscated country houses, and we smiled the smile of happiness. Then one day I said something I would better have left unsaid. I was expelled from the Party and had to leave the circle.

That is when I became aware of the magic qualities of the circle. Leave a row and you can always go back to it. The row is an open formation. But once a circle closes, there is no return. It is no accident that the planets move in a circle and when a stone breaks loose from one of them it is drawn inexorably away by centrifugal force. Like a meteorite broken loose from a planet, I too fell from the circle and have been falling ever since. Some people remain in the circle until they die, others smash to pieces at the end of a long fall. The latter (my group) always retain a muted nostalgia for the circle dance. After all, we are every one of us inhabitants of a universe where everything turns in circles.

At one or another of those anniversaries of God knows what, the streets of Prague were once again crowded with young people dancing in rings. I wandered from one to the next, stood up as close as I could to them, but I was forbidden entrance. It was June 1950, the day after Milada Horakova had been hanged. She had been a National Assembly representative of the Socialist Party, and a Communist court had charged her with plotting to overthrow the state. She was hanged together with Zavis Kalandra, Czech surrealist and friend to André Breton and Paul Éluard. And knowing full well that the day before in their fair city one woman and one surrealist had been hanged by the neck, the young Czechs went on dancing and dancing, and they danced all the more frantically because their dance was the manifestation of their innocence, the purity that shone forth so brilliantly against the black villainy of the two public enemies who had betrayed the people and its hopes.

André Breton did not believe that Kalandra had betrayed the people and its hopes, and called on Éluard (in an open letter written in Paris on June 13, 1950) to protest the absurd accusation and try to save their old Prague friend. But Éluard was too busy dancing in the gigantic ring encircling Paris, Moscow, Warsaw, Prague, Sofia, and Athens, encircling all the socialist countries and all the Communist parties of the world; too busy reciting his beautiful poems about joy and brotherhood. After reading Breton's letter, Éluard took two steps in place, one step forward, he shook his head, refusing to stand up for a man who had betrayed the people (in the June 19, 1950, issue of the magazine *Action*), and instead, recited in a metallic voice:

The Angels

> We shall fill innocence
> With the strength we have
> So long been lacking
> We shall never again be alone.

And as I walked through the streets of Prague passing rings of laughing, dancing Czechs, I knew I belonged to Kalandra, not to them, to Kalandra who had also broken away from the circular trajectory and fallen, fallen, fallen right into a convict's coffin, but even though I did not belong to them, I could not help looking on with envy and nostalgia, I could not take my eyes off them. And that is when I saw him, right in front of me!

He had his arms around their shoulders and was singing those two or three simple notes and lifting first one leg, then the other. Yes, there was no doubt about it. The toast of Prague. Paul Éluard! And suddenly the people he was dancing with stopped singing and went on with their movements in absolute silence while he intoned one of his poems to the rhythm of their feet:

> We shall flee rest, we shall flee sleep,
> We shall outstrip dawn and spring
> And we shall fashion days and seasons
> To the measure of our dreams.

And then suddenly they were all singing the three or four simple notes again, speeding up the steps of their dance, fleeing rest and sleep, outstripping time, and filling their innocence with strength. Everyone was smiling, and Éluard leaned down to a girl he had his arm around and said,

> A man possessed by peace never stops smiling.

And she laughed and stamped the ground a little harder and rose a few inches above the pavement, pulling the others along with her, and before long not one of them was touching the ground, they were taking two steps in place and one step forward without touching the ground, yes, they were rising up over Wenceslaus Square, their ring the very image of a giant wreath taking flight, and I ran off after them down on the ground, I kept looking up at them, and they floated on, lifting first one leg, then the other, and down below—Prague with its cafés full of poets and its jails full of traitors, and in the crematorium they were just finishing off one Socialist representative and one surrealist, and the smoke climbed to the heavens like a good omen, and I heard Éluard's metallic voice intoning,

Love is at work it is tireless,

and I ran after that voice through the streets in the hope of keeping up with that wonderful wreath of bodies rising above the city, and I realized with anguish in my heart that they were flying like birds and I was falling like a stone, that they had wings and I would never have any.

7

Seventeen years after his execution Kalandra was completely rehabilitated, but several months later Russian tanks invaded Bohemia, and right away there were tens of thousands of new people charged with betraying the people and its hopes, the minority was jailed, the majority thrown out of work, and two years later (in other words, exactly twenty years after Éluard rose up over Wenceslaus Square) one of the newly accused (myself) was writing an astrology column for an illustrated weekly aimed at Czech youth. A year after my article on Sagittarius (which sets the date at December 1972) a young man I didn't know came to see me. He handed me an envelope without saying a word. I tore it open and read the letter, but it took some time before I realized it was from R. Her handwriting was completely different. She must have been extremely upset when she wrote it. She had tried to formulate her sentences in such a way that only I could understand them, with the result that even I missed quite a bit. In fact, all I did understand was that now, a year after the fact, my identity had been discovered.

At that time I had a one-room apartment in Prague on Bartolomejska—a short street, but a famous one. All the buildings except two (one of which I lived in) belong to the police. Looking out from my large fourth-floor window I could see the towers of the Prague Castle up above the roofs and the police courtyards down below me, the glorious history of the Czech kings above, the history of glorious Czech prisoners below. They had all passed through those courtyards: Kalandra, Horakova, Clementis, and my friends Sabata and Hubl.

The young man (everything led me to believe he was R.'s fiancé) looked around gingerly. He obviously suspected the police had bugged my apartment. We nodded at one another—we still had not exchanged a word—and went out into the street. We walked awhile in silence. Not until we reached noisy Narodni Avenue did he tell me that R. wished to see me. A friend of his, whom I did not know, was willing to lend us his apartment in a Prague suburb for a secret meeting.

So the next day I took a long tram ride to the outskirts of Prague. My hands were frozen, and the rows of identical apartment houses were totally deserted in the midmorning hours. Finally I found the right one, took the elevator to the third floor, looked through the names on the door, and rang the bell. The apartment was silent. I rang again, but no one answered. I went back down to the street and walked around the building for an hour on the assumption R. was late and I would spot her on the empty sidewalk walking up from the tram stop. But no one came. I took the elevator back up to the third floor and rang the bell again. Several seconds later I heard the sound of water flushing from inside the apartment. All at once I felt as though an ice cube of anxiety had been thrust into the pit of my stomach. Deep down in my own body I felt the fear of that girl unable to open the door because anxiety had upset her bowels.

She opened the door. She was pale but smiling, and she tried to be as nice as always. She made several awkward jokes on the order of Well, here we are, finally alone in an empty apartment. We sat down, and she told me she had recently been called in by the police. They had spent an entire day questioning her. The first two hours they asked her about a lot of unimportant things, and she felt she was master of the situation. She joked with them and asked them flippantly if they thought she was going to skip lunch for such nonsense. That was when they asked her, Who writes your astrology articles? She blushed and tried to say something about the famous physicist whose name she was not at liberty to divulge. Do you know Milan Kundera? they asked. She said she did. Was there anything wrong with that? Nothing at all, they answered. But did you happen to know that Mr. Kundera is interested in astrology? No, she didn't. So you don't know anything about it, they laughed. All Prague is talking about it and you don't know a thing? She went back to her nuclear physicist for a while, but then one of them began shouting at her to stop lying.

She told them the truth. They'd decided to do a good, readable astrology column, but didn't have anyone to write it, and since she knew me, she asked me to help them out. She was sure she hadn't broken any law. She was right, they told her. She hadn't broken any law. But she had infringed on in-house regulations prohibiting dealings with certain people who had proved themselves unworthy of the confidence of either Party or state. She pointed out that nothing terrible had happened: Mr. Kundera's name had remained hidden behind a pseudonym and couldn't possibly have offended anyone. As for the fees he received, well, they weren't even worth mentioning. Again they agreed with her: nothing serious *had* happened, and now all they were going to do was write it up and ask her to sign it, and she wouldn't have a thing to worry about.

She signed, and two days later the editor-in-chief called her in and told her she was fired, effective immediately. The same day she went to Czechoslovak Radio, where she had friends who had long been trying to lure her over to them. They greeted her with open arms, but the next day when she came back to take care of the formalities, the head of personnel, who liked her very much, met her with an unhappy look on his face. "How could you have done a thing like that? Your life is ruined. There's nothing I can do for you."

At first she was afraid to talk to me. The police made her promise not to breathe a word about the interrogation to anyone. But when she got another summons from them (she was due there the next day), she decided she had to see me in secret so we could agree on a story and avoid contradicting each other if I happened to be called in too.

Please don't misunderstand. R. was no crybaby. She was simply young and not particularly knowledgeable about the ways of the world. This first blow had caught her unawares, and she would never forget it. I realized I had been chosen as a mailman to deliver people warnings and punishments, and I began to feel afraid of myself.

"Do you think they know about the thousand crowns you got for that horoscope?"

"Don't worry. Nobody who spent three years studying Marxism-Leninism is going to admit to having horoscropes drawn up for himself."

She laughed, and even though the laugh lasted no more than half a second, I took it as a modest promise of salvation. It was just the kind of laughter I was yearning for when I wrote those stupid little articles about Pisces, Virgo, and Aries, just the kind of laughter I saw as my reward, and it never came. In the meantime, all the critical posts in the word, all the general staffs, had been occupied by angels; they had taken over the left and the right, Arab and Jew, Russian general and Russian dissident. They looked down on us from all sides with their icy stares stripping us of the motleys we wear for happy-go-lucky mystification and reducing us to common cheats who work at magazines for socialist youth even though we have no faith in either youth or socialism, who write horoscopes for editors-in-chief even though we consider both editor-in-chief and horoscope to be ridiculous, who waste our time on trivialities when everyone else (the left and the right, Arab and Jew, Russian general and Russian dissident) is fighting for the future of mankind. We felt the weight of their stares turning us into insects to be crushed underfoot.

I mastered my anxiety and tried to come up with the most rational plan for R. to follow the next day at the police. Several times during our talk she got up and went to the bathroom. Each time she came back accompanied by the sound of water flushing and a look of embarrassed panic. That brave girl was ashamed of her fear. That graceful woman was ashamed of her insides acting up before the eyes of a stranger.

8

Twenty-five or so students of various nationalities sat at their desks looking up bemusedly at a very excited Michelle and Gabrielle. Standing before the podium where Madame Raphael sat, they each held several sheets of paper—the text of their report—and an odd cardboard object with a rubber band hanging from it.

"We are going to talk about *Rhinoceros* by Ionesco," said Michelle, and bent her head down to slip the cardboard cone decorated with bits and pieces of colored paper over her nose and fasten it around the back of her head with the rubber band. Gabrielle followed suit. Then the girls turned and looked at each other and began letting out short, shrill, breathy sounds.

The class had no trouble figuring out that the girls had two points to make: (1) that a rhinoceros has a horn over its nose and (2) that Ionesco's play is meant to be funny. They had decided to make both points using not only words, but their bodies as well.

The long cones bounced up and down on their faces as they talked, and the class froze into a sort of sympathetic embarrassment. It was as if a man had stood up in front of the class and shown off his amputated arm.

The only enthusiastic response to the idea came from Madame Raphael, who answered her pets' shrill, breathy sounds with her own version.

The girls nodded their long noses happily, and Michelle launched into her part of the report.

One of the students was a young Israeli girl named Sarah. Several days before she had asked the two Americans if they would let her look at their notes (everyone knew they took down every word Madame Raphael said), but they had refused. "Don't cut class to go to the beach." Ever since, she had detested them, and she was glad to see them making fools of themselves.

Michelle and Gabrielle took turns reading their analysis of *Rhinoceros,* their long cardboard cones sticking out like vain prayers. Sarah realized what a shame it would be to let this kind of opportunity go by. During a short pause when Michelle had turned to Gabrielle to indicate she was on, Sarah left her seat and started walking toward the two girls. Instead of saying her part, Gabrielle trained the orifice of her astonished cardboard nose on Sarah. Sarah went up to them, walked around in back of them (the extra noses seemed to have weighed down their heads to such an extent they were unable to turn and watch what was going on behind their backs), took aim, kicked Michelle in the behind, took aim again, and kicked Gabrielle. Whereupon she returned to her seat with great calm—no, great dignity.

For a moment there was absolute silence.

Then tears started rolling down Michelle's cheeks and, a split second later, down Gabrielle's.

Then the class broke into unrestrained laughter.

Then Sarah sat down again.

Then Madame Raphael, who had at first been surprised and shocked, caught on: Sarah's little misdemeanor had been a prearranged part of a carefully prepared student joke in the interest of getting closer to the work (in teaching works of art, we must move beyond older theoretical approaches and embrace such modern methodologies as practical applications, nonverbal analysis, classroom happenings!), and since she could not see her darlings' tears (they were facing the class and so had their backs to her), she threw her head back and burst into a laughter of joyous acquiescence.

Hearing their beloved teacher laughing behind their backs,

Michelle and Gabrielle felt betrayed. Teardrops fell from their eyes like water from a faucet. The feeling of humiliation was so painful they began writhing as if overcome with stomach cramps.

Madame Raphael took her darlings' writhing for a dance, and all at once a force more powerful than her professorial dignity ejected her from her chair. She laughed so hard she cried, and her body began twitching. With her arms wide open she swung her head back and forth on her neck like an upside-down bell in the hands of a sexton ringing an urgent call to mass. She went up to the writhing girls and took Michelle by the hand. Now all three of them were standing in front of the classroom writhing, the tears streaming down their cheeks. Madame Raphael took the requisite steps and lifted first one leg, then the other. Still crying, the girls made a timid attempt at following her. By now their cardboard noses were dripping wet, but they twisted and turned and hopped in place. Then Madame Raphael took Gabrielle's hand and made a little circle in front of the classroom. Now all three of them were holding hands, doing their steps and kicks, and moving round and round the classroom floor. They lifted first one leg, then the other, and imperceptibly their faces distorted with weeping turned into faces distorted with laughter.

As they laughed and danced and their cardboard noses jiggled, the class looked on in mute horror. By then, however, the dancing women were paying no attention to anyone else, they were completely caught up in themselves and their rapture. All at once Madame Raphael stamped a little harder than before and rose a few inches above the classroom floor. Her next step did not touch the ground. She pulled her two friends up after her, and before long all three of them were circling above the floor and moving slowly upward in a spiral. No sooner did their hair touch the ceiling than it yielded to them, and up they went through the opening. First their cardboard noses vanished, then only three pairs of shoes remained, and finally the shoes vanished as well, leaving the stupefied students with nothing but the brilliant, fading laughter of the three archangels from on high.

9

My meeting with R. in the borrowed apartment was a turning point for me. It was then I came to grips with the idea that I had become a bearer of ill tidings and could not go on living among the people I loved if I wanted no harm to come to them. The only thing left for me to do was leave my country.

But I have another reason for remembering my last meeting with R. I had always been fond of her in the most innocent, asexual way. It was as if her body was always entirely hidden behind her radiant mind, the modesty of her behavior, and her taste in dress. She had never offered me the slightest chink through which to view the glow of her nakedness. And now suddenly the butcher knife of fear had slit her open. She was as open to me as the carcass of a heifer slit down the middle and hanging on a hook. There we were, sitting side by side on a couch in a borrowed apartment, the gurgling of the water filling the empty toilet tank in the background, and suddenly I felt a violent desire to make love to her. Or to be more exact, a violent desire to rape her. To throw myself on her and take possession of her with all her intolerably exciting contradictions, her impeccable outfits, her rebellious insides, her reason and her fear, her pride and her misery. It was contradictions like those, I felt, that made up her true essence—that treasure, that nugget of gold, that diamond buried deep within her. I felt like leaping on her and tearing it out of her. I felt like engulfing her—her shit and her ineffable soul.

But I also felt two anxious eyes on me (anxious eyes in a knowing face), and though the more anxious those eyes, the greater my desire, nonetheless, the more anxious those eyes, the more ridiculous, absurd, scandalous, incomprehensible, inconceivable it all became.

When I left the borrowed apartment that day and walked out into the deserted street of the housing development (she stayed upstairs awhile for fear someone might see us together), I could think of nothing but my monumental desire to rape that fine girl, my friend. The desire has remained with me, trapped like a bird in a pouch, a bird that wakes up now and then and flaps its wings.

Perhaps that wild desire to rape R. was merely a desperate attempt to grab at something during the fall. Because from the day they excluded me from the circle, I have not stopped falling, I am still falling, all they have done is give me another push to make me fall farther, deeper, away from my country and into the void of a world resounding with the terrifying laughter of the angels that covers my every word with its din.

Sarah is out there somewhere, I know she is, my Jewish sister Sarah. But where can I find her?

Quotations are from the following works: Annie Leclerc, *Parole de femme*, 1976; Paul Éluard, *Le Visage de la paix*, 1951; and Eugène Ionesco, *Le Rhinocéros*, 1959.

PART FOUR
Lost Letters

1

According to my calculations there are two or three new fictional characters baptized on earth every second. As a result, I am always unsure of myself when it comes time for me to enter that vast crowd of John the Baptists. But what can I do? I have to call my characters something, don't I? Well, this time, just to make it clear my heroine belongs to me and me alone (and means more to me than anyone ever has), I am giving her a name no woman has ever had before: Tamina. I picture her as tall and beautiful, thirty-three, and a native of Prague.

I can see her now, walking down a street in a provincial town in the west of Europe. Yes, you're right. Prague, which is far away, I call by its name, while the town my story takes place in I leave anonymous. It goes against all rules of perspective, but you'll just have to put up with it.

Tamina has a job as a waitress in a small café belonging to a married couple. The café brought in so little money the husband took a job somewhere else and they hired Tamina to take his place. The difference between the miserable salary he earned at his new job and the even more miserable salary they gave Tamina was their only profit.

Tamina serves the customers their coffee and Calvados (there are never very many of them; the café is invariably half-empty), and then goes back to her place behind the bar. There is almost always someone sitting on a bar stool wanting to talk to her. They all like her. She is a good listener.

But does she really listen? Or does she just look on, silent and preoccupied? I can't quite tell, and it really doesn't matter that much. What does matter is that she never interrupts anybody. You know what it's like when two people start a conversation. First one of them does all the talking, the other breaks in with "That's just like me, I . . ." and goes on talking about himself until his partner finds a chance to say, "That's just like me, I . . . "

The "That's just like me, I . . .'s" may look like a form of agreement, a way of carrying the other party's idea a step further, but that is an illusion. What they really are is a brute revolt against brute force, an attempt to free one's ear from bondage, a frontal attack the objective of which is to occupy the enemy's ear. All man's life among men is nothing more than a battle for the ears of others. The whole secret of Tamina's popularity is that she has no desire to talk about herself. She offers no resistance to the forces occupying her ear; she never says, "That's just like me, I . . . "

2

Bibi is ten years younger than Tamina. For nearly a year now she has been telling Tamina about herself on a day-to-day basis. Not too long ago (and that was when it actually all began) Bibi told Tamina that she and her husband were thinking of going to Prague that summer.

Suddenly Tamina seemed to awaken from a sleep of several years. Bibi went on talking, but Tamina (uncharacteristically) cut her off. "If you do go to Prague, Bibi," she said, "could you go to my father's and bring me back something? Oh, nothing big. Just a little package. Small enough to slip into your suitcase."

"You name it," said Bibi, ready and willing.

"You don't know how grateful I'd be," said Tamina.

"You can count on me," said Bibi, and they both talked some more about Prague. Tamina's cheeks were burning.

Then Bibi changed the subject. "I want to write a book."

Tamina thought of her package back in Czechoslovakia, and realizing she could not afford to lose Bibi's friendship, she offered her ear once again. "A book? What about?"

Bibi's year-old daughter was toddling around under her mother's bar stool, making a lot of noise.

"Sh!" Bibi said to the floor, and inhaled thoughtfully on her cigarette. "About the world as I see it."

The child's squeals were more and more acute.

"You mean you'd really dare to write a book?" asked Tamina.

"Why not?" said Bibi. She was thoughtful again. "Of course I need a few pointers about how a book gets written. Do you happen to know Banaka?"

"No. Who is he?" asked Tamina.

"A writer," said Bibi. "He lives somewhere around here. I've got to meet him."

"What has he written?"

"I don't know," said Bibi, and then added thoughtfully, "Maybe I ought to try reading something by him."

3

What came through the receiver, instead of the exclamation of joy and surprise she might have expected, was a cold "Well, what do you know. After all these years."

"You know I'm low on funds," Tamina apologized. "It costs a lot to call."

"Well, you could still write. A stamp doesn't cost that much, does it? I can't remember the last time I got a letter from you."

Realizing she was off to a bad start, she gave in and asked her mother-in-law how she was and what she had been doing. Only then could she bring herself to say, "There's a favor I'd like to ask of you. When we left the country, we left behind a small package."

"Package?"

"Yes. You and Mirek locked it in his father's desk. He always had his drawer there, remember? And he gave the key to you."

"I don't know anything about a key."

"But Mother, you've got to have it! Mirek gave it to you. I'm absolutely positive. I was there."

"You didn't give me a thing."

"It's been a long time. Maybe you've forgotten. All I'm asking is that you look around and see if you have the key. I'm positive you'll find it."

"And what am I supposed to do with it?"

"Just look and see if the package is still there."

"Where could it have gone to? You put it there, didn't you?"

"Yes."

"Then why do I have to open the drawer? What do you think? I've been tampering with your notebooks?"

Tamina was stunned. How did her mother-in-law know there were notebooks in the drawer? They were all wrapped up and carefully sealed with gummed tape. But she did not let her mother-in-law know she was surprised. "That's not what I mean. All I want is for you to make sure everything's there. Next time I call I'll tell you more."

"Why can't you tell me any more now?"

"I can't talk now, Mother. It costs too much."

"Well, why did you call me in the first place if it costs so much?" She was in tears now.

"Don't cry, Mother," said Tamina. She knew her tears by heart. Whenever her mother-in-law had wanted anything from them, she would burst into tears. It was her way of preferring charges, her most aggressive weapon.

The receiver shook with her sobs. "Goodbye, Mother," said Tamina. "I'll call again soon."

Tamina did not dare hang up before her mother-in-law stopped weeping and said goodbye. But the weeping went on and on, and every tear was expensive.

Tamina hung up.

"That was an awfully long call you just made," said her boss's wife in her mournful voice, pointing to the timer. She multiplied the time by the rate to Czechoslovakia, and Tamina was horrified at how much it came to. She had to count every penny to make it to next payday. But she paid right up without flinching.

4

Tamina and her husband had left Czechoslovakia illegally. They had signed up with the official state travel agency for a group tour to the Yugoslav coast, but once there, they abandoned the group and crossed over to the West via Austria.

To avoid being conspicuous, they took only one large suitcase apiece. At the last moment they had not dared to include the bulky package containing their letters to each other and Tamina's notebooks. If an official of her occupied country had opened her suitcase during a customs check, he would have immediately suspected something. Why would anyone bring along the entire archive of his private life for a two-week vacation by the sea? And because they did not wish to leave the package in their own apartment, which they knew would be appropriated by the state after their departure, they stashed it outside Prague in the apartment of Tamina's mother-in-law, in her late father-in-law's old and virtually unused desk.

Tamina's husband had fallen seriously ill abroad, and all she could do was sit by and watch as death slowly took him. When he died, they asked her whether she wanted him to be buried or cremated. She told them to burn him. They asked her whether she wanted to keep him in an urn or have his ashes scattered. Since she had no home and was afraid she would be forced to carry her husband around for the rest of her life like so much hand luggage, she had his ashes scattered.

I picture the world growing up around Tamina like a circular wall, and I picture her as a small patch of grass down below. The only rose growing on that patch of grass is the memory of her husband.

Or I picture Tamina's present (which consists of serving coffee and lending an ear) as a raft drifting on the water, with her sitting on it and looking back, looking only back.

Lately she has begun noticing with desperation that the past is growing paler and paler. All she has left of her husband is his passport picture. The other pictures remain behind in their appropriated apartment in Prague. Every day she looks at the grimy, dog-eared picture showing her husband full face (like a criminal in a mug shot). It is not a good likeness. Every day she spends some time in a sort of spiritual exercise, trying to remember what he looked like in profile, then half profile, then quarter profile, going over the lines of his nose and chin, and every day she is horrified at new fuzzy spots where her memory hesitates about which way to go.

During these exercises she tried to evoke his skin, its color, and all its minor blemishes: tiny warts, protuberances, freckles, veins. It was difficult, almost impossible. The colors her memory used were unrealistic. They could not do justice to human skin. As a result, she developed her own special technique of calling him to mind. Whenever she sat across from a man, she would use his head as a kind of sculptor's armature. She would concentrate all her attention on him and remodel his face inside her head, darkening the complexion, adding freckles and warts, scaling down the ears, and coloring the eyes blue.

But all her efforts only went to show that her husband's image had disappeared for good. When they first began dating, he had asked her to keep a diary taking both their lives into account. (He was ten years older than she was and had some idea of how poor the human memory can be.) She refused at first, saying it would make a mockery of their love. She loved him too much to admit that what she thought of as unforgettable could ever be forgotten. Finally, of course, she did as he asked, but without enthusiasm. The notebooks showed it: they had many empty pages, and the entries were fragmentary.

5

She had spent eleven years with her husband in Bohemia, and eleven notebooks remained behind with her mother-in-law. Shortly after her husband's death she bought a notebook and divided it into eleven parts. She had succeeded in reconstructing many half-forgotten events and situations, but she had no idea where to enter them. She had lost all sense of chronology.

The first thing she wanted to do, therefore, was to bring back memories that would serve as reference points in the flow of time and provide a basic framework for the past as she recreated it. Their vacations, for example. They must have had eleven of them, but she could remember only nine. Two had been irretrievably lost.

She tried to enter each of those nine reconstructed vacations into one of the eleven sections of her notebook. But she could do so with certainty only when something out of the ordinary had happened during the year. In 1964 Tamina's mother had died, and they had had a sad few weeks in the Tatras, a month later than usual. And she knew that the year after that they had gone to Bulgaria, to the sea. She also remembered the vacations they took in 1968 and 1969 because they were the last ones they had in Czechoslovakia.

But if she could do a fairly good job of reconstructing most of their vacations (chronology excluded), she was completely at a loss when it came to Christmas and New Year's. Of eleven Christmases she could recall only two, of twelve New Year's Eves, five.

She also tried to conjure up all the pet names he had ever called her. Her real name he used only for the first two weeks or so. His tenderness was like a machine for churning out terms of endearment. As quickly as they seemed to wear, he would make up new ones for her. During the twelve years they had known each other, she had had twenty or thirty of them, each one belonging to a definite period in their lives.

But how can she reconstruct the lost link between a pet name and the rhythm of time? Only in rare instances does she succeed. She can remember the days after her mother's death, for example, when, as if trying to wake her from a dream, her husband whispered her name into her ear with great urgency (her name at that time and that moment). That name she remembers perfectly, and she can enter it with confidence under the year 1964. But all the other names are soaring freely, madly, outside time, like birds escaped from an aviary.

That is why she so desperately wants that package of note-books and letters back.

She is aware, of course, that there are many unpleasant things in the notebooks—days of dissatisfaction, quarrels, even bore-dom. But that is not what counts. She has no desire to turn the past into poetry, she wants to give the past back its lost body. She is not compelled by a desire for beauty, she is compelled by a desire for life.

There she sits on a raft, looking back, looking only back. The sum total of her being is no more than what she sees in the distance, behind her. And as her past begins to shrink, disappear, fall apart, Tamina begins shrinking and blurring.

She longs to see the notebooks so she can fill in the fragile framework of events in the new notebook, give it walls, make it a house she can live in. Because if the shaky structure of her memories collapses like a badly pitched tent, all Tamina will have left is the present, that invisible point, that nothing moving slowly toward death.

6

Then why did she wait so long to ask her mother-in-law to send the package?

Correspondence with foreign countries goes through the hands of the secret police in Czechoslovakia, and Tamina could not resign herself to the idea of police officials sticking their noses into her private life. Besides, her husband's name (which was still her name) would definitely have remained on the blacklists, and the police are always on the lookout for any document dealing with the lives of their adversaries, even dead ones. (Tamina was far from wrong on this point: police files are our only claim to immortality.)

In other words, Bibi is her only hope, and she will do anything to stay in good with her. Bibi wants to meet Banaka. She ought to be familiar with the plot of at least one of his books, Tamina thinks. Some time during their talk she's got to come up with something like "Oh yes, that's just the way you put it in your book!" or "You know, you're just like your characters." Tamina knows that Bibi doesn't have a single book in her apartment and that reading bores her to tears. She needs to find out what Banaka writes about and prepare her for her talk with him.

Hugo, one of the café's regulars, might have some idea. "Do you know Banaka?" she asked, putting his coffee down in front of him.

Hugo had bad breath, but otherwise Tamina found him quite personable: quiet, shy, five or so years younger than she. He would come to the café once a week and divide his time between looking voraciously through the books he brought with him and looking voraciously at Tamina standing behind the bar.

"Yes, I do," he said.

"Could you tell me what any one of his books is about?"

"Look, Tamina," said Hugo, "nobody, but nobody, has ever read a thing he's written. At least, nobody has ever admitted it. He's a second-rate, third-rate, tenth-rate writer, and everyone knows it. Banaka is so much the victim of his own reputation that, believe me, he himself has nothing but scorn for people who read his books."

She gave up trying to get hold of his books, but she still made it her business to arrange a meeting with him. From time to time she lent her apartment, which was empty during the day, to a young married Japanese girl named Joujou for her trysts with a professor of philosophy who also happened to be married. The professor knew

Banaka, and Tamina made the lovers promise to bring him on a day Bibi was going to be there.

When Bibi found out, her reaction was, "Maybe Banaka's good-looking and your sex life's finally going to look up."

7

That's right. Tamina had not made love since her husband's death. Not on principle. Her fidelity beyond the grave actually seemed quite ludicrous to her, and she certainly never boasted about it. But whenever she imagined taking her clothes off in front of a man (and she imagined it often), she would see her husband's image. She knew she would see him when she made love. She knew she would see his face and his eyes watching her.

It was obviously incongruous, it was just plain silly, and she knew it. She did not believe in the life after death of her husband's soul, nor did she feel she would be offending his memory if she took a lover. There was nothing she could do about it.

It even occurred to her, strange as it may seem, that it would have been much easier if she had been unfaithful to her husband while he was alive. He had been happy, successful, energetic; she had felt much the weaker of the pair. It had always seemed to her she couldn't hurt him if she tried.

But now things were different. Now she would be hurting someone who couldn't fight back, who was as dependent on her as a child. She was the only person her dead husband had in the world, the only one!

That is why the minute she even thought about the possibility of physical love with someone else, the image of her husband appeared before her eyes, and with it a terrible longing for him, and with that longing a great desire to cry.

8

Banaka was ugly—not the type to awaken a woman's dormant sensuality. Tamina poured him some tea, and he thanked her very respectfully. Everyone was having a good time talking about nothing in particular when Banaka turned to Bibi with a smile and said, "I hear you want to write a book. What about?"

"Very simple," said Bibi. "A novel. About how I view the world."

"A novel?" asked Banaka in a voice clearly tinged with disapproval.

"Well, it doesn't have to be a novel," she said, unsure of herself.

"Think of what goes into a novel, after all," he said. "All those different characters. Do you really mean to say you know all there is to know about them? How they look, think, dress? What kinds of backgrounds they come from? Come on, admit it. You couldn't care less about all that."

"You're right," admitted Bibi. "I couldn't care less."

"You know," he went on, "novels are the fruit of the human illusion that we can understand our fellow man. But what do we know about each other?"

"Nothing," said Bibi.

"True," said Joujou.

The professor of philosophy acquiesced with a nod of the head.

"The only thing we *can* do," said Banaka, "is to give an account of our own selves. Anything else is an abuse of power. Anything else is a lie."

"True, how true!" Bibi agreed enthusiastically. "I don't want to write a novel. That wasn't what I meant. What I want to do is exactly what you've been saying: write about myself, an account of my life. And I won't hide the fact I live an absolutely ordinary, everyday life and nothing special has ever happened to me."

Banaka smiled. "What difference does that make? Look at me. Seen from the outside, even I don't seem so special."

"Right!" cried Bibi. "Right! Look at me *from the outside* and I don't seem special. *From the outside!* Because it's what goes on in me, *on the inside,* that's worth writing about, that people will want to read about."

Tamina kept filling their cups with tea. She was glad that the two men, who had descended from the Olympus of the mind to her apartment, were being nice to her friend.

The professor of philosophy sucked on his pipe, hiding behind the smoke as if ashamed of himself.

"Ever since Joyce," he said, "we have been aware of the fact that the greatest adventure in our lives is the absence of adventure. Odysseus fought at Troy, made his way home on a ship he himself piloted, had a mistress on every island—no, such is not the life we live. Homer's *Odyssey* now takes place within man. Man has internalized it. The islands, the sea, the sirens seducing us, and Ithaca calling us home—they have all been reduced to voices within us."

"Yes, yes! That's just the way I feel!" exclaimed Bibi. "That's why I wanted to ask you how to go about it, Mr. Banaka. Very often I have the feeling my whole body is bursting with a desire to express itself. To speak. To say something. Sometimes I think I'll go off my rocker or explode I get so keyed up. You must know the feeling, Mr. Banaka. I want to tell the story of my life, my emotions. They're really quite unique. Really they are. But sit me down in front of a piece of paper and I lose all my ideas. So I figure it must be a problem of technique. There must be something you know that I don't know. Your books are so terrific. . . . "

9

You are hereby excused from the lecture the two Socrateses gave the young woman on the art of writing. I want to talk about something else instead. Recently I took a taxi from one end of Paris to the other and got a garrulous driver. He couldn't sleep at night. He had a bad case of insomnia. It all began during the war. He was a sailor. His ship sank. He swam three days and three nights. Finally he was saved. For several months he had wavered between life and death, and though he eventually recovered, he had lost the ability to sleep.

"I live a third more life than you," he said, smiling.

"And what do you do with the extra third?" I asked.

"I write," he answered.

I asked him what he wrote.

His life story. The story of a man who swam three days at sea, held his own against death, lost the ability to sleep, but preserved the strength to live.

"Is it for your children? A family chronicle?"

"My kids don't give a damn." He laughed bitterly. "No, I'm making a book out of it. I think it could do a lot of people a lot of good."

My talk with the taxi driver gave me sudden insight into the nature of a writer's concerns. The reason we write books is that our kids don't give a damn. We turn to an anonymous world because our wife stops up her ears when we talk to her.

You may ask whether the taxi driver was merely a graphomaniac. Let us define our terms. A woman who writes her lover four letters a day is not a graphomaniac, she is simply a woman in love. But my friend who xeroxes his love letters so he can publish them someday—my friend is a graphomaniac. Graphomania is not a desire to write letters, diaries, or family chronicles (to write for oneself or one's immediate family); it is a desire to write books (to have a public of unknown readers). In this sense the taxi driver and Goethe share the same passion. What distinguishes Goethe from the taxi driver is the result of the passion, not the passion itself.

Graphomania (an obsession with writing books) takes on the proportions of a mass epidemic whenever a society develops to the point where it can provide three basic conditions:

1. a high enough degree of general well-being to enable people to devote their energies to useless activities;
2. an advanced state of social atomization and the resultant general feeling of the isolation of the individual;
3. a radical absence of significant social change in the internal development of the nation. (In this connection I find it symptomatic that in France, a country where nothing really happens, the percentage of writers is twenty-one times higher than in Israel. Bibi was absolutely right when she claimed never to have experienced anything *from the outside.* It is this absence of content, this void, that powers the motor driving her to write.)

But the effect transmits a kind of flashback to the cause. If general isolation causes graphomania, mass graphomania itself reinforces and aggravates the feeling of general isolation. The invention of printing originally promoted mutual understanding. In the era of graphomania the writing of books has the opposite effect: everyone surrounds himself with his own writings as with a wall of mirrors cutting off all voices from without.

10

"Tamina," said Hugo one day while she was having a chat with him in the empty café, "I know I don't stand a chance, so I promise not to make a play for you, but will you have dinner with me on Sunday?"

The package is with her mother-in-law in a provincial town, and Tamina needs to get it to her father in Prague so Bibi can pick it up. At first glance, nothing could be simpler, but it is going to take a lot of time and money to make her point to people who are old and headstrong. Long-distance calls are expensive, and Tamina earns barely enough to cover her room and board.

"All right," agreed Tamina, remembering that Hugo had a telephone.

He picked her up in his car and took her to a restaurant in the country.

Tamina's precarious position should have made it easy for him to play the conquering sovereign, but behind the poorly paid waitress he saw the mysterious foreigner and widow. He felt unsure of himself. Her kindness was like a suit of armor, a bulletproof vest. He wanted to attract her attention, captivate her, climb into her head!

He had tried to come up with something interesting for her. Before reaching their destination, they stopped off at a zoo on the grounds of a beautiful country château. They walked among monkeys and parrots against a backdrop of Gothic towers, completely alone except for a rustic-looking gardener sweeping fallen leaves from the broad paths. They passed a wolf, a monkey, a tiger, and came to a large fenced-in field where the ostriches were.

There were six of them. When they saw Tamina and Hugo, they ran right up to them. All bunched together near the wire fence, they stretched out their long necks, stared, and opened and closed their broad, flat beaks. They opened and closed them feverishly, at an incredible speed, as if taking part in a debate and trying to outtalk one another, but the beaks were hopelessly mute and did not make the slightest sound.

The ostriches were like messengers who had learned their vital message by heart, but whose vocal cords had been slit by the enemy, so that when they finally reached their goal, all they could do was move their mouths.

Tamina stared at them, bewitched, as they talked and talked, more and more urgently, and when she and Hugo left, they ran along the fence after them, still clicking their beaks and warning her about something, but what—she did not know.

11

_____

"It was like something out of a terrifying fairy tale," said Tamina, cutting her pâté. "They seemed to have something very important to tell me. But what? What did they mean to say?"

Hugo explained to her that they were young and that that was the way young ostriches behaved. The last time he'd been there, the same six ostriches had run up to the fence and opened their mute beaks.

Tamina was still on edge. "You know, I left something behind in Czechoslovakia. A package with some papers in it. If I had it sent, the police might confiscate it. Bibi is going to Prague this summer. She promised to bring it back with her. And now I'm afraid those ostriches were trying to give me a warning, tell me that something's gone wrong with the package."

Hugo knew Tamina was a widow and her husband had been forced to emigrate for political reasons. "Political documents?" he asked.

Tamina had long since realized that if she wanted to make her life comprehensible to people here she had to simplify it. It would have been impossibly complicated to explain why private letters and diaries might be confiscated and why she set such great store by them. So all she said was, "That's right. Political documents."

All of a sudden she was afraid Hugo would want to know something more about the documents, but no, nothing of the sort. Did anybody ever ask her anything? Sometimes people would _tell_ her what they thought about her country, but no one was interested in her own experiences.

"Does Bibi know they're political documents?" asked Hugo.

"No," said Tamina.

"That's good," said Hugo. "Don't tell her they have anything to do with politics. She'd get scared at the last minute and leave them behind. People are afraid of everything, Tamina. Make sure Bibi thinks it's something completely unimportant and prosaic. Your love letters, for example. That's it. Tell her the package is full of love letters!" Hugo got a good laugh out of that one. "Love letters! That's it! That's something well within her reach, something she can grasp."

So Hugo thinks love letters are unimportant and prosaic, thought Tamina. It never occurs to anybody that she might have loved someone and the love meant something to her.

"If for some reason her trip falls through," added Hugo, "you can always count on me. I'll go get them."

"Thank you," Tamina said sincerely.

"I'd go get them for you even if they threw me in jail."

"Don't be silly," protested Tamina. "Nothing like that could possibly happen." Then she tried to make him see that foreign tourists in Czechoslovakia run no risks whatsoever. The only risk was for Czechs themselves, and they weren't even aware of it anymore. Suddenly she was making a long and impassioned speech. She knew the country inside out, and I can tell you—everything she said was true.

An hour later she was holding the receiver of Hugo's telephone up to her ear. She had no better luck with her mother-in-law this time than the last. "You never gave me any key! You always hid everything from me! Why bring up all those bad memories again?"

12

If Tamina's memories mean so much to her, why doesn't she just go back to Czechoslovakia? Emigrants who left the country illegally after 1968 have been offered amnesty and urged to return.

What is Tamina afraid of? Certainly she is too insignificant to be in any kind of danger!

Yes, she could go back without fear. And yet she couldn't.

Everyone at home had betrayed her husband. If she went back, she would be afraid of betraying him too.

When they pushed him farther and farther down the ladder and finally fired him, nobody stood up for him. Not even his friends. Of course Tamina knew that deep down they were with him and it was only fear that kept them from speaking out. But the very fact that they were really with him made them all the more ashamed of their fear, and when they met him in the street, they pretended they didn't see him. Both husband and wife took to avoiding people just to be tactful, to keep them from feeling ashamed of themselves. Before long they felt like lepers. When they escaped from Czechoslovakia, his former colleagues signed a public declaration condemning and slandering her husband. Clearly they did it only so as not to lose their jobs the way he had lost his. But they did it, and the chasm they thus created between themselves and the two émigrés was a chasm Tamina wished never to cross again.

That first morning after their escape, when they woke up in a small hotel in the Alps and realized they were alone, cut off from the world which had been their entire life to that point, she felt liberated, relieved. They were in the mountains, mercifully alone. They were surrounded by unbelievable silence. For Tamina, it was an unexpected gift, and she suddenly saw that if her husband had to leave Czechoslovakia to escape persecution, she had to leave to find silence; silence for her husband and herself; silence for love.

When her husband died, she had an abrupt attack of homesickness, of nostalgia for the country in which a decade of their life together had left traces everywhere. In a spontaneous burst of sentimentality she sent death notices to about ten friends. She did not receive a single response.

A month later she spent all of the money they had scraped together on a trip to the seashore. She put on her bathing suit and swallowed a whole vial of tranquilizers. Then she swam far out to sea. She thought the pills would make her very tired and she would drown. But the cold water and her strong strokes (she had always been a first-rate swimmer) prevented her from falling asleep, and the pills were apparently weaker than she had expected.

She swam back to the beach, went up to her room, and slept for twenty hours straight. When she awoke, she felt peaceful and quiet. She resolved to live in silence and for silence.

13

Bibi's television set shed its silver-blue light on Tamina, Joujou, Bibi, and her husband, Dédé, a traveling salesman who had returned the day before from a four-day absence. The room smelled vaguely of urine. On the screen a large, round, ancient, bald head was being asked a provocative question by an invisible master of ceremonies: "There are some shocking erotic confessions in your memoirs."

It was a regular program on which a popular master of ceremonies chatted with a panel of authors whose books had been published the previous week.

The large bald head smiled complacently. "Shocking? No, not in the least. Exact mathematics, that's all. Figure it out for yourself. The first time I had sex I was fifteen"—the round old head looked proudly from one panel member to the next—"that's right, fifteen. I am now sixty-five. That means a sex life of fifty years' duration. Assuming I have made love on the average of twice a week —a very modest estimate—that means a hundred times a year or five thousand times so far. Let's go on. If an orgasm lasts five seconds, I have twenty-five thousand seconds of orgasm to my credit. Which comes to a total of six hours and fifty-six minutes. Not bad, eh?"

Everyone in the room nodded seriously except Tamina, who was picturing the bald-headed old codger undergoing a continual orgasm: twisting, writhing, he grabs at his heart, within a quarter of an hour his false teeth fall out, and five minutes later he falls down dead. She burst out laughing.

"What's so funny?" asked Bibi, annoyed. "That's a pretty good score, six hours fifty-six minutes of orgasm."

"For years I didn't know what an orgasm was," said Joujou. "But in the past few years I've been having them very regularly."

Everyone began talking about Joujou's orgasm. Soon another face, this one filled with indignation, appeared on the screen.

"What's he so angry about?" wondered Dédé.

"It's very important," the writer on the screen was saying, "very important. It's all here in my book."

"What's so important?" asked Bibi.

"That he spent his childhood in the village of Rourou," said Tamina.

The man who spent his childhood in the village of Rourou had a long nose weighing him down like an anchor. His head sank lower and lower, and once or twice it appeared ready to fall off the screen onto the floor. The nose-heavy face was extremely agitated. "It's all here in my book. My entire creative self is wound up in that simple village, and anyone who fails to understand that will misunderstand everything I've ever written. That's where I wrote my first few poems, after all. Yes, I consider it of prime importance."

"Some men," said Joujou, "never give me an orgasm."

"And don't forget," said the writer, looking more and more agitated, "that that's where I first rode a bicycle. That's right. It's all here in my book. It's a symbol. For me, the bicycle represents man's first step from the world of the patriarchs to the world of civilization. The first flirtation with civilization. A virgin flirting before her first kiss. Still a virgin, yet a party to sin."

"That's true," said Joujou. "Tanaka, a girl I work with, had her first orgasm on a bicycle when she was still a virgin."

They all began talking about Tanaka's orgasm, and Tamina asked Bibi whether she could make a telephone call.

14

In the adjoining room the urine smell was stronger. Bibi's daughter was sleeping there.

"I realize you're not on speaking terms with her," whispered Tamina, "but there's no other way for me to get it. You'll just have to go there and take it from her. If she can't find the key, have her break open the drawer. She has some things of mine. Letters. I have a right to get them back."

"Don't make me talk to her. Please, Tamina."

"Pull yourself together and do it for me, will you, Daddy? She's scared stiff of you. She wouldn't dare say no."

"You know what? If your friends come to Prague, let me give them a fur coat to take back to you. That's more important than a bunch of old letters."

"But I don't want a fur coat. All I want is that package!"

"Talk louder! I can't hear you!" said her father, but his daughter was whispering on purpose. She did not want Bibi to hear her speaking Czech and making a long-distance call that she, the owner of the telephone, would have to pay for, second by expensive second.

"It's the package I want, not your coat!"

"So you still don't have your priorities straight."

"Look, Daddy, this call is awfully expensive. Go see her. Please."

It was hard to keep the conversation going. Tamina's father kept asking her to repeat things, and obstinately refused to visit her mother-in-law.

"Why not call your brother?" he finally suggested. "Ask him to go see her. He can bring me the package."

"But he doesn't even know her!"

"That's just it." Her father laughed. "If he did, he'd never dream of going."

Tamina thought it over quickly. It wasn't such a bad idea to have her brother go see her mother-in-law. He was the energetic type, forceful. But Tamina didn't want to call him. Since she'd been abroad, they hadn't exchanged a single letter. He had a very well-paying job, and the only way he'd held on to it was by cutting off all relations with his émigrée sister.

"I can't call him, Daddy. Could you explain it to him? Could you? Please, Daddy!"

15

Daddy was small and sickly, and when he walked along the street with Tamina, he looked so proud he seemed to be presenting the entire world with a monument to the heroic night when he created her. He had never liked his son-in-law and constantly waged war against him. When he offered to send her a fur coat (which he must have inherited from some relative or other), he was moved by their old rivalry rather than any anxiety over his daughter's health. He wanted her to choose her father (the fur coat) over her husband (the package of letters).

Tamina was horrified at the idea that the fate of her package was in the hostile hands of her mother-in-law and her father. The more she thought about it, the more she had the feeling that her notebooks were being read by outsiders, and it seemed to her that the outsiders' eyes were like rain washing away inscriptions on a stone wall. Or light ruining a print by hitting photographic paper before it goes into the developer.

She realized that what gave her written memories value, meaning, was that they were meant for *her alone*. As soon as they lost that quality, the intimate chain binding her to them would be broken, and instead of reading them with her own eyes, she would be forced to read them from the point of view of an audience perusing an impersonal document. Then the woman who wrote them would lose her identity, and the striking similarity that would nonetheless remain between her and the author of the notes would be nothing but a parody, a mockery. No, she could never read her notes once they had been read by someone else.

That was why she had become so impatient and yearned to get her hands on those notebooks and letters as quickly as possible, before the image of the past they contained was destroyed.

16

One day Bibi came into the café and sat down at the bar. "Hi, Tamina," she said. "Give me a whiskey."

Usually Bibi ordered coffee, and every once in a while she would have some port. By ordering whiskey, she was making it clear that something was wrong.

"How's the writing coming along?" asked Tamina, pouring the drink into a glass.

"I'd be doing better if I was in a better mood," said Bibi, tossing it down and ordering a second one.

Some more customers came in, and Tamina asked them all what they wanted. Then she came back to the bar, gave her friend her second whiskey, and went away to take care of the new arrivals. When she was back again, Bibi told her, "I'm down on Dédé. When he gets back from his trips, he spends two whole days in bed. For two days he doesn't change out of his pajamas! Wouldn't that drive you out of your skull? And the worst part of it is he's always hot to fuck. He can't seem to get it through his head that fucking means nothing to me. Nothing. I've got to get away from that guy. Always thinking about his stupid vacation. Lying in bed in his pajamas with an atlas propped up in front of him. First he wanted to go to Prague. Well, he's over that now. Now he's picked up on some book about Ireland, and he's all fired up about Ireland."

"You mean you're going to Ireland on your vacation?" asked Tamina with a lump in her throat.

"Are *we* going to Ireland? *We* are going nowhere. I'm staying right here and writing. I won't budge. I don't need him. He's not the least interested in me. Here I am, writing away, and do you think he even asks what I'm writing about? I've finally realized we have nothing more to say to one another."

Tamina wanted to say, "So you're not going anymore," but the lump in her throat had grown bigger, and she could not speak.

Just then in came Joujou, the Japanese girl. Hopping up on the bar stool next to Bibi's, she said, "Could you do it in public?"

"What do you mean?" asked Bibi.

"Well, here in the café, on the floor, in front of everybody. Or during a movie in a movie theater."

"Oh, shut up!" Bibi yelled down to the foot of the bar stool, where her daughter was making a racket. Then she looked up and said, "Why not? There's nothing unnatural about it, is there? Why should I be ashamed about something natural?"

Tamina started debating with herself again about whether she should ask Bibi about her trip to Prague, but the question was superfluous. She knew very well, it was only too clear: Bibi would never go to Prague.

The owner's wife came out of the kitchen and smiled at Bibi. "How are you?" she asked, shaking her hand.

"What we need is a revolution," said Bibi. "Something's got to happen. Something's just got to happen around here."

That night Tamina had a dream about the ostriches. There they were, standing by the fence, jabbering away at her. She was terrified of them. She could not move. All she could do was watch their mute beaks, hypnotized. She kept her lips tightly pressed together. She had a golden ring in her mouth, and she feared for its safety.

17

Why do I picture her with a golden ring in her mouth?

There's nothing I can do about it. That's just the way I see her. And suddenly something I once read comes back to me: "a soft, clear, metallic tone, like a golden ring falling into a silver basin."

When Thomas Mann was very young, he wrote a naive, intriguing story about death. In the story death is beautiful, as it is beautiful to all those who dream of it very young, when it is still unreal and enchanting, like the bluish voice of far-off places.

A young man, mortally ill, gets off a train at an unknown station. He walks into the town without knowing its name and takes rooms in the house of an old woman whose forehead is covered with eczema. No, I do not wish to go into what took place in the rented rooms. I only wish to recall a single minor occurrence: walking around the front room, the ill young man had the feeling that "in between the sounds made by his footsteps he heard another sound in the rooms on either side—a soft, clear, metallic tone—but perhaps it was only an illusion. Like a golden ring falling into a silver basin, he thought. . . ."

That minor acoustic event is never developed or explained in the story. From the standpoint of the action alone it could have been omitted without any loss. The sound simply happened; all by itself; just like that.

The reason I think Thomas Mann sounded that "soft, clear, metallic tone" was to create silence, the silence he needed to make the beauty audible (because the death he was speaking of was *beauty-death*), and if beauty is to be perceptible, it needs a certain minimal degree of silence (a perfect criterion of which happens to be the sound of a golden ring falling into a silver basin).

(Yes, I know. You haven't the slightest idea what I'm talking about. Beauty has long since disappeared. It has slipped beneath the surface of the noise—the noise of words, the noise of cars, the noise of music, the noise of signs—we live in constantly. It has sunk as deep as Atlantis. The only thing left of it is the word, whose meaning loses clarity from year to year.)

The first time Tamina heard that silence (as precious as the splinter of a marble statue from sunken Atlantis) was when she woke up after escaping from Czechoslovakia in that Alpine hotel deep in the woods. The second time she heard it was when she was swimming through the ocean, her stomach full of tranquilizers that instead of death brought her unexpected peace. She means to hold on to that silence with her body, within her body. That is why I see her in her dream standing up against a wire fence with a golden ring in her tightly closed mouth.

She is standing across from six long necks with tiny heads and flat beaks that open and close noiselessly. She does not understand them. She does not know whether they are threatening, warning, appealing, or begging. And because she does not know, she feels immense anxiety. She is afraid something will happen to the golden ring (that tuning fork of silence), and she keeps it tightly closed away in her mouth.

Tamina will never know what they came to tell her. But I do. They did not come to warn or scold or threaten her. They are not at all concerned with her. They came, each one of them, to tell her about themselves. About how they ate, how they slept, how they ran up to the fence, and what they saw on the other side. About how they had spent their important childhood in the important village of Rourou. About how their important orgasm had lasted six hours. About how they saw a woman on the other side of the fence and she was wearing a knitted shawl over her head. About how they swam, fell ill, and then recovered. About how they had been young, ridden bicycles, and eaten a sack of grass that day. There they are, standing face to face with Tamina, telling her their stories, all at the same time, belligerently, pressingly, aggressively, because there is nothing more important than what they want to tell her.

18

Several days later Banaka turned up at the café dead drunk. He sat on a bar stool, fell off twice, climbed back up twice, ordered a Calvados, and then put his head down on the counter. Tamina noticed he was crying.

"What's the matter, Mr. Banaka?" she asked him.

Banaka looked up at her tearfully and pointed to his chest. "I'm nothing, do you understand? Nothing. I don't exist!"

Then he went to the men's room and from there straight outside without paying.

When Tamina told Hugo about it, he showed her a page of newsprint with several book reviews including a short note on Banaka's works—four lines of ridicule.

The episode of Banaka pointing to his chest and crying out of existential anguish reminds me of a line from Goethe's *West-East Divan:* "Is one man alive when others are alive?" Deep within Goethe's query lies the secret of the writer's creed. By writing books, the individual becomes a universe (we speak of the universe of Balzac, the universe of Chekhov, the universe of Kafka, do we not?). And since the principal quality of a universe is its uniqueness, the existence of another universe constitutes a threat to its very essence.

Two shoemakers can live together in perfect harmony (provided their shops are not on the same block). But once they start writing books on the lot of the shoemaker, they will begin to get in each other's way; they will start to wonder, Is one shoemaker alive when others are alive?

Tamina feels that the eyes of a single outsider are enough to destroy the worth of her personal diaries, while Goethe thinks that if a single individual *fails* to set eyes on his lines, that individual calls his—Goethe's—entire existence into question. The difference between Tamina and Goethe is the difference between human being and writer.

A person who writes books is either all (a single universe for himself and everyone else) or nothing. And since *all* will never be given to anyone, every one of us who writes books is *nothing*. Ignored, jealous, deeply wounded, we wish the death of our fellow man. In that respect we are all alike: Banaka, Bibi, Goethe, and I.

The proliferation of mass graphomania among politicians, cab drivers, women on the delivery table, mistresses, murderers, criminals, prostitutes, police chiefs, doctors, and patients proves to me that every individual without exception bears a potential writer within himself and that all mankind has every right to rush out into the streets with a cry of "We are all writers!"

The reason is that everyone has trouble accepting the fact he will disappear unheard of and unnoticed in an indifferent universe, and everyone wants to make himself into a universe of words before it's too late.

Once the writer in every individual comes to life (and that time is not far off), we are in for an age of universal deafness and lack of understanding.

19

Now Hugo was her only hope. When he invited her to dinner again, she was very happy to accept.

Sitting across the table from her, Hugo can think of one thing only: Tamina continues to escape him. He feels unsure of himself with her and cannot bring himself to make a frontal attack. And the more he suffers from the fear of trying for something modest and well defined, the more he wants to conquer the world, the infinity of the undefined, the undefinedness of the infinite. He takes a magazine out of his pocket, opens it, and hands it to her. The page he has opened to consists of a long article signed with his name.

He goes off on a long tirade about the magazine: true, it doesn't have a very large readership outside the town where they live, but it's a good theoretical journal, and the people who put it together have the courage of their convictions and will go far. Hugo talks on and on, his words straining to be a metaphor for erotic aggressivity, a show of strength. They have all the enchanting verve of the abstract rushing in to replace the futility of the concrete.

As Tamina watches Hugo, she begins to remodel his face. What was first a spiritual exercise has now become no more than a habit. She cannot look at a man any other way. It takes a good deal of effort, she needs to mobilize all her imagination, but all at once Hugo's brown eyes really do turn blue. Tamina keeps her eyes fixed on his. To keep the blue from dissipating, she has to concentrate all the force of her stare on it.

Hugo finds the stare unnerving, so he steps up his patter. His eyes are a beautiful blue, and his hairline is receding gradually at the temples until the only hair he has left in front is a narrow triangle pointing down.

"I've always directed my criticism at our Western world, but the injustice here in our midst tends to make us wrongly indulgent with respect to other countries. Thanks to you, yes, thanks to you, Tamina, I have come to realize that the problem of power is the same everywhere, in your country and ours, East and West. We must be careful not to replace one type of power with another; we must reject the very *principle* of power and reject it everywhere."

The sour smell from Hugo's mouth as he leaned across the table to her threw off her concentration. Once again his forehead was overgrown with thick wavy hair. But he went on telling her that she was the reason he understood everything.

"What do you mean?" she interrupted him. "We've never even talked about it."

At that point Hugo had only one blue eye left, and even it was slowly turning brown.

"You didn't have to tell me anything. All I had to do was think about you."

The waiter leaned down to serve them the first course.

"I'll read it when I get home," said Tamina, stuffing the

magazine into her bag. "Bibi isn't going to Prague," she added.

"I knew she wouldn't," said Hugo. "But don't worry, Tamina. Remember my promise. *I'll* go for you."

20

—————————————————————————————

"I've got some good news for you: I had a talk with your brother, and he's going to your mother-in-law's this Saturday."

"Really? Did you explain everything to him? Did you tell him that if she can't find the key he should force it open?"

By the time Tamina put down the receiver, she felt drunk.

"Good news?" asked Hugo.

"Yes," she said, nodding.

She could still hear her father's voice in her ears, cheerful and energetic. She had maligned him, she told herself.

Hugo got up and went over to the bar. He took out two small glasses and poured some whiskey. "You can call Prague from my place whenever you like, Tamina. All I can say is what I've said before. I feel good with you, even though I know you'll never sleep with me."

He had forced himself to say "I know you'll never sleep with me" just to prove to himself he could stand face to face with this inaccessible woman and say certain things (though carefully couched in the negative), and he felt almost reckless.

Tamina stood up and walked over to Hugo to take the glass from his hand. She was thinking about her brother: even though they were no longer on speaking terms, they were still friends, still willing to help each other.

"Here's hoping everything works out!" said Hugo, emptying his glass.

Tamina drank down her whiskey too, and put her glass on the table. She was just about to go back to her chair when Hugo put his arms around her.

She did nothing to stop him, she only turned away her head.

Her mouth twisted, her forehead wrinkled.

He had taken her in his arms without knowing quite how it happened. At first, he was afraid of his own audacity, and if Tamina had pushed him away, he would have timidly pulled back and practically apologized to her. But Tamina did not push him away, and her contorted face, her head straining away from him, aroused him greatly. The few women he had known up to then never had any particularly strong reaction to his caresses. If they made up their minds to make love with him, they took off their clothes and waited calmly, almost indifferently, to see what he would do with them. By contorting her face, Tamina had given their embrace a meaning he had never dreamed of before. He began hugging her madly and trying to tear her clothes off.

But why did Tamina refuse to defend herself?

She had been fearing the day this would happen for three years now. For three years she had lived under its hypnotic stare. And now it had come, exactly the way she had imagined it. That was why she refused to defend herself. She accepted it the way one accepts the inevitable.

All she could do was turn away her head. But that did no good. Her husband's image followed her around the room as she turned her face. It was a giant image of a grotesquely giant husband, a husband much larger than life, yet just what she had imagined for three years.

When she was finally naked, Hugo, excited by what he took to be her excitement, was stupefied to discover that Tamina's genitals were dry.

21

She had once undergone minor surgery without anesthesia and forced herself to conjugate English irregular verbs all the way through it. Now she tried the same technique, concentrating all her attention on the notebooks, on how they would soon be safe and sound with her father, and this nice guy Hugo would bring them back to her.

Nice guy Hugo had been going at it fast and furious for a while when she felt him raise himself up on his forearms and start to thrash his hips in all directions. She realized he was dissatisfied with her response, she was not excited enough for him, he was trying to penetrate her from different angles and find that mysterious point of sensitivity she was holding back from him somewhere deep within her.

She had no desire to watch his laborious efforts, and turned her head away again. She tried to discipline her thoughts and bring them back to her notebooks. She forced herself to go over the order of their vacations in the incomplete version she had managed to reconstruct: the first one at a small lake in Bohemia, next Yugoslavia, then a small lake in Bohemia again, a spa—but the order still wasn't clear. In 1964 they'd gone to the Tatras and the year after that to Bulgaria, but after that things got hazy. In 1968 they'd spent their entire vacation in Prague, the following year they'd gone to a spa, and then they emigrated and had their last vacation in Italy.

Hugo withdrew from her and tried to turn her body over. She realized he wanted her to kneel on all fours. Suddenly she remembered that Hugo was younger than she was, and she was ashamed. But she tried to deaden all her feelings and submit to him with total indifference. Then she felt the rough thrusts of his body on her backside. She realized he was trying to dazzle her with his strength and endurance, fighting a decisive battle, putting himself to the test, proving he could subdue her and was worthy of her.

She did not know that Hugo could not see her. A glance at Tamina's backside (at the open eye of her handsome, mature backside, an eye staring out pitilessly at him) had so aroused him that he quickly shut his eyes, slowed down his thrusts, and started breathing deeply. Now he too was doing his best to train his mind on something else (the only thing the two had in common) and sustain the act of love a bit longer.

In the midst of all this Tamina saw a huge face of her husband on Hugo's white wall and quickly shut her eyes. Once again she began going through the vacations like irregular verbs: first the vacation at the lake, then Yugoslavia, the lake, and the spa—or was it the spa, Yugoslavia, and the lake?—then the Tatras, then Bulgaria, then things got hazy, then Prague, the spa, and finally Italy.

Hugo's heavy breathing wrenched her away from her memories. She opened her eyes and saw her husband's face on the white wall.

At the same moment, Hugo opened his eyes, and seeing the eye of Tamina's backside, he felt a bolt of ecstasy run through him.

22

When Tamina's brother went to see her mother-in-law, he did not have to force the drawer. It was unlocked and had all eleven notebooks in it. But they were loose, not tied up in a package. The letters were loose too, a shapeless pile of papers. Tamina's brother stuffed both letters and notebooks into a small suitcase and delivered it to their father.

Tamina asked her father over the phone to wrap everything up and seal it carefully, and—most important—she requested that neither he nor her brother read a word.

He assured her, almost offended, that he would never dream of following her mother-in-law's example by reading something that was none of his business. But I know (and so does Tamina) that there are certain sights no one can resist—automobile accidents, for instance, and other people's love letters.

So Tamina's intimate writings were finally in safekeeping with her father. But did they still have value for her? Hadn't she said a hundred times over that the eyes of outsiders were like the rain that washes away inscriptions?

Well, she was wrong. She longed to see them more than ever, they meant even more to her. They had been ravaged and defiled, she had been ravaged and defiled; she and her memories were sisters in a common fate. She loved them even more.

But she still felt humiliated.

Once very long ago—when she was about seven—an uncle of hers happened to come into her room when she was naked. She was terribly ashamed. Then her shame turned to defiance. She made a solemn, childish vow never to set eyes on him again in her whole life. No matter what anyone did—scold her, yell at her, laugh at her —she refused to look at him when he came on his frequent visits.

Now here she was in a similar situation. She was grateful to her father and her brother, but she never wanted to see them again. She was clearer about it than ever before: she would never go back to them.

23

Hugo's unexpected sexual success brought with it an equally unexpected letdown. Even though he could now make love to her whenever he liked (she could hardly refuse after giving in the first time), he felt he had failed to make her really his, to dazzle her. How could a naked body under his body be so indifferent, so out of reach, so distant, so foreign? And here he'd wanted to make her a part of his inner world, that grandiose universe made up of his blood and thoughts!

"I want to write a book, Tamina," he said, sitting across from her in a restaurant. "A book about love. That's right, about you and me, about the two of us, our most intimate feelings, in diary form, the diary of our two bodies. That's right, I want to sweep away all taboos and give a no-holds-barred account of what I am and what I think. It will be a political book too, a political story about love and a love story about politics. . . ."

Tamina just sits there watching him. Suddenly he cannot bear the look on her face anymore and loses the thread of what he is saying. He'd wanted to whisk her off to the universe of his blood and thoughts, and there she sat, completely and utterly enclosed in her own world. His words, falling on deaf ears, become more cumbersome, less fluent: " . . . a love story about politics, that's right, because what we need is to create a world on a human scale, our scale, the scale of our bodies, your body, Tamina, my body, that's right, so man can find a new way of kissing, a new way of loving. . . ."

The words become more and more cumbersome, they are like hunks of tough, gristly meat. Hugo gives up. Tamina is beautiful, and he hates her. He feels she is taking unfair advantage of him, using her émigrée widow past, looking down on everyone from a skyscraper of false pride. And Hugo thinks enviously of his own tower, the one he is trying to put up across the way from her skyscraper, the one she refuses to notice—a tower made of one published article and the book he has in mind about their love.

"When are you going to Prague?" Tamina asks him.

Hugo realizes she has never loved him and the only reason she is with him is that she needs someone to go to Prague. He is overcome by an irresistible desire to get back at her. "I thought you'd have figured it out for yourself by now. You've read my article, haven't you?"

"Yes, I have," she answers.

He does not believe her. And even if she has read it, it hasn't made any impression on her. Hugo realizes that the one big feeling he can muster is fidelity to his unrecognized, forsaken tower (the tower of the published article and the book he has in mind about his love for Tamina), and he is willing to go to war for that tower and force Tamina to acknowledge its presence and marvel at its elevation.

"Well, then you know it deals with the problem of power. I analyze the machinery of power. I refer to what's going on right now in your country. And I don't mince words."

"Don't tell me you really think they know about your article in Prague!"

Hugo is wounded by her irony. "You've been living abroad a long time now. You've forgotten how far your police will go. That article has been very well received. I've gotten a lot of letters about it. Your police know all about me. I'm positive they do."

Tamina makes no reply; she just sits there looking more and more beautiful. Good God, he'd go to Prague a hundred times and back if only she'd give his universe the slightest bit of recognition, the universe he had hoped to whisk her off to, the universe of his blood and thoughts! And suddenly he changes his tone. "Tamina," he says sadly, "I know you're angry because I can't go to Prague. At first I figured I could hold off for a while with the article, but then I realized I had no right to keep it to myself, understand?"

"No," says Tamina.

Hugo knows that everything he is saying is ridiculous and can only put him in a position he has absolutely no desire to be in, but he can't retreat now, and it is driving him to despair. His face breaks out in red blotches, and his voice cracks. "You don't understand? I don't want things to end up here the way they did there! If everybody holds off for a while, we'll be slaves before we know it!"

At that moment Tamina was overcome by a wave of revulsion. She jumped up from her chair and ran into the ladies' room, her stomach rising to her throat. She kneeled down in front of the toilet bowl and vomited, and her body writhed and shook as if she were sobbing. Before her eyes was the image of that boy's balls, prick, and pubic hair. She could smell the sour breath from his mouth, feel the pressure of his thighs on her backside. It occurred to her that she was no longer able to remember what her husband's genitals looked like—in other words, the memory of revulsion was stronger than the memory of tenderness (God yes, the memory of revulsion is stronger than the memory of tenderness!) —and that soon all she'd have left in her miserable head was this boy with bad breath. And she vomited, writhed and shook, and vomited.

When she came out of the ladies' room, her mouth (still full of that sour smell) was sealed shut.

He was embarrassed. He wanted to walk her home, but she would not say a word, her lips were sealed (as in the dream, when she had a golden ring in her mouth).

When he spoke to her, all she did was walk faster, and soon he had nothing left to say and just walked alongside her awhile in silence. Finally he stopped. She walked straight ahead, without looking around.

She went on serving coffee and never made another call to Czechoslovakia.

PART FIVE
Litost

Who Is Kristyna?

Kristyna is a woman in her thirties. She has a child, a butcher husband with whom she lives in perfect harmony, and an on-again-off-again affair with the local mechanic, who makes love to her once in a long while after hours in the rather cramped conditions of the garage. Small-town life does not particularly lend itself to extramarital love, or, rather, it requires inordinate ingenuity and courage, qualities with which Kristyna is not abundantly endowed.

Which is why she was so utterly confused by her meetings with the student. He had come to town to spend the summer vacation with his mother, and after staring at her twice behind the counter in the butcher's shop, he had gone up and spoken to her at the local swimming place, and was so charmingly shy that Kristyna, accustomed as she was to her butcher and her mechanic, could not resist. The only time she had dared touch another man since her marriage (a good ten years by then) was in the security of a locked garage amid dismantled cars and balding tires, and suddenly she made up her mind to accept a rendezvous out in the open and expose herself to the danger of prying eyes. Even though the places they chose for their walks were quite remote and the probability of their being recognized practically nonexistent, Kristyna's heart would pound and she would be consumed with titillating fear. The more bravely she faced the danger, the more reserved she was with the student. He did not get very far with her—a few fast hugs and tender kisses. She would wriggle out of his arms and press her legs together whenever he ran his hand along her body.

It was not that she did not want him; it was just that she had fallen in love with his gentle shyness and wanted to preserve it for herself. No man had ever expounded his philosophy of life or dropped names of great poets and thinkers to her. The student, poor boy, had nothing else to talk about. The range of his seductive patter was so limited that he was unable to adjust it to

women of different social levels. Besides, he did not feel particularly handicapped in this case, because quotations from the
philosophers would make a much stronger impression on a simple butcher's wife than on a fellow student. What he failed to
see was that while a well-chosen quote might charm her soul, it
also placed a barrier between him and her body. She had a vague
fear that by surrendering her body to the student, she would
drag their relationship down to the level of her relationship with
the butcher or mechanic and she would never hear another word
about Schopenhauer.

With the student she felt a modesty she had never
known before; with the butcher and the mechanic she could say
whatever she pleased and even laugh at it. For instance, that
they had to be very careful about making love because the doctor who'd delivered her child had told her not to have any more
—it could be dangerous to her health or even fatal. All this happened a long time ago, when abortions were strictly forbidden
and women had no access to birth control. The butcher and the
mechanic had no trouble understanding her fears, and before she
allowed them to enter her, she would make a playful show of
checking to see they had taken the necessary precautions. But
whenever she imagined going through it with her angel, who had
come down from a cloud where he hobnobbed with Schopenhauer, she froze completely. I therefore conclude that her reserve
had two motivations: to keep the student as long as possible in
the enchanting realm of tenderness and timidity, and to avoid
repelling him as long as possible with the mundane directions
and details that her notion of physical love required.

All his fine words notwithstanding, the student was adamant.
No matter how tightly she squeezed her thighs together, he kept a
firm grip on her backside, a grip implying that a man who quotes
Schopenhauer does not necessarily mean to give up a body he finds
desirable.

When his vacation came to an end, the lovers realized they
would find it hard not to see each other for a whole year. The only
possibility was for Kristyna to think up an excuse to go to Prague.

They both knew what her visit would mean. The student lived in a tiny attic room, and she would have no choice but to spend the night.

What Is *Litost*?

Litost is a Czech word with no exact translation into any other language. It designates a feeling as infinite as an open accordion, a feeling that is the synthesis of many others: grief, sympathy, remorse, and an indefinable longing. The first syllable, which is long and stressed, sounds like the wail of an abandoned dog.

Under certain circumstances, however, it can have a very narrow meaning, a meaning as definite, precise, and sharp as a well-honed cutting edge. I have never found an equivalent in other languages for this sense of the word either, though I do not see how anyone can understand the human soul without it.

Let me give an example. One day the student went swimming with his girlfriend. She was a top-notch athlete; he could barely keep afloat. He had trouble holding his breath underwater, and was forced to thrash his way forward, jerking his head back and forth above the surface. The girl was crazy about him and tactfully kept to his speed. But as their swim was coming to an end, she felt the need to give her sporting instincts free rein, and sprinted to the other shore. The student tried to pick up his tempo too, but swallowed many mouthfuls of water. He felt humiliated, exposed for the weakling he was; he felt the resentment, the special sorrow which can only be called *litost*. He recalled his sickly childhood—no physical exercise, no friends, nothing but Mama's ever-watchful eye—and sank into utter, all-encompassing despair. On their way back to the city they took a shortcut through the fields. He did not say a word. He was wounded, crestfallen; he felt an irresistible desire to beat her. "What's wrong with you?" she asked him, and he went into a tirade about how the undertow on the other side of the river was very dangerous and he had told her not to swim over there and she could have drowned—then he slapped her face. The girl burst out crying, and when he saw the tears running down her face, he took pity on her and put his arms around her, and his *litost* melted into thin air.

Or take an instance from the student's childhood: the violin lessons that were forced on him. He was not particularly gifted, and his teacher would stop him and point out his mistakes in a cold, unbearable voice. It humiliated him, he felt like crying. But instead of trying to play in tune and make fewer mistakes, he would make mistakes on purpose. As the teacher's voice became more and more unbearable, enraged, he would sink deeper and deeper into his bitterness, his *litost.*

Well then, what is *litost?*

Litost is a state of torment caused by a sudden insight into one's own miserable self.

One of the standard remedies for personal misery is love. The recipient of an absolute love cannot be miserable. All his faults are redeemed by love's magic eyes, which make even uncoordinated thrashing and a head jerking back and forth above the water look charming.

The absolute quality of love is actually a desire for absolute identification. We want the woman we love to swim as slowly as we do; we want her to have no past of her own to look back on happily. But as soon as the illusion of absolute identity falls apart (the girl looks back happily on her past or picks up speed), love turns into a permanent source of that great torment we call *litost.*

Anyone with broad experience in the general imperfectability of mankind is fairly well protected against its excesses. He accepts insights into his own miserable self as ordinary and uninteresting. *Litost,* in other words, is characteristic of immaturity. It is one of the ornaments of youth.

Litost works like a two-stroke motor. First comes a feeling of torment, then the desire for revenge. The goal of revenge is to make one's partner look as miserable as oneself. The man can't swim, but the woman cries when slapped. It makes them feel equal and keeps their love alive.

Since revenge can never reveal its true motivation (the student can't tell the girl he slapped her because she swam too fast), it must plead false ones. In other words, *litost* is unthinkable without a kind of passionate hypocrisy: the young man proclaims he was frantic at the thought of his girl drowning, and the child plays agonizingly off-key, feigning hopeless ineptitude.

I was originally going to call this chapter *Who Is the Student?* But even if it now deals with the emotion I call *litost,* it still is very much about the student as well. In fact, the student represents *litost* incarnate. No wonder the girl he was in love with finally left him. There is nothing particularly pleasant about having your face slapped for knowing how to swim.

The butcher's wife from his hometown entered his life in the form of a giant-sized bandage ready-made for his wounds. She admired him, worshiped him. When he talked to her about Schopenhauer, she never tried to make her own independent personality felt by raising objections (as did the girlfriend of inglorious memory); and when she looked at him, he was so moved by her emotion he seemed to see tears welling up in her eyes. We must also bear in mind that he had not made love since breaking up with his girlfriend.

Who Is Voltaire?

Voltaire is a lecturer at the university, a witty and aggressive young man whose eyes glare maliciously into the faces of his adversaries—reason enough for his nickname.

He liked the student, which was no mean distinction; he was very particular about the company he kept. One day, after a seminar, he went up to the student and asked if he was free the following evening. Too bad, the very time Kristyna was due to arrive. It took the student all the courage he could muster to tell Voltaire he was busy. But Voltaire wouldn't hear of it. "You can put it off, can't you?

You won't regret it." Apparently the best poets in the country were getting together at the Writers' Club, and Voltaire, who would be there too, wanted the student to meet them.

And yes, the great poet whom Voltaire was writing a monograph on, the one he was always going to visit—he would be there too. He was ill and walked on crutches, so he was hardly ever seen in society, and the chance to meet him was all the more valuable.

The student knew the work of all the poets taking part, and had memorized entire pages by the great poet. Nothing would have pleased him more than to spend an evening in their company. But then he remembered he hadn't slept with a woman for months, and told Voltaire again he would not be able to make it.

Voltaire refused to accept the idea that anything could be more important than meeting great men. A woman? Couldn't it be postponed? His glasses were alive with sparks of irony. But all the student could see was the butcher's wife slipping out of his hands that whole month, and hard as it was to do, he shook his head. Kristyna meant as much to him at that moment as all his country's poetry.

The Compromise

She arrived in the morning. During the day she did the errand that served as her alibi. The student had arranged to meet her in the evening at a restaurant he had selected himself. When he entered, he was shocked to find the main room overflowing with drunks. The small-town fairy princess of his vacation was sitting in the corner near the rest rooms at a table meant for dirty dishes. She was dressed in her awkward Sunday best, the stereotype of a provincial lady visiting the capital after a long absence and looking forward to its joys. She was wearing a hat, some large beads, and black high-heeled pumps.

The student felt his cheeks burning—with disappointment, not excitement. Against the backdrop of a small town populated by butchers, mechanics, and pensioners, Kristyna had stood out as she never could in the Prague of pretty students and hairdressers. With her laughable beads and discreet gold tooth (in the upper left corner of her mouth) she seemed to personify the antithesis of the youthful, jeans-clad beauty that had been rejecting him so cruelly for the past few months. He wended his way insecurely over to her table, taking his exasperation, his *litost,* along with him.

If the student was disappointed, so was Kristyna. The restaurant the student had invited her to had a nice name—the King Wenceslaus—and Kristyna, a stranger to Prague, assumed it would be a high-class establishment where he would wine and dine her, their first stop on a whirlwind tour of Prague by night. When she saw that the King Wenceslaus was on the same level as the place the mechanic went for beer and that she would have to wait for the student in the corner near the rest rooms, what she felt instead of the delicate ineffable emotion I have called *litost* was good old everyday anger. By which I mean that instead of feeling miserable and humiliated, she felt that her student did not know how to behave. She lost no time in telling him so either. Her face was livid, and she used the same language with him she used with the butcher.

There they stood, face to face, she loud and voluble in her abuse, he weak in his defense. His antipathy toward her rose sharply. All he wanted was to take her back to his room, hide her from everybody's sight, and test whether the intimacy of their hideaway would bring back the lost magic. She refused. It wasn't every day she got to Prague. She wanted to see things, go places, have a good time. Those black heels and colored beads were adamant about their rights.

"This is usually a great place," said the student. "All the best people come here." He wanted to make the butcher's wife feel she couldn't begin to understand what counted in Prague and what didn't. "Unfortunately, there isn't any room today, so I'll have to take you somewhere else." But every other place turned out to be just as crowded, it took a long time to go from one to the next, and Kristyna looked unbearably funny with her hat and beads and shiny gold tooth. As they walked through streets overflowing with young women, the student realized he would never forgive himself for missing an evening with the greats of his country to spend an evening with Kristyna. On the other hand, he did not wish to make an enemy of her; as I have pointed out, he had not made love in a long time. The only way he could resolve the dilemma was to come up with a brilliant compromise.

Finally they found a free table at an out-of-the-way café. The student ordered two apéritifs and looked mournfully into Kristyna's eyes. Life here in Prague was full of unexpected events, he told her. Yesterday, for example, he had had a phone call from the country's most famous poet.

Kristyna stiffened when he said the poet's name. She had memorized his poetry in school, after all, and people we memorize in school have something unreal, incorporeal, about them. Even while they are alive, they belong to the exalted gallery of the immortals. Kristyna could not believe that the student actually knew him personally.

Of course he did, declared the student. He was even writing his thesis on him, a monograph that had a good chance of being published. The only reason he hadn't told her about it before was that he didn't want her to think he was showing off, but now he had to tell her because the poet had unexpectedly put an obstacle in their path. There was a private get-together of poets at the Writers' Club that evening, and only a very few critics and insiders had been invited. It was an extremely important meeting. There was sure to be a debate, and would the sparks fly! But obviously he wasn't planning to attend. He'd been so looking forward to his meeting with her!

In my sweet, strange country, poets still exercise a charm over the hearts of women, and Kristyna now admired the student more than ever. She also felt a maternal desire to give him advice and defend his interests. With laudable and unanticipated naiveté she announced it would be a shame for the student to miss the meeting the great poet was going to attend.

The student said he had tried to persuade them to let her come along with him because he knew she would enjoy seeing the great poet and his friends, but unfortunately it wasn't possible. Even the great poet wasn't bringing his wife. It was strictly for specialists. At first the student hadn't really thought of going, but now he realized Kristyna might be right. Yes, it was actually a good idea. Supposing he did drop by for an hour or so. She could wait for him at his apartment, and when he got back, there would be just the two of them.

Leaving behind the lure of the theaters and nightclubs, Kristyna followed the student up to his attic apartment. For a while she felt the same disappointment as when she had stepped into the King Wenceslaus. It hardly deserved to be called an apartment; it didn't even have an entrance hall. It was more like a cubbyhole with a couch and desk. But she had lost confidence in her own judgment; she had entered a world with a mysterious scale of values she could not fathom. So she quickly made her peace with the uncomfortable, dirty room, and mobilized all her feminine talent to make herself at home in it. The student asked her to take her hat off. He kissed her, sat her down on the couch, and showed her his modest library so she would have something to read while he was away.

All of a sudden she had an idea. "You don't happen to have one of his books, do you?" She meant the great poet.

Yes, the student had one of his books.

"Well, maybe you could give it to me," she went on very hesitantly, "and ask him to write me a dedication."

The student's face lit up. The great poet's dedication would make up for the theater and nightclubs. She had given him a bad conscience, and he was willing to do anything for her. Just as he expected, her magic had returned in the privacy of the attic. The girls strolling through the streets had vanished, and the charm of her modesty quietly filled the room. His disappointment melted slowly away, and he left for the club calm and content at the thought of the coming evening's exciting double program.

The Poets

The student waited for Voltaire in front of the Writers'
Club, and the two of them went upstairs together. As soon as they
passed through the cloakroom into the vestibule, they heard an
exuberant din. Voltaire opened the door to the dining room, and
before the student's eyes was his country's poetry sitting around a
large table.

I watch them from a distance of two thousand kilometers.
It is now the autumn of 1977. For eight years my country has been
drowsing in the sweet, strong embrace of the Russian empire, Voltaire has been thrown out of the university, and my books are banned
from all public libraries, locked away in the cellars of the state. I held
out a few years and then got into my car and drove as far west as
I could, to the Breton town of Rennes, where the very first day I
found an apartment on the top floor of the tallest high-rise. When
the sun woke me the next morning, I realized that its large picture
windows faced east, toward Prague.

Now I watch them from my tower, but the distance is too
great. Fortunately the tear in my eye magnifies like the lens of a
telescope and brings their faces closer. Now I can make out the great
poet, the undisputed center of attention. Although he is certainly
more than seventy, his face is still handsome, his eyes wise and lively.
His crutches are leaning up against the table next to him.

I see them against the night lights of Prague the way it was
fifteen years ago, before their books had been locked away in the
cellars of the state, when they could all have a happy, raucous time
together around a large table laden with bottles. I like them all and
wouldn't feel right picking random names for them from the telephone book. If I do have to hide their faces behind the masks of
assumed names, I might as well make them a gift of it, a decoration,
an honor.

If the students call the lecturer Voltaire, what is to stop

me from calling the great and greatly revered poet Goethe?

And the poet across from him Lermontov.

And the one with the dreamy black eyes Petrarch.

But along with Verlaine, Yesenin, and several others not particularly worth mentioning, there is a man who must be there by mistake. It is absolutely plain (I can see it from two thousand kilometers) that the muse of poetry has never yet bestowed her favors on him, that he does not even care for verse. His name is Boccaccio.

Voltaire took two chairs from the wall, pushed them over to the bottle-laden table, and introduced the student to the poets. All the poets nodded civilly in his direction, all but Petrarch, who was so engrossed in an argument with Boccaccio that he did not even notice him. "Women always get the better of us," he said, summing up. "I could go on about it for weeks."

"That's a bit much," said Goethe. "How about ten minutes' worth?"

Petrarch's Story

"The most unbelievable thing happened to me a week ago. My wife had just taken a bath. She was wearing a red negligee and had let down her long golden hair. She looked beautiful. At ten past nine there was a ring at the door. I opened it and saw a girl pressing up against the wall. I recognized her right away. Once a week I go to a girls' school that has a poetry club. The girls are all secretly in love with me.

" 'What are you doing here?' I asked her.

" 'There's something I have to tell you!'

" 'And what might that be?'

" 'I have something terribly important to tell you!'

" 'Look,' I said, 'it's late and you can't come in now. Go downstairs and wait for me at the door to the basement.'

"I went back to the bedroom and told my wife that somebody had rung the wrong bell. Then I added nonchalantly that I had to go down to the basement for coal, and picked up two empty buckets. That was a tactical error. My gallbladder had been bothering me all day, and I'd spent some of it in bed. The sudden burst of energy must have raised her suspicions."

"You have gallbladder problems?" asked Goethe with interest.

"And have for many years," said Petrarch.

"Why don't you have an operation?"

"Not on your life," said Petrarch.

Goethe nodded sympathetically.

"Where did I leave off?" Petrarch asked.

"You're having gallbladder problems and you've picked up two coal buckets," prompted Verlaine.

"I found the girl waiting at the door to the basement," Petrarch continued, "and invited her down with me. And as I shoveled coal into the buckets, I tried to find out what she wanted. She kept repeating that she *had* to see me. I couldn't get anything else out of her.

"Suddenly I heard steps coming down the staircase. I grabbed the bucket I had filled, and ran up out of the basement right into my wife. 'Here,' I said, handing her the bucket. 'I'm going back down to fill the other one.' My wife went upstairs with the bucket, and I went down to the basement and told the girl we couldn't stay there and she'd better go and wait for me outside. I shoveled the bucket full of coal and ran back up to the apartment with it. I gave my wife a kiss and told her to go lie down, I was going to take a bath before bed. She got into bed, and I turned on the water in the bathtub. The water made a good loud noise against the bottom of the tub. I took off my slippers and went out into the hall in my stocking feet. The shoes I had worn that day were next to the front door. I left them there as proof I hadn't left the house. Then I took another pair of shoes out of the closet, put them on, and slipped out of the apartment."

"We all know what a great poet you are, Petrarch," interrupted Boccaccio, "but now for the first time I see the strategist in you, the clever tactician blinded by passion. That little maneuver with the slippers and two pairs of shoes was a stroke of genius!"

Everyone agreed with Boccaccio and showered Petrarch with praise, which clearly flattered him.

"Anyway, there she was outside, waiting for me," he went on. "I did what I could to calm her. I told her I had to go in and invited her back the next morning when I knew for certain my wife would be at work. There's a tram stop right in front of our building, and I tried to talk her into getting on a tram. But when one finally came, she burst into hysterics and tried to run back into the building."

"You should have pushed her under the tram," said Boccaccio.

"Friends," said Petrarch almost ceremoniously, "there are times when a man is forced to be brutal with a woman. So I said to her, 'If you won't go home by yourself, I'll lock you out of the building. Keep in mind this is my home. I can't go turning it into a stable!' And don't forget, gentlemen, that all the time I was arguing with her down there in front of the building, the water was running in the bathroom and the bathtub could overflow any minute!

"I turned and made a dash to the front door. The girl took off behind me. Unfortunately, there were some other people going in the door at just that time and the girl slipped in with them. I ran up those stairs like a sprinter! I could hear her footsteps just behind me. We live four flights up, and it was tough going, but I was faster. I slammed the door in her face just in the nick of time. Then I ripped the doorbell wires down from the wall so nobody could hear her ringing—I was positive she'd lean on that bell for all she was worth —and ran into the bathroom on tiptoe."

"The tub hadn't overflowed?" asked Goethe anxiously.

"I turned off the water at the last minute. Then I went back to have another look at the door. I opened the peephole and saw her standing there motionless, staring at the door. Gentlemen, I was scared. I was afraid she'd stand there all night."

Boccaccio Makes Trouble

"You're an incorrigible idolizer, you know that, Petrarch?" said Boccaccio, interrupting him. "I can just imagine the type of girl who would join a poetry club and invoke you as her Apollo. You couldn't get me near her. A woman poet is twice a woman. More than a misogynist like me can bear."

"Tell me, Boccaccio," said Goethe, "why do you make so much of being a misogynist?"

"Because only the best of men are misogynists."

All the poets reacted to these words with hooting and booing, and Boccaccio was forced to raise his voice. "Now, don't misunderstand me. The misogynist doesn't despise women; he dislikes womankind. From time immemorial men have been divided into two large categories: idolizers—also known as poets—and misogynists—or, rather, gynophobes. Idolizers or poets worship the traditional feminine values like feelings, house and home, motherhood, fertility, divine flashes of hysteria, and the divine voice of nature in us; misogynists or gynophobes experience mild terror at the thought of them. The idolizer worships womankind in a woman; the gynophobe prefers the woman to womankind. And keep one thing in mind: a woman can be happy only with a misogynist. No woman has been happy with any of you!"

There was a fresh round of hooting and booing.

"The idolizer or poet may give a woman drama, passion, tears, and worries; he will never give her contentment. I knew one once. He worshiped his wife. Then he began worshiping somebody else's. He refused to humiliate the former by deceiving her or the latter by sleeping with her on the sly. So he made a clean breast of it to his wife and asked her to help him. She couldn't take it and fell ill, and he began weeping all the time, so much so that the other woman finally put her foot down and broke up with him. One day he lay down on the tram rails to end it all, but unfortunately the driver saw him from far off, and my idolizer got stuck with a fifty-crown ticket for disturbing traffic."

"Liar! Boccaccio's a liar!" shouted Verlaine.

"The story Petrarch's just told you is cut from the same cloth," countered Boccaccio. "What has your wife of the golden tresses done to make you take a hysterical girl like that so seriously?"

"What do you know about my wife?" shouted Petrarch. "My wife is my faithful companion! There are no secrets between us!"

"Then why did you change your shoes?" asked Lermontov.

But Petrarch stuck to his guns. "Friends," he said, "at that crucial moment when the girl was standing out in the hall and I didn't have the faintest idea what to do, I went straight to the bedroom and made a clean breast of it all to my wife."

"Just like my idolizer!" laughed Boccaccio. "The clean-breast syndrome! The idolizer's first reflex! I'll bet you asked her to help you, too."

Petrarch's voice was tenderness itself. "Yes, I did ask her to help. She'd never refused me before, she didn't then. She went to the door herself. I stayed back in the bedroom. I was scared."

"I'd have been scared too," said Goethe sympathetically.

"Well, she came back perfectly calm. She'd looked through the peephole into the hall, opened the door, and found nobody. It looked as though I'd made the whole thing up. But suddenly behind us we heard a loud noise, followed by the sound of shattering glass. As you know, we live in an old apartment house, the kind with galleries around the courtyard on each floor. Anyway, when no one answered the girl's ringing, she picked up an iron bar from somewhere and walked along the gallery smashing all our windows, one after the other. We stood there watching her from inside—helpless, horror-struck. And then we saw three white shadows appear on the other side of the dark gallery. It was the old ladies from the apartment across the way. They'd been awakened by the sound of the glass shattering, and had run out in their nightgowns, all eyes and ears, hoping for a scandal. Just picture it: a beautiful young girl holding an iron bar surrounded by the ominous shadows of three witches!

"Anyway, after she broke the last window, she climbed through it into the room.

"I wanted to go up and speak to her, but my wife put her arms around me and begged me not to. 'She'll kill you!' There stood the girl in the middle of our bedroom, iron bar in hand, Joan of Arc with sword, stunning, majestic. I tore myself away from my wife's embrace and began walking toward her. As I came closer, the girl's face lost its intimidating expression; it became gentle, suffused with a heavenly peace. I snatched the bar from her, threw it down on the floor, and grabbed her by the hand."

Insults

"I don't believe a word of it," said Lermontov.

"It didn't happen quite the way Petrarch told it, of course," said Boccaccio, interrupting again, "but I do believe it happened. The girl was a hysteric, and any normal man in his place would have long since given her a healthy slap or two. Idolizers or poets have always been prime booty for hysterics. Hysterics know that idolizers will never slap them. Idolizers are helpless when faced with a woman because they've never left their mothers' shadows. They see an envoy from their mothers in every woman and immediately give in. Their mothers' skirts hang over them like the firmament." He liked this last sentence so much he tried a few variations on it. "See that expanse up there over your heads, all you poets? Well, that's no sky, it's your mothers' enormous skirts. You all live under your mothers' skirts!"

"What's that you said?" bellowed Yesenin with incredible force, jumping out of his chair. He was teetering. He had drunk the most of anyone all evening. "What's that you said about my mother? What's that you said?"

"I wasn't talking about your mother," said Boccaccio mildly. He knew that Yesenin was living with a famous ballerina thirty years his elder and in fact felt genuinely sorry for him. But the spittle was ready on Yesenin's lips, and he bent over and let it fly. He was too drunk; it landed on Goethe's collar. Boccaccio took out a handkerchief and wiped it off the great poet.

Exhausted by the act of spitting, Yesenin collapsed into his chair.

"Let me tell you what she said to me, friends," continued Petrarch. "It was unforgettable, like a prayer, a litany. 'I'm a simple girl, a perfectly ordinary girl. I have nothing to give you, but I have come at love's behest. I want you to feel'—by now she was squeezing my hand—'real love, I want you to taste it once in your life.'"

"And what did your wife say to this herald of love?" asked Lermontov, his voice heavy with irony.

"What Lermontov wouldn't give for a woman to break his windows!" Goethe laughed. "He'd even pay her to do it!"

Lermontov threw Goethe a hostile glance, and Petrarch took up again. "My wife? You're wrong if you think this is all just one of Boccaccio's silly stories, Lermontov. The girl turned to my wife with her heavenly eyes and said—again like a prayer, a litany—'Don't be angry, I know you are good and I love you as I love him, I love you both.' Then she took her hand too."

"If that had been a scene from one of Boccaccio's silly stories, I would have nothing against it," said Lermontov. "But no, it's much worse. It's bad poetry."

"You're just jealous," Petrarch shouted at him. "You've never been alone in a room with two beautiful women who love you! Do you have any idea how beautiful my wife is when her golden hair flows down over her red negligee?"

When Lermontov responded with a malicious laugh, Goethe decided to punish him for his general ill will. "Nobody doubts you're a great poet, Lermontov," he said, "but why are you so full of complexes?"

Lermontov was thunderstruck. "You shouldn't have said that, Johann," he said to Goethe, scarcely containing himself. "That was the worst thing you could have said. A low blow."

Now Goethe, a great lover of peace and harmony, would never have gone any farther, but his biographer, our four-eyed Voltaire, laughed and said, "Everybody knows about your complexes, Lermontov," and went on to analyze his poetry, which lacked Goethe's grace, Petrarch's passion. He even began analyzing individual metaphors, arguing wittily that Lermontov's inferiority complex was the font of his imagination and that it came from a childhood marked by poverty and the oppressive influence of an authoritarian father.

Just then Goethe leaned over to Petrarch and whispered in a stage whisper that filled the room and was heard by everyone, including Lermontov, "No, no. He's got it all wrong. The trouble with Lermontov is he doesn't get enough ass."

The Student Stands Up for Lermontov

All this time the student had sat quietly, pouring himself wine (a discreet waiter noiselessly removed the empty bottles and brought back full ones) and straining to catch every word of the scintillating conversation. He needed all his wits to keep up with the poets' giddy gyrations.

He tried to decide which of them he liked best personally. He worshiped Goethe no less than Kristyna did, no less than the entire country, for that matter. He was fascinated by Petrarch and his burning eyes. But strangely enough, he felt closest to the muchmaligned Lermontov. It was Goethe's last remark that decided him. Suddenly he saw that even a great poet (and Lermontov really was a great poet) could have the same problems as an insignificant student such as himself. He glanced at his watch and realized he had better be going if he did not want to end up like Lermontov.

But somehow he couldn't tear himself away from the great poets, and instead of going back to Kristyna, he went to the men's room. He was standing there staring at the white tile and thinking when suddenly he heard Lermontov's voice next to him saying, "You heard them. They're not very *subtle*, you know what I mean? Not very *subtle*."

He said the word "subtle" as if it were in italics. Yes, some words are not like others; they have a special meaning known only to initiates. The student did not know why Lermontov said the word "subtle" as if it were in italics, but I, who am among the initiates, know that Lermontov once read Pascal's *pensée* about subtle minds and geometrical minds, and since then he had divided all mankind into those who are subtle and those who are not.

"Or do you think they are subtle?" he challenged the mute student.

Buttoning his fly, the student noticed that, just as the Countess N. P. Rostopchina noted in her diary, Lermontov had very short legs. The student was extremely grateful to him. He was the first great poet ever to honor him with a serious question and request a serious answer.

"Not the least bit subtle," he said.

Lermontov turned around on his short legs and said, "No, not the slightest bit." And raising his voice he added, "But I have my *pride*. Understand? I have my *pride*."

He pronounced the word "pride" in italics too, an italics implying that only a fool could put Lermontov's pride on a level with a girl's pride in her beauty or a shopkeeper's in his wares. No, his was a special pride, exalted and richly deserved.

"I've got my pride!" shouted Lermontov as he and the student walked back into the room. They sat down just in time to hear Voltaire deliver an encomium to Goethe. Lermontov was seething. He stood up again—which instantly made him a head taller than everyone else—and said, "Now I'm going to tell you why I'm so proud. Now I'm going to tell you what I'm so proud about. There are only two poets in this country: Goethe and me."

"You may be a great poet," Voltaire countered immediately, "but if you go around saying things like that about yourself, you're a very small man!"

Lermontov was so startled he could only stutter, "Well, why shouldn't I say them?" and he repeated "I've got my pride!" a few more times. Soon Voltaire was roaring with laughter, and the others began to join in.

The student saw his chance. He stood up the way Lermontov had, looked around at everyone present, and said, "You don't understand Lermontov. A poet's pride is very different from ordinary pride. Only the poet himself can know the true worth of what he writes. Others don't understand it until much later, they may never understand. A poet has got to have his pride. Without it he would betray his life's work."

Even though they had been roaring with laughter a minute before, they suddenly saw the student's point. In fact, they had every bit as much pride as Lermontov, they were simply ashamed to say so. They did not realize that when the word "pride" is pronounced with the proper emphasis, there is nothing laughable about it, it is witty and noble. So they were grateful to the student for giving them such useful advice, and one or another of them—it may have been Verlaine—even applauded him.

Goethe Turns Kristyna into a Queen

When the student took his seat, Goethe turned to him with a friendly smile and said, "Now there's a boy who knows his poetry!"

The others had sunk back into their drunken debates, so the student was left face to face with the great poet. He wanted to make the best of the precious opportunity, but suddenly did not know what to say. While his mind searched desperately for a suitable response, Goethe just sat there smiling at him, and since he was unable to come up with anything, all he did was smile back. And then all at once the thought of Kristyna came to his aid.

"Lately I've been going with a girl, I mean, a young woman, who is the wife of a butcher."

Goethe liked the idea and laughed a friendly laugh.

"She worships you. She's given me a book of yours for you to autograph."

"Let me have it," said Goethe, and taking the book of his

poems from the student, he opened it to the title page. "Tell me something about her," he went on. "What does she look like? Is she beautiful?"

Face to face with Goethe the student could not lie. He confessed that the butcher's wife was no beauty. Besides, she'd come to Prague in the most ridiculous outfit. She'd walked all over the city wearing a string of beads around her neck and the kind of formal black pumps that had been out of style for ages.

Goethe was sincerely interested. "Wonderful," he said with a tinge of nostalgia.

So the student went even further and admitted that the butcher's wife had one gold tooth that shone in her mouth like a golden fly.

Goethe laughed exuberantly and did the student one better. "Like a solitaire."

"Like a lighthouse," laughed the student.

"Like a star," smiled Goethe.

The butcher's wife was actually a typical small-town product, said the student, but that was what had attracted him to her.

"And well I understand you," said Goethe. "A mismatched outfit, a slightly defective denture, an exquisite mediocrity of the soul—those are the details that make a woman real, alive. The women you see on posters or in fashion magazines—the ones all the women try to imitate nowadays—how can they be attractive? They have no reality of their own; they're just the sum of a set of abstract rules. They aren't born of human bodies; they hatch ready-made from the computers. Let me tell you, my friend, your small-town butcher's wife is the perfect woman for a poet. Congratulations!"

He bent over the title page of the book, took out his pen, and began to write. He was in ecstasy, in a trance, his face glowed with love and understanding. He filled the entire page.

Taking back the book, the student blushed with pride. The words Goethe had written to this woman he did not know were beautiful and sad, nostalgic and sensual, humorous and wise. The student was certain that more beautiful words had never been addressed to any woman. He ached at the very thought of her. Poetry had cast a cloak of sublime words over her ridiculous street clothes. She had turned into a queen.

The Poet Descending

The next time the waiter came in, it was without a new bottle. He had come to ask the poets to get ready to leave. The building would be closing in a few minutes, and the janitor was threatening to lock them in and leave them there until morning.

He had to repeat it many times—loudly and softly, to the entire assembly and to each of them individually—before the poets finally realized he was not in fact joking. Petrarch had a sudden vision of his wife in her red negligee and jumped up from the table as if someone had kicked him in the behind.

Suddenly Goethe spoke in a voice of boundless sorrow. "You go ahead. Leave me here. I'll stay here." They looked over at the crutches leaning against the table next to him and tried to talk him into leaving with them, but he just shook his head.

They all knew his wife, a harsh, dour woman; they were all afraid of her. They knew that if Goethe did not come home on schedule, she would make a terrible scene in front of everybody. "Be reasonable, Johann," they begged him. "You've got to go home." And they gingerly clutched him under the arms and tried to lift him out of his chair. But the king of Olympus was heavy and their arms were far from bold. He was at least thirty years their senior and the father of them all, and now that they had to pick him up and hand him his crutches, they all felt uncomfortable and small. Besides, he kept repeating he wanted to stay.

Nobody wanted to let him stay, but Lermontov took advantage of the situation to show how much cleverer he was than the others. "Why not leave him here? I'll watch over him till morning. Don't you see? When he was young, he stayed away from home for weeks on end. All he wants is to bring back his youth! Don't you see, you idiots? What do you say, Johann? How about the two of us stretching out on the rug with this bottle of wine and holing up here till morning? The rest of them can go to hell, and Petrarch can go back to his red negligee and flowing blond tresses!"

But Voltaire knew it wasn't a desire to recapture lost youth that kept Goethe from leaving. Goethe was ill, he was not allowed to drink. When he did, his legs refused to carry him. Voltaire took hold of both crutches and told the others to forget their reserve. And so the weak arms of the drunken poets gripped Goethe's armpits and hoisted him off the chair. Then they carried him, or rather dragged him (Goethe's feet sometimes touched the floor, sometimes dangled over it like a child's when its parents swing it back and forth), across the room into the vestibule. But Goethe was heavy and the poets were drunk, so they lowered him to the floor halfway through the vestibule. "Friends," he wailed, "let me die right here, on this spot."

Voltaire lost his temper and shouted at everyone to pick him up again immediately. The poets suddenly felt ashamed of themselves. Some of them took hold of Goethe's arms, others of his legs, and they picked him up and carried him out of the vestibule onto the stairs. They all carried him together. Voltaire carried him, Petrarch carried him, Verlaine carried him, Boccaccio carried him, and even the very unsteady Yesenin held onto Goethe's legs, if only to keep himself from falling.

The student also tried to lend a hand. He knew it was a once-in-a-lifetime opportunity. But he couldn't. Lermontov had become too attached to him. He had a firm grip on his arm and kept finding things to talk to him about.

"Not only do they lack subtlety," he was telling the student, "they can't do anything right. Mama's boys, that's what they are. Look how they're carrying him. They'll drop him for sure. When have they ever worked with their hands? Did you know I once worked in a factory?"

(We must not forget that all heroes of that age and country had put in their time at a factory, either voluntarily—out of revolutionary fervor—or under duress, as a punishment. In either case they were equally proud. They felt that at the factory they had earned their personal kiss from the noble goddess of the Hard Life.)

Holding him by his arms and legs, the poets carried their patriarch down the stairs. The staircase was square in design. It had many right-angle turns, and turning made special demands on their strength and skill.

"Do you have any idea what it takes to carry beams, my boy?" Lermontov continued. "You've never done it, you're a student. But they haven't either. Look at the rotten job they're doing! He's going to fall!" He turned to them and shouted, "Turn him the other way around, you idiots! He'll fall if you go on like that! Never done a thing with your hands, have you!" And arm in arm with the student, he came slowly down the stairs after the tottering poets, whose anguish grew greater as Goethe grew heavier. Finally they got him out onto the sidewalk and up against a lamppost. Petrarch and Boccaccio kept him from keeling over while Voltaire went out into the street and tried to hail a cab.

"Do you have any idea what you're witnessing?" said Lermontov to the student. "You're just a student, you don't know what life is, but what a fantastic scene! The poet descending. Do you have any idea what a poem it would make?"

In the meantime Goethe had slid to the ground and Petrarch and Boccaccio had propped him back up.

"Look at that, will you?" said Lermontov to the student. "They can't even hold him up their arms are so weak. What do they know about life? 'The Poet Descending.' A magnificent title, don't you think? I've been working on two books lately, two completely different books. One is purely classical in form: rhymes, a clear-cut meter. The second is in free verse. I'm going to call it *Poetic Reports.* The final poem will be 'The Poet Descending,' and a grim poem it will be. Grim, but honest. *Honest.*"

That was the third word Lermontov had pronounced in italics. It meant the opposite of everything that was mere ornament and wit. It meant the opposite of Petrarch's dreams and Boccaccio's games. It meant the pathos of labor and a passionate belief in the aforenamed goddess of the Hard Life.

Verlaine, intoxicated by the night air, was standing on the

sidewalk, looking up at the sky and singing. Yesenin had sat down against the wall of the building and fallen asleep. Voltaire, still waving his arm in the street, finally managed to flag down a taxi. He tried to get Petrarch to climb in next to the driver. Petrarch was the only one with a chance of mollifying Mrs. Goethe. But Petrarch put up a frenzied self-defense. "Why me? I'm scared stiff of her!"

"You see?" said Lermontov to the student. "When the time comes to give a friend a hand, he runs the other way. There isn't a single one of them capable of talking to the wife." He leaned into the car. Goethe, Boccaccio, and Voltaire were squeezed together in the back seat. "Friends," he said, "I'm going with you. You can leave Mrs. Goethe to me." And he climbed in next to the driver.

Petrarch Objects to Boccaccio's Laughter

Once the poet-laden taxi had disappeared into the distance, the student remembered he'd better be getting back to Kristyna.

"Well, I'll be on my way," he said to Petrarch.

Petrarch nodded, took his arm, and walked off with him in the wrong direction.

"You know, you're very perceptive," he said. "You were the only one in a position to listen to what the others were saying."

"That girl standing in the middle of the room like Joan of Arc with her sword—I could repeat it all, word for word."

"And those winos didn't even let me finish! They're not interested in anything but themselves."

"Or when your wife was afraid the girl was going to kill you and you went up to her and her expression became suffused with heavenly peace. It was like a minor miracle."

"*You're* the poet, my friend. You, not them." Petrarch was taking the student in the direction of his apartment at the other end of the city. "How did it end?" asked the student.

"My wife took pity on her and let her spend the night with us. And you know what happened? My mother-in-law, who sleeps in a storage room on the other side of the kitchen and gets up very early—when she saw all the windows broken, she went and found some glaziers who happened to be working in the building next door, and all the panes were back in place before we even woke up. There wasn't a trace left of the night before. The whole thing felt like a dream."

"And the girl?" asked the student.

"She slipped out before morning too."

Petrarch stopped abruptly in the middle of the street and gave him an almost hostile look. "You know, friend, I'd be terribly upset if you thought of my story as a Boccaccian anecdote ending up in bed. There's something you must learn. Boccaccio's a real bastard. Boccaccio never understands anybody, because understanding means merging, identifying. That is the secret of poetry. We burn in the woman we adore, we burn in the thought we espouse, we burn in the landscape that moves us."

Listening ardently to Petrarch, the student saw the image of his Kristyna before him. And only hours before he had doubted her. Now he felt ashamed of those doubts. They belonged to the worse (Boccaccian) side of his personality. They were the fruit of his cowardice, not his strength. They made him see how much he feared entering wholly into a love relationship, how much he feared burning in the woman he loved.

"Love is poetry, poetry is love," said Petrarch, and the student promised himself he would love Kristyna with a great and all-consuming love. First Goethe had clothed her in royal vesture, now Petrarch had injected fire into her heart. The night to come would be blessed by both poets.

"Laughter, on the other hand," continued Petrarch, "is an explosion that tears us away from the world and drops us into frigid solitude. A joke is a barrier between man and the world. A joke is an enemy of love and poetry. So let me tell you again—and don't you forget it—Boccaccio doesn't know a thing about love. Love can't be laughable. Love has nothing in common with laughter."

"Yes!" said the student enthusiastically. He saw the world as divided in two: half love, half joke. He knew that he belonged, and would always belong, to Petrarch's army.

The Angels Hover over the Student's Couch

She had not paced the room nervously, she had not lost her temper, she had not pouted or pined by the open window. She was curled up in her nightgown under his blanket. He woke her with a kiss on the lips, and to quell any reproaches she might have, he quickly went through the events of the unbelievable gathering, at which Boccaccio and Petrarch had locked horns so dramatically and Lermontov had offended all the other poets.

She showed no interest in his account and interrupted him mistrustfully. "I bet you forgot all about the book."

When he handed her the book with Goethe's long dedication, she couldn't believe her eyes. She read those unlikely flights of fancy several times through. They seemed to embody the whole of her equally unlikely adventure with the student: their summer together, their secret walks along unexplored wooded paths, all the delicacy and tenderness that seemed so removed from her life.

Meanwhile the student had undressed and climbed into bed beside her. She clutched him and pressed him to her breast. It was an embrace the likes of which he had never before experienced. It was strong, sincere, fervent, like a mother's, like a sister's, like a friend's—and passionate. Lermontov had repeatedly used the word "honest" that evening, and the student felt there could be no better synthetic term for her embrace, encompassing as it did a myriad of qualifiers.

The student's body told him it was exceptionally well disposed toward making love. It was in such dependable, durable, and firm condition he did not need to rush things and savored the long, sweet, motionless embrace.

First she gave him deep, sensual French kisses, then sisterly pecks all over his face. Fondling her gold tooth with his tongue, he recalled Goethe's words: she didn't hatch ready-made from a computer, she was born of a human body! She was a woman for a poet!

He felt like shouting for joy. Then he went over Petrarch's statement about how love was poetry and poetry love and understanding meant merging with one's partner and burning in her. (Yes, all three poets were there with him, hovering over his bed like angels—singing, rejoicing, and granting him their blessings.) By now the student was so overflowing with emotion that the time had come to move on from the Lermontovian honesty of a motionless embrace to the act of love itself. He turned over onto Kristyna's body and tried to spread her legs with his knees.

But what's this? Kristyna resists! She presses her legs together with the same obstinacy as on their summer walks in the woods!

He wanted to ask her why, but couldn't bring himself to speak. Kristyna was so shy, so delicate, that the workings of love lost their names in her presence. The only language he dared use was the language of breathing and touching. Weren't they beyond cumbersome words? Wasn't he burning in her? Weren't they burning with a single flame? And so over and over in obstinate silence he tried forcing his knee between her tightly closed thighs.

She was silent too, she too was afraid to speak; she preferred making her position clear by means of kisses and caresses. But when he tried prying apart her thighs for the twenty-fifth time—a particularly brutal attempt—she came out with, "No, please don't. It would kill me."

"What?" he said, breathing deeply.

"It would kill me. Really. It would kill me," she repeated, giving him another deep kiss and pressing her thighs together tightly.

The student felt a mixture of despair and bliss. On the one hand, he felt a wild need to make love to her; on the other, he could cry for joy at the thought that she loved him as no one had ever loved him. She loved him so much she could die; she loved him so much she was afraid to make love to him; if she did, she would never be able to live without him, she would die of longing and desire. He was happy, blissfully happy. Suddenly, unexpectedly, undeservedly, he had attained all he had ever wished for—that boundless love compared to which the entire earth with all its waters and all its dry land is as nothing.

"I understand. I feel just the same!" he whispered to her, stroking and kissing her, almost weeping with love. But all these tender emotions did nothing to gratify his physical desire, which was becoming painful, nearly unbearable. So he kept trying to insert his knee between her thighs and clear a path through to her genitals, more mysterious to him at that moment than the Holy Grail.

"No you don't. Not you; it won't happen to you. I'm the one it will kill!" said Kristyna.

He imagined a sensual pleasure so boundless as to kill him, and whispering "We'll die together! Let's die together!" over and over, he persisted in his unsuccessful attempts to force open her thighs with his knee.

They had nothing more to say. All they could do was cling to one another, she shaking her head and he storming the fortress of her thighs. In the end, he capitulated and submissively turned over on his back next to her. Instantly she seized the scepter of his love, upright in her honor, and squeezed it with all her splendid honesty: strongly, sincerely, fervently, like a mother, like a sister, like a friend—and passionately.

The student felt both the bliss of boundless love and the despair of a body rejected. The butcher's wife did not let go of his weapon, but rather than make the few simple motions that would simulate the physical act he so longed for, she held it in her hand like something rare, something precious, something to be preserved, kept stiff and hard for a long, long time.

But enough of that night, which lasted without substantial change almost until morning.

The Sordid Light of Morning

Since they did not fall asleep until late, they did not wake up until noon. They both had headaches. They didn't have much time left together because Kristyna's train was leaving shortly. They didn't speak. Kristyna packed her nightgown and Goethe's book into her bag, and put on her impossible black pumps and her impossible necklace.

As if the sordid light of morning had broken the seal of silence and a day of prose had followed on the night of poetry, Kristyna told the student quite matter-of-factly, "I hope you're not angry about last night. It really *could* have killed me. The doctor told me after my first child that I should never get pregnant again."

"Do you really think I would have made you pregnant?" asked the student with a desperate look in his eye. "What do you take me for?"

"That's what they all say. Always so sure of themselves. I know what happens to my girlfriends. The young ones like you are the most dangerous. And when it happens, that's it."

He told her with desperation in his voice that he'd had plenty of experience and would never have given her a child. "You're not going to put me in the same category as the small fry your friends run around with, are you?"

"I guess you're right," she said almost apologetically. The student had made his point. She believed him. He was no country bumpkin and probably knew the ways of love better than all the mechanics in the world. Maybe she had been wrong to put up so much resistance. But she wasn't sorry she had. A quick roll in the hay (Kristyna could not picture physical love as anything but hurried and short) was nice enough, but it could be dangerous and might make her feel unfaithful. The night she'd had with the student was infinitely better.

Even while they were on their way to the station, she was

looking forward to sitting in her compartment and running it over in her mind. With the down-to-earth egotism of a simple woman she kept telling herself she had experienced something that "no one could take from her": she had spent the night with a boy who had always seemed unreal, elusive, distant, and had held him the whole night through by his upright member. Yes, all night! Now there's something she'd never experienced before! She might never see him again, but she'd never really expected to go on seeing him. She was happy to have at least one permanent thing to remember him by: Goethe's book with that unbelievable dedication, proof positive that her adventure had not been a dream.

The student, on the other hand, was in despair. If only he had said one sensible sentence, if only he had called a spade a spade, he could have had her. She was afraid he would get her pregnant, and he thought she was frightened by the boundless horizons of their love! Peering deep into the abyss of his stupidity, he felt like scream-ing with laughter—tearful, hysterical laughter.

He wends his way from the station to his loveless wasteland, with *litost,* frustration, at his side.

Further Notes for a Theory of *Litost*

I have used two incidents from the life of the student to illustrate the two basic reactions we may have to our own *litost.* Should our counterpart prove weaker than ourselves, we merely insult him under false pretenses, just as the student insulted his girlfriend when she swam too fast.

Should our counterpart prove stronger, we are forced to choose a circuitous route—the backhanded slap, murder by means of suicide. The little boy plays out of tune so long that the teacher can't stand it anymore and throws him out the window. And as the boy falls, during his flight, he rejoices in the thought that the mean old teacher will be accused of murder.

These are the two classic reactions, and if the former occurs most commonly among couples, married or unmarried, the latter is a main ingredient of what we call the history of mankind. Everything our teachers once called heroism may well be nothing more than the form of *litost* I have illustrated with the example of the young boy and his violin teacher. The Persians conquer the Peloponnesus, and the Spartans make one tactical error after another. Just as the little boy refuses to play in tune, they refuse to take reasonable action; blinded by tears of rage, they can neither fight more efficiently nor surrender nor take to their heels and run. They let spite—*litost*—kill them to a man.

It occurs to me in this connection that it is no accident the concept of *litost* first saw the light of day in Bohemia. The history of the Czechs—a history of never-ending revolts against stronger enemies, a history of glorious defeats setting the course of world history in motion but causing the downfall of its own people—is the history of *litost*. When in August of the year 1968 thousands of Russian tanks occupied this small, wonderful country, I saw the following example of graffiti on the walls of one of its towns: *We Do Not Want Compromise, We Want Victory*. You must understand that by this time the only choice was among several varieties of defeat, but the town in question rejected compromise and would settle for nothing but victory. That was not reason talking; that was the voice of *litost!* Rejecting compromise means *ipso facto* choosing the worst of defeats, but that is exactly what *litost* is after. A man obsessed with *litost* revenges himself by destroying himself. The little boy was smashed to smithereens on the sidewalk, but his immortal soul will eternally rejoice in the fact that the teacher hanged himself from the hasp of the open window.

But how can the student hurt Kristyna? She is safely on the train before he can do anything Theoreticians are acquainted with this phenomenon and call it "impacted *litost.*"

Nothing can be worse. The student's *litost*, his disillusionment, was like a tumor growing minute by minute, and he did not know how to treat it. Since he could not take revenge, he hoped at least for consolation. That was what made him think of Lermontov. He remembered how Goethe had insulted him, how Voltaire had humiliated him, and how Lermontov had shouted over and over that he had his pride, as if all the poets around the table were violin teachers and he was trying to provoke them to throw him out the window.

The student needed Lermontov's fraternal support. He thrust his hands deep into his pockets and felt a large piece of folded paper. It was a sheet torn from a notebook with the message "I'm waiting. I love you. Kristyna. Midnight."

He put two and two together. The jacket he was wearing had been hanging in his room yesterday. The belated message only went to confirm what he already knew. He had lost Kristyna's body because of his own stupidity. He was filled to bursting with his *litost,* and had nowhere to release it.

In the Depths of Despair

It was late afternoon, and the student assumed the poets had slept off the effects of the drinking bout and would be at the Writers' Club. He ran up the stairs and past the cloakroom, then headed to the right, toward the restaurant. Because he was still new there, he stopped at the entrance, looking around uneasily. At the other end of the room he saw Petrarch and Lermontov sitting with two people he did not know. There was an empty table nearby, and he went and took a seat at it. Nobody paid any attention to him. He even had the feeling that Petrarch and Lermontov had glanced over without recognizing him. Waiting for his cognac, he painfully ran the infinitely sad and infinitely beautiful text of Kristyna's message through his head. "I'm waiting. I love you. Kristyna. Midnight."

He sipped at the cognac a full twenty minutes, but the sight of Petrarch and Lermontov not only failed to comfort him, it made him even sadder. Everyone had abandoned him—Kristyna *and* the poets. All he had left was a large sheet of paper with "I'm waiting. I love you. Kristyna. Midnight" on it. He felt like standing and waving it high over his head so everyone could see, so everyone could know that he, the student, had been loved, loved with a boundless love.

He called the waiter over and paid. Then he lit another cigarette. He was not particularly anxious to stay, but he had a horror of going back to an empty room where no woman was waiting. Just as he finally ground the stub into the ashtray, Petrarch caught sight of him and waved from his table. But it was too late. Rancor (that's right, *litost*) was calling him away from the club and back to his joyless solitude. He stood up, and at the last minute took Kristyna's love note out of his pocket. It would no longer give him any pleasure. If he left it behind, someone might notice it and learn that the student sitting there had been loved with a boundless love.

He turned in the direction of the door and began his exit.

Sudden Glory

"Wait!" came a voice from behind. The student turned around. Petrarch waved and went up to him. "Going so soon?" he asked, and apologized for not having recognized him right away. "I'm always completely out of it the day after."

The student said he hadn't wanted to interfere because he didn't know the other gentlemen at Petrarch's table.

"Oh, they're morons," said Petrarch to the student, and walked back with him to the table the student had just left. The student stared in anguish at the large sheet of paper lying innocently on the table. If only it had been a tiny scrap, but no—a large sheet like that made it impossible to ignore the clumsy premeditation with which it had been forgotten there.

Petrarch, his black eyes burning with curiosity, went straight for it. "What's this?" he said, looking it over. "Isn't it yours, my friend?"

The student was inept in the role of a man embarrassed at having left a confidential note behind. He tried to tear the paper out of Petrarch's hands.

But Petrarch had begun reading it aloud. "I'm waiting. I love you. Kristyna. Midnight."

He looked the student in the eyes and asked, "Midnight? Not yesterday, I hope."

"Yes, yesterday," said the student, lowering his eyes. He had stopped trying to grab the paper out of Petrarch's hands.

By then Lermontov was making his way over to the table on his short legs. "Glad to see you," he said, shaking the student's hand. Then, glancing back at the table he had come from, he added, "A real bunch of morons," and sat down with Petrarch and the student.

Petrarch immediately read Lermontov the text of the message. He read it several times through and with a lilting, sonorous voice, as if it were a line of poetry.

It occurs to me that in situations where we can't give a good slap to a girl who swims too fast or let ourselves be massacred by the Persians, when there is no way out of our heart-rending *litost*, then poetry comes to our aid.

What remains of this complete and utter fiasco? Only the poetry. The words Goethe inscribed in the book that Kristyna took home with her and the words on the lined sheet of paper that have earned the student unexpected glory.

"Admit it, my boy," said Petrarch, clasping the student's hand. "Confess. You write poetry! You're a poet!"

The student lowered his eyes and admitted that Petrarch was right.

And Lermontov Is Alone Again

It was Lermontov the student came to the Writers' Club to see, but from that time forth he was lost to Lermontov and Lermontov to him. Lermontov hates happy lovers. He frowned and started in disdainfully about the poetry of saccharine feelings and big words. About how a poem must be as honest as an object crafted by a worker's hands. He scowled at Petrarch and the student, he was peevish with them. We know what the trouble was. Goethe knew it too. Not enough ass. The terrible *litost* that comes from not getting enough ass.

Now who was in a better position to understand Lermontov than the student? But all that incorrigible imbecile can see is the poet's saturnine face, all he can hear is his vitriolic talk. And he takes it personally.

I watch them from afar, from my high-rise in France. Petrarch and the student get up to leave. They bid Lermontov a cold farewell. And Lermontov is all by himself again.

Dear Lermontov, the genius of that special torment which in my sad country bears a name evoking the plaint of an abandoned dog, the name of *litost.*

PART SIX
The Angels

In February 1948, Communist leader Klement Gottwald stepped out on the balcony of a Baroque palace in Prague to address the hundreds of thousands of his fellow citizens packed into Old Town Square. It was a crucial moment in Czech history. There were snow flurries, it was cold, and Gottwald was bareheaded. The solicitous Clementis took off his fur cap and set it on Gottwald's head.

Neither Gottwald nor Clementis knew that every day for eight years Franz Kafka had climbed the same staircase they had just climbed to get to the balcony. During the days of the Austro-Hungarian Monarchy the building had housed a German secondary school. Another thing they did not know was that on the ground floor of the same building Hermann Kafka, Franz's father, had kept a shop whose sign had a jackdaw painted next to his name, *kafka* being the Czech word for jackdaw.

Gottwald, Clementis, and all the others did not know about Kafka, and Kafka knew they did not know. Prague in his novels is a city without memory. It has even forgotten its name. Nobody there remembers anything, nobody recalls anything. Even Josef K. does not seem to know anything about his previous life. No song is capable of uniting the city's present with its past by recalling the moment of its birth.

Time in Kafka's novel is the time of a humanity that has lost all continuity with humanity, of a humanity that no longer knows anything nor remembers anything, that lives in nameless cities with nameless streets or streets with names different from the ones they had yesterday, because a name means continuity with the past and people without a past are people without a name.

Prague, as Max Brod used to say, is the city of evil. After the defeat of the Czech Reformation in 1621 the Jesuits tried to re-educate the nation in the true Catholic faith by overwhelming the city with the splendor of Baroque cathedrals. The thousands of stone saints looking out from all sides—threatening you, following you, hypnotizing you—are the raging hordes of occupiers who invaded Bohemia three hundred and fifty years ago to tear the people's faith and language from their hearts.

The street Tamina was born on was called Schwerin. That was during the war, and Prague was occupied by the Germans. Her father was born on Cernokostelecka Avenue—the Avenue of the Black Church. That was during the Austro-Hungarian Monarchy. When her mother married her father and moved there, it bore the name of Marshal Foch. That was after World War I. Tamina spent her childhood on Stalin Avenue, and when her husband came to take her away, he went to Vinohrady—that is, Vineyards—Avenue. And all the time it was the same street; they just kept changing its name, trying to lobotomize it.

There are all kinds of ghosts prowling these confused streets. They are the ghosts of monuments demolished—demolished by the Czech Reformation, demolished by the Austrian Counterreformation, demolished by the Czechoslovak Republic, demolished by the Communists. Even statues of Stalin have been torn down. All over the country, wherever statues were thus destroyed, Lenin statues have sprouted up by the thousands. They grow like weeds on the ruins, like melancholy flowers of forgetting.

2

If Franz Kafka was the prophet of a world without memory, Gustav Husak is its creator. After T. G. Masaryk, who is known as the liberator-president (all his monuments without exception have been demolished), after Benes, Gottwald, Zapotecky, Novotny, and Svoboda, Husak, the seventh president of my country, is known as *the president of forgetting*.

The Russians brought him into power in 1969. Not since

1621 has the history of the Czech people experienced such a massacre of culture and thought. Everybody everywhere assumes that Husak simply tracked down his political opponents. In fact, however, the struggle with the political opposition was merely an excuse, a welcome opportunity the Russians took to use their intermediary for something much more substantial.

I find it highly significant in this connection that Husak dismissed some hundred and forty-five Czech historians from universities and research institutes. (Rumor has it that for each of them —secretly, as in a fairy tale—a new monument to Lenin sprang up.) One of those historians, my all but blind friend Milan Hubl, came to visit me one day in 1971 in my tiny apartment on Bartolomejska Street. We looked out the window at the spires of the Castle and were sad.

"The first step in liquidating a people," said Hubl, "is to erase its memory. Destroy its books, its culture, its history. Then have somebody write new books, manufacture a new culture, invent a new history. Before long the nation will begin to forget what it is and what it was. The world around it will forget even faster."

"What about language?"

"Why would anyone bother to take it from us? It will soon be a matter of folklore and die a natural death."

Was that hyperbole dictated by utter despair?

Or is it true that a nation cannot cross a desert of organized forgetting?

None of us knows what will be. One thing, however, is certain: in moments of clairvoyance the Czech nation can glimpse its own death at close range. Not as an accomplished fact, not as the inevitable future, but as a perfectly concrete possibility. Its death is at its side.

3

Six months later Hubl was arrested and sentenced to many years' imprisonment. My father was dying at the time.

During the last ten years of his life my father gradually lost the power of speech. At first he simply had trouble calling up certain words or would say similar words instead and then immediately laugh at himself. In the end he had only a handful of words left, and all his attempts at saying anything more substantial resulted in one of the last sentences he could articulate: "That's strange."

Whenever he said "That's strange," his eyes would express infinite astonishment at knowing everything and being able to say nothing. Things lost their names and merged into a single, undifferentiated reality. I was the only one who by talking to him could temporarily transform that nameless infinity into the world of clearly named entities.

His unusually large blue eyes still stared out of his handsome old face as intelligently as before. I often took him for walks. We would walk once around the block. That was all he had strength for. He had trouble walking. He took tiny steps, and as soon as he felt the least bit tired, his body would tilt forward, and he would lose his balance. We often had to stop so he could lean his forehead against the wall and rest.

During the walks we talked about music. When Father could speak normally, I hadn't asked him many questions. Now I wanted to make up for it. So we talked about music. It was an unusual conversation. One of the participants knew nothing but a lot of words, the other knew everything but no words.

Through the ten years of his illness Father worked steadily on a long study of Beethoven's sonatas. He wrote somewhat better than he spoke, but even while writing he would suffer more and more memory lapses until finally no one could understand the text—it was made up of words that did not exist.

Once he called me into his room. The variations from the Opus 111 sonata were open on the piano. "Look," he said, pointing to the music (he had also lost the ability to play the piano), "look." Then, after a prolonged effort, he managed to add, "Now I know!" He kept trying to explain something important to me, but the words he used were completely unintelligible, and seeing that I didn't understand him, he looked at me in amazement and said, "That's strange."

I knew what he wanted to talk about, of course. He had been involved with the topic a long time. Beethoven had felt a sudden attachment to the variation form toward the end of his life. At first glance it might seem the most superficial of forms, a showcase for technique, the type of work better suited to a lacemaker than to Beethoven. But Beethoven made it one of the most distinguished forms (for the first time in the history of music) and imbued it with some of his finest meditations.

True, all that is well known. But what Father wanted to know was what we are to make of it. Why did he choose variations? What lay behind his choice?

That is why he called me into his room, pointed to the music, and said, "Now I know!"

4

The silence of my father, whom all words eluded, the silence of the hundred and forty-five historians, who have been forbidden to remember, that myriad-voiced silence resounding from all over my country forms the background of the picture against which I paint Tamina.

She went on serving coffee at the café in a small town in Western Europe. But she no longer moved in the aura of friendly civility that used to draw in customers. She no longer had any desire to lend them her ear.

One day when Bibi was sitting at the counter on a bar stool

and her baby girl was crawling around on the floor screaming and yelling, Tamina lost her patience. She waited a minute to give Bibi a chance to quiet the child down and then said, "Can't you stop her from making such a racket?"

Bibi took offense. "What makes you hate children so much?"

There is no reason to think that Tamina hated children. Besides, she detected a completely unexpected hostility in Bibi's voice. Without quite knowing how it came about, she stopped seeing her.

Then one morning Tamina did not show up for work. It had never happened before. The owner's wife went to see if anything was wrong. She rang her doorbell, but nobody answered. She went back the next day, and again—no answer. She called the police. When they broke down the door, all they found was a carefully maintained apartment with nothing missing, nothing suspicious.

Tamina did not report to work the next few days either. The police came back on the case, but uncovered nothing new. They filed Tamina away with the Permanently Missing.

5

On the fateful day, a young man in jeans sat down at the counter. Tamina was all alone in the café at the time. The young man ordered a Coke and sipped the liquid slowly. He looked at Tamina; Tamina looked out into space.

Suddenly he said, "Tamina."

If that was meant to impress her, it failed. There was no trick to finding out her name. All the customers in the neighborhood knew it.

"I know you're sad," he went on.

That didn't have the desired effect either. She knew that there were all kinds of ways to make a conquest and that one of the surest roads to a woman's genitals was through her sadness. All the same she looked at him with greater interest than before.

They began talking. What attracted and held Tamina's attention was his questions. Not what he asked, but the fact that he asked anything at all. It had been so long since anyone had asked her about anything. It seemed like an eternity! The only person who had ever really interrogated her was her husband, and that was because love is a constant interrogation. In fact, I don't know a better definition of love.

(Which means that no one loves us better than the police, my friend Hubl would object. Absolutely. Since every apex has its nadir, love has the prying eye of the police. Sometimes people confuse the apex with the nadir, and I wouldn't be surprised if lonely people secretly yearn to be taken in for cross-examination from time to time to give them somebody to talk to about their lives.)

6

The young man looks into her eyes and listens to what she has to say and then tells her that what she calls remembering is in fact something different, that in fact she is under a spell and watching herself forget.

Tamina nods her head in agreement.

The young man goes on. When she looks back sadly, it is no longer out of fidelity to her husband. She no longer even sees her husband; she simply looks out into space.

Into space? Then what makes it so hard for her to look back?

It's not the memories, explains the young man; it's remorse. Tamina will never forgive herself for forgetting.

"But what can I do?" asks Tamina.

"Forget your forgetting," says the young man.

"Any advice on how to go about it?" Tamina laughs bitterly.

"Haven't you ever felt like getting away from it all?"

"Yes, I have," admits Tamina. "Very much so. But where can I go?"

"How about a place where things are as light as the breeze,

where things have no weight, where there is no remorse?"

"Yes," says Tamina in a dreamy voice, "a place where things weigh nothing at all."

And as in a fairy tale, as in a dream (no, it *is* a fairy tale, it *is* a dream!), Tamina walks out from behind the counter where she has spent several years of her life, and leaves the café with the young man. There is a red sports car parked out front. The young man climbs in behind the wheel and offers Tamina the seat next to him.

7

I understand the remorse Tamina felt. When my father died, I had a bad case of it too. I couldn't forgive myself for asking him so little, for knowing so little about him, for losing him. In fact, it was that very remorse which suddenly made me see what he must have meant to tell me the day he pointed to the Opus 111 sonata.

Let me try to explain it by means of an analogy. The symphony is a musical epic. We might compare it to a journey leading through the boundless reaches of the external world, on and on, farther and farther. Variations also constitute a journey, but not through the external world. You recall Pascal's *pensée* about how man lives between the abyss of the infinitely large and the infinitely small. The journey of the variation form leads to that *second* infinity, the infinity of internal variety concealed in all things.

What Beethoven discovered in his variations was another space and another direction. In that sense they are a challenge to undertake the journey, another *invitation au voyage*.

The variation form is the form of maximum concentration. It enables the composer to limit himself to the matter at hand, to go straight to the heart of it. The subject matter is a theme, which often consists of no more than sixteen measures. Beethoven goes as deeply into those sixteen measures as if he had gone down a mine to the bowels of the earth.

The journey to the second infinity is no less adventurous than the journey of the epic, and closely parallels the physicist's descent into the wondrous innards of the atom. With every variation Beethoven moves farther and farther from the original theme, which bears no more resemblance to the final variation than a flower to its image under the microscope.

Man knows he cannot embrace the universe with all its suns and stars. But he finds it unbearable to be condemned to lose the second infinity as well, the one so close, so nearly within reach. Tamina lost the infinity of her love, I lost my father, we all lose in whatever we do, because if it is perfection we are after, we must go to the heart of the matter, and we can never quite reach it.

That the external infinity escapes us we accept with equanimity; the guilt over letting the second infinity escape follows us to the grave. While pondering the infinity of the stars, we ignore the infinity of our father.

It is no wonder, then, that the variation form became the passion of the mature Beethoven, who (like Tamina and like me) knew all too well that there is nothing more unbearable than losing a person we have loved—those sixteen measures and the inner universe of their infinite possibilities.

8

This entire book is a novel in the form of variations. The individual parts follow each other like individual stretches of a journey leading toward a theme, a thought, a single situation, the sense of which fades into the distance.

It is a novel about Tamina, and whenever Tamina is absent, it is a novel for Tamina. She is its main character and main audience, and all the other stories are variations on her story and come together in her life as in a mirror.

It is a novel about laughter and forgetting, about forgetting and Prague, about Prague and the angels. By the way, it is not the least bit accidental that the name of the young man sitting at the wheel is Raphael.

The countryside gradually turned into a wilderness. The farther they went, the less green there was, the more ocher; the fewer fields and trees, the more sand and clay. Suddenly the car swerved from the highway onto a narrow road that almost immediately came to an end at a steep incline. The young man stopped the car. They got out. Standing on the edge of the incline, they could see the thin stripe of a clay riverbank about thirty feet below them. The water was murky brown and went on forever.

"Where are we?" asked Tamina with a lump in her throat. She wanted to tell Raphael that she felt like going back, but she didn't dare. She was afraid he would refuse, and if he did, it would only make her more anxious.

There they stood, on the edge of the slope, water in front of them, clay all around them, wet clay with no grass cover, the kind of land good for mining. And in fact there was an abandoned bulldozer not far off.

Suddenly Tamina had a sense of *déjà vu:* this looked exactly like the terrain around where her husband had last worked in Czechoslovakia. After they fired him from his original job, he had found work as a bulldozer operator about seventy-five miles outside of Prague. During the week he lived at the site in a trailer, and since he could come into Prague to see her only on Sundays, she once made the trip out there during the week to visit him. They went for a walk through just this kind of countryside—the ocher and yellow of wet, clayey, grassless, treeless soil beneath them, the low, gray clouds above. They walked side by side in rubber boots that sank into the mud and slipped. They were alone in the world, the two of them, full of anguish, love, and desperate concern for each other.

That same sense of despair now invaded her, and she was glad for the lost fragment from the past it had suddenly, unexpectedly returned to her.

The memory had been completely lost. This was the first time it had come back to her. It occurred to her that she should put it down in her notebook. She even knew the exact year!

Again she felt like telling the young man she wanted to go back. No, he was wrong to tell her that her grief was all form and no content! No, no, her husband was still alive in her grief, just lost, that's all, and it was her job to look for him! Search the whole world over! Yes, yes! Now she understood. Finally! We will never remember anything by sitting in one place waiting for the memories to come back to us of their own accord! Memories are scattered all over the world. We must travel if we want to find them and flush them from their hiding places!

She was about to tell all that to the young man and ask him to drive her back when they suddenly heard a whistling sound down below.

9

Raphael grabbed Tamina by the hand. He had a strong grip, so there could be no thought of escape. A narrow, slippery path zigzagged down the incline, and he led her along it.

On the shore, where seconds before there had been no trace of anyone, stood a boy of about twelve. He was holding the painter of a rowboat bobbing up and down at the edge of the water. He smiled at Tamina.

She looked around at Raphael. He was smiling too. She looked back and forth from one to the other. Then Raphael began to laugh. The boy followed suit. It was a strange laugh—nothing funny had happened, after all—and yet pleasant and infectious. It was a challenge to Tamina to forget her anxieties, it was a promise of something vague—joy, perhaps, or peace. And since Tamina wanted to shed her misery, she laughed obediently with them.

"You see?" Raphael said to her. "There's nothing to be afraid of."

When Tamina stepped into the boat, it began to pitch under her. She sat on the seat nearest the stern. It was wet. She was wearing a light summer dress, and the moisture went right through to her bottom. It felt slimy, and again she was overcome by anxiety.

The boy pushed the boat away from the shore and picked up the oars. Tamina turned around. Raphael stood on the shore looking after them and smiling. Tamina thought she detected something unusual in that smile. Yes! Smiling, he shook his head ever so slightly! He shook his head ever so slightly.

10

Why didn't Tamina ask where she was going?

You don't ask where you're going if you don't care about the destination!

She watched the boy sitting across from her, rowing. He looked weak to her. The oars were too heavy for him.

"How about letting me take over for a while?" she suggested, and the boy nodded eagerly and gave up the oars.

They changed places. Now he was sitting in the stern watching Tamina row. He pulled a small tape recorder out from under the seat. The air was suddenly filled with electric guitars and voices. The boy began jerking his body in rhythm. Tamina looked on in disgust. The child was swaying his hips as provocatively as an adult. She found it obscene.

She lowered her eyes so as not to see him. The boy turned up the volume and began singing along softly. When Tamina looked up at him again for a minute, he asked her, "Why aren't you singing?"

"I don't know the song."

"What do you mean, you don't know it?" he asked, still jerking in time to the music. "Everybody knows it."

Tamina began to feel tired. "How about taking over for a while now?" she said.

"No, you keep rowing," he answered, laughing.

But Tamina was really tired. She shipped the oars and took a rest. "Will we be there soon?"

The boy pointed ahead. Tamina turned to look. They were quite close to the shore now. It differed enormously from the landscape they had left behind. It was green—all grass and trees.

In no time the boat had touched bottom. There were ten or so children playing ball on the shore, and they looked over curiously. Tamina and the boy stepped out of the boat. The boy tied it to a stake. Beyond the sandy shore stretched a long double row of plane trees. After a ten-minute walk along the path between the trees they came to a sprawling, low, white building. There were a number of large, strange, colored objects out front—she wondered what they were used for—and several volleyball nets. It struck Tamina that there was something not quite right about them. Yes, they were very close to the ground.

The boy put two fingers into his mouth and whistled.

11

Out came a girl who could not have been more than nine. She had a charming little face and walked with her stomach coquettishly protruding like the virgins in Gothic paintings. She glanced at Tamina with no special interest and with the look of a woman secure in her beauty and not beneath emphasizing it by a show of indifference to everything not touching her directly.

She opened the door to the white building. They walked directly into a large room full of beds (there was no sort of foyer or hallway). She looked around for a while, apparently counting beds, and then pointed to one. "That's where you sleep."

"You mean I'm going to sleep in a dormitory?" Tamina protested.

"A child doesn't need a room to itself."

"What do you mean? I'm not a child!"

"We're all children here!"

"But there must be some grownups!"

"No, no grownups."

"Then what am I doing here?" Tamina shouted.

The child did not notice her excitement and went back to the door. Just before going out, she turned and said, "I've put you in with the squirrels."

Tamina did not understand.

"I've put you in with the squirrels," repeated the child with the voice of a dissatisfied teacher. "All the children are assigned to groups with animal names."

Tamina refused to talk about the squirrels. She wanted to go back. She asked what had happened to the boy who had brought her over.

The girl made believe she had not heard what Tamina said, and went on with her remarks.

"I don't care about any of that!" shouted Tamina. "I want to go back! Where is that boy?"

"Stop shouting!" No adult could have been more imperious than that beautiful child. "I don't understand you," she went on, shaking her head to show how amazed she was. "Why did you come here if you want to leave?"

"I didn't want to come here!"

"Now, now, Tamina, don't lie. Nobody takes such a long journey without knowing where it ends. You must learn not to lie."

Tamina turned her back to the child and ran out to the tree-lined path. When she reached the shore, she looked for the boat at its mooring, where the boy had tied it an hour before. But the boat was nowhere to be seen—nor the stake, for that matter.

She began to run. She wanted to inspect the entire shore. But the sandy beach soon turned into swampland, and she had to make a detour before coming back to the water. The shoreline followed an even curve, and after about an hour's search (with no trace of the boat or any possible pier), she found herself back at the point where the tree-lined path came out on the beach. She realized she was on an island.

She walked slowly back along the path to the dormitory, where she found a group of ten children—boys and girls between the ages of six and twelve—standing in a circle. When they saw her, they all cried out, "Tamina, come and play with us!"

They opened the circle to let her in.

Just then she remembered Raphael smiling and shaking his head.

She was struck with terror, and ignoring the children, she ran straight into the dormitory and curled up on her bed.

12

Her husband died in a hospital. She stayed with him as much as she could, but he died in the night, alone. When she arrived the next day and found his bed empty, the old man he had shared the room with said to her, "You should file a complaint. The way they treat the dead!" There was fear in his eyes. He knew he hadn't long to live. "They took him by the legs and dragged him along the floor. They thought I was asleep. I saw his head bump against the threshold."

Death has two faces. One is nonbeing; the other is the terrifying material being that is the corpse.

When Tamina was very young, death would appear to her only in the first form, the form of nothingness, and the fear of death (a rather vague fear, in any case) meant the fear that someday she would cease to be. As she grew older, that fear diminished, almost disappeared (the thought that she would one day stop seeing trees or the sky did not scare her in the least), and she paid more and more attention to the second, material side of death. She was terrified of becoming a corpse.

Being a corpse struck her as an unbearable disgrace. One

minute you are a human being protected by modesty—the sanctity of nudity and privacy—and the next you die, and your body is suddenly up for grabs. Anyone can tear your clothes off, rip you open, inspect your insides, and—holding his nose to keep the stink away—stick you into the deepfreeze or the flames. One of the reasons she asked to have her husband cremated and his ashes thrown to the winds was that she did not want to torture herself over the thought of what might become of his dearly beloved body.

And when a few months later she contemplated suicide, she decided to drown herself somewhere far out at sea so that the only witnesses to the disgrace of her dead body would be fish, mute fish.

I have mentioned Thomas Mann's story before. A young man with a mortal illness boards a train and takes rooms in an unknown city. In one room there is a wardrobe, and every night a painfully beautiful naked woman steps out of it and tells him a long bittersweet tale, and the woman and her tale are death.

They are the sweet bluish death of nonbeing. Because nonbeing is infinite emptiness, and empty space is blue, and there is nothing more beautiful and comforting than blue. It is no mere coincidence that Novalis, the poet of death, loved blue and sought it out wherever he went. Death's sweetness is blue.

Granted, the nonbeing of Mann's young hero was beautiful, but what happened to his body? Did they drag him by the legs over the threshold? Did they slit his belly down the middle? Did they toss him into a hole or into the flames?

Mann was twenty-six at the time, and Novalis died before the age of thirty. I am unfortunately older, and unlike them I can't help thinking of what happens to the body. The trouble is, death is not blue, and Tamina knows it as well as I do. Death is terrible drudgery. It took my father several days of high fever to die, and from the way he was sweating I could see he was working hard. Death took all his concentration; it seemed almost beyond his powers. He couldn't even tell I was sitting at his bedside; he had no time to notice. The work he was putting in on death had completely drained him. His concentration was as focused as that of a rider driving his horse to a far-off destination, pressing his final burst of energy.

Yes, he was riding horseback.

Where was he going?

Somewhere far away to hide his body.

No, it is no coincidence that all poems about death depict it as a journey. Mann's young hero boards a train, Tamina climbs into a red sports car. Man has an infinite desire to go off and hide his body. But the journey is in vain. When his ride is done, they find him in bed and bang his head on the threshold.

13

Why is Tamina on a children's island? Why is that where I imagine her?

I don't know.

Maybe it's because on the day my father died the air was full of joyful songs sung by children's voices.

Everywhere east of the Elbe, children are banded together in what are called Pioneer organizations. They wear red kerchiefs around their necks, go to meetings like grownups, and now and then sing the "Internationale." They also have a nice custom of tying one of their red kerchiefs around the neck of a very special grownup and giving him the title Honorary Pioneer. The grownups like it very much, and the older the grownup is, the more he enjoys receiving the red kerchief from the children for his coffin.

They've all received one—Lenin, Stalin, Masturbov and Sholokhov, Ulbricht and Brezhnev. And that day Husak was receiving his at a festive ceremony in the Prague Castle.

Father's temperature had gone down a bit. It was May, and I opened the window facing the garden. From the house opposite us a television broadcast of the ceremony made its way through the blossoming branches of the apple trees. We heard the children singing in their high-pitched voices.

The doctor happened to be making his rounds. He bent over Father, who by now was incapable of a single word, and then turned to me and said in a normal tone of voice, "He's in a coma. His brain is decomposing." I saw Father's large blue eyes open even wider.

When the doctor left, I was so embarrassed I wanted to say something, right away, to push the doctor's words out of his mind. So I pointed out the window and said, "Hear that? What a joke! Husak is being named an Honorary Pioneer!"

And Father began to laugh. He laughed to let me know that his brain was alive and I could go on talking and joking with him.

Suddenly Husak's voice came to us through the apple trees. "Children! You are the future!"

And then, "Children! Never look back!"

"Let me close the window," I said. "We've heard enough of him, haven't we?" I gave Father a wink, and looking at me with his infinitely beautiful smile, he nodded his head.

Several hours later his fever shot up again. He mounted his horse and rode it hard the next few days. He never saw me again.

14

But what could she do now that she was there among the children? The ferryman had disappeared and taken the boat with him, and she was surrounded by an endless expanse of water.

She would fight.

It's sad, so sad. In the small town in the west of Europe she never lifted a finger. Did she really mean to fight there, among the children (in the world of things without weight)?

And how did she plan to go about it?

On the day she arrived, the day she refused to play and ran off to the impregnable fortress of her bed, she had felt their nascent hostility in the air. It scared her. She wanted to forestall it and decided to try to win them over, which meant she would have to identify with them, accept their language. She would volunteer for all their games, offer them her own ideas and her superior physical strength, and take them by storm with her charm.

To identify with them she had to give up her privacy. That first day she had refused to go into the bathroom with them. She was ashamed to wash with all of them looking on. Now she washed with them every day.

The large, tiled bathroom stood at the center of the children's lives and secret thoughts. Against one wall were ten toilet bowls, on the other ten sinks. While one team turned up its nightgowns and sat on the toilets, another stood naked in front of the sinks. The ones sitting on the toilets watched the naked ones at the sinks, the naked ones at the sinks looked over their shoulders at the ones on the toilets, and the whole room was full of a secret sensuality, which prompted in Tamina a vague memory of something long forgotten.

While Tamina sat on the toilet in her nightgown, the naked tigers standing at the sinks were all eyes. When the toilets flushed, the squirrels would stand up and take off their long nightgowns, and the tigers would leave the sinks for the bedroom, passing the cats on their way to the newly vacated toilets, where they in turn would watch Tamina with her black pubis and large breasts as she and the rest of the squirrels stood at the sinks.

She felt no shame. She felt that her mature sexuality made her a queen among all those whose pubic regions were smooth.

15

_____

Apparently, then, the journey to the island was not a plot against her, as she had originally thought when she first saw the dormitory and her bed. On the contrary, she felt as though she had finally come to the place she had always longed to be; she had slipped back in time to a point where her husband did not exist in either memory or desire and where consequently she felt neither pressure nor remorse.

She, who had always had such a well-developed sense of modesty (modesty was the faithful shadow of love), now exhibited herself naked to scores of foreign eyes. At first she found it distressing and unpleasant, but she soon grew accustomed to it. Her nakedness was no longer immodest; it had lost all meaning, it had become (or so she thought) drab, mute, dead. A body whose every inch was part of the history of love had lost its meaning, and in that lack of meaning was peace and quiet.

But if her adult sensuality was on the wane, a world of other pleasures had slowly begun to emerge from her distant past. Buried memories were coming to the fore. This, for example (it is no wonder that she had long since forgotten it; Tamina the adult would have found it unbearably improper and grotesque): in her very first year of elementary school she'd had a crush on her beautiful young teacher and dreamed for months on end of being allowed to go to the bathroom with her.

And now here she was, sitting on the toilet, smiling and half-closing her eyes. She imagined herself as the teacher and the little freckled girl sitting beside her and curiously peeking over at her as Tamina the child. She so identified with the sensuous eyes of the little freckled girl that she suddenly felt the shudder of an old half-awakened feeling of arousal in the farthest depths of her memory.

16

Thanks to Tamina the squirrels won nearly all the games, and they decided to reward her handsomely. All prizes and penalties were given out in the bathroom, and Tamina's prize was that she be waited on hand and foot there. In fact, she would not be allowed to touch herself. Everything would be done for her by her devoted servants, the squirrels.

Here is how they served her. First, while she was on the toilet they wiped her carefully; next, they stood her up, flushed the toilet, took off her nightgown, and led her over to the sink; then, they all tried to wash her breasts and pubis and see what she looked like between her legs and feel what it was like to touch. Now and then she tried to push them away, but it wasn't easy. She couldn't be mean to a bunch of children who were really just following the rules of their own game and thought they were rewarding her with their services.

Finally they took her back to her bed, where again they found all kinds of nice little excuses to press up against her and stroke her all over. There were so many of them swarming around her that she could not tell whose hand or mouth belonged to whom. She felt their pressing and probing everywhere, but especially in those areas where she differed from them. She closed her eyes and felt her body rocking, slowly rocking, as in a cradle. She was experiencing a strange, gentle sort of climax.

She felt the pleasure of it tugging at the corners of her lips. She opened her eyes again and saw a child's face staring at her mouth and telling another child's face, "Look! Look!" Now there were two faces leaning over her, avidly following the progress of her twitching lips. They might as well have been examining the workings of an open watch or a fly whose wings had been torn off.

But her eyes seemed to see something completely different from what her body felt, and she could not quite make the connection between the children leaning over her and the quiet, cradlelike pleasure she was experiencing. So she closed her eyes again and rejoiced in her body, because for the first time in her life her body was taking pleasure in the absence of the soul, which, imagining nothing and remembering nothing, had quietly left the room.

17

This is what my father told me when I was five: a key signature is a king's court in miniature. It is ruled by a king (the first step) and his two right-hand men (steps five and four). They have four other dignitaries at their command, each of whom has his own special relation to the king and his right-hand men. The court houses five additional tones as well, which are known as chromatic. They have important parts to play in other keys, but here they are simply guests.

Since each of the twelve notes has its own job, title, and function, any piece we hear is more than mere sound: it unfolds a certain action before us. Sometimes the events are terribly involved (as in Mahler or—even more—Bartók or Stravinsky): princes from other courts intervene, and before long there is no telling which court a tone belongs to and no assurance it isn't working undercover as a double or triple agent. But even then the most naive of listeners can figure out more or less what is going on. The most complex music is still *a language*.

That is what my father told me. What follows is all my own. One day a great man determined that after a thousand years the language of music had worn itself out and could do no more than rehash the same message. Abolishing the hierarchy of tones by revolutionary decree, he made them all equal and subjected them to a strict discipline: none was allowed to occur more often than any other in a piece, and therefore none could lay claim to its former feudal privileges. All courts were permanently abolished, and in their place arose a single empire, founded on equality and called the twelve-tone system.

Perhaps the sonorities were more interesting than they had been, but audiences accustomed to following the courtly intrigues of the keys for a millennium failed to make anything of them. In any case, the empire of the twelve-tone system soon disappeared. After Schönberg came Varèse, and he abolished notes (the tones of the human voice and musical instruments) along with keys, replacing them with an extremely subtle play of sounds which, though fascinating, marks the beginning of the history of something other than music, something based on other principles and another language.

When in my Prague apartment Milan Hubl held forth on the possibility of the Czech nation disappearing into the Russian empire, we both knew that the idea, though legitimate, went beyond us and that we were speaking of the *inconceivable*. Even though man is mortal, he cannot conceive of the end of space or time, of history or a nation: he lives in an illusory infinity.

People fascinated by the idea of progress never suspect that every step forward is also a step on the way to the end and that behind all the joyous "onward and upward" slogans lurks the lascivious voice of death urging us to make haste.

(If the obsession with the word "onward" has become universal nowadays, isn't it largely because death now speaks to us at such close range?)

In the days when Arnold Schönberg founded his twelve-tone empire, music was richer than ever before and intoxicated with its freedom. No one ever dreamed the end was so near. No fatigue. No twilight. Schönberg was audacious as only youth can be. He was legitimately proud of having chosen the only road that led "onward." The history of music came to an end in a burst of daring and desire.

18

If it is true that the history of music has come to an end, what is left of music? Silence?

Not in the least. There is more and more of it, many times more than in its most glorious days. It pours out of outdoor speakers, out of miserable sound systems in apartments and restaurants, out of the transistor radios people carry around the streets.

Schönberg is dead, Ellington is dead, but the guitar is eternal. Stereotyped harmonies, hackneyed melodies, and a beat that gets stronger as it gets duller—that is what's left of music, the eternity of music. Everyone can come together on the basis of those simple combinations of notes. They are life itself proclaiming its jubilant "Here I am!" No sense of communion is more resonant, more unanimous, than the simple sense of communion with life. It can bring Arab and Jew together, Czech and Russian. Bodies pulsing to a common beat, drunk with the consciousness that they exist. No work of Beethoven's has ever elicited greater collective passion than the constant repetitive throb of the guitar.

One day, about a year before my father's death, the two of us were taking a walk around the block, and that music seemed to be following us everywhere. The sadder people are, the louder the speakers blare. They are trying to make an occupied country forget the bitterness of history and devote all its energy to the joys of everyday life. Father stopped and looked up at the device the noise was coming from, and I could tell he had something very important to tell me. Concentrating as hard as he could on putting what was on his mind into words, he finally came out with: "The idiocy of music."

What did he mean? Could he possibly have meant to insult music, the love of his life? No, what I think he wanted to tell me was that there is a certain *primordial state of music,* a state prior to its history, the state before the issue was ever raised, the state before the play of motif and theme was ever conceived or even contemplated. This elementary state of music (music minus thought) reflects the inherent idiocy of human life. It took a monumental effort of heart and mind for music to rise up over this inherent idiocy, and it was this glorious vault arching over centuries of European history that died out at the peak of its flight like a rocket in a fireworks display.

The history of music is mortal, but the idiocy of the guitar is eternal. Music in our time has returned to its primordial state, the state after the last issue has been raised and the last theme contemplated—a state that follows history.

When Karel Gott, the Czech pop singer, went abroad in 1972, Husak got scared. He sat right down and wrote him a personal letter (it was August 1972 and Gott was in Frankfurt). The following is a verbatim quote from it. I have invented nothing.

Dear Karel,
We are not angry with you. Please come back. We will do everything you ask. We will help you if you help us . . .

Think it over. Without batting an eyelid Husak let doctors, scholars, astronomers, athletes, directors, cameramen, workers, engineers, architects, historians, journalists, writers, and painters go into emigration, but he could not stand the thought of Karel Gott leaving the country: Because Karel Gott represents music minus memory, the music in which the bones of Beethoven and Ellington, the dust of Palestrina and Schönberg, lie buried.

The president of forgetting and the idiot of music deserve one another. They are working for the same cause. "We will help you if you help us." You can't have one without the other.

19

But even in the tower where the wisdom of music reigns supreme we sometimes feel nostalgic for that monotonous, heartless shriek of a beat which comes to us from outside and in which all men are brothers. Keeping exclusive company with Beethoven is dangerous in the way all privileged positions are dangerous.

Tamina was always a little ashamed of admitting she was happy with her husband. She was afraid people would hate her for it.

As a result, she is not quite sure where she stands. First she feels that love is a privilege and all privileges are undeserved and that's why she has to pay. Being here with the children is a form of punishment.

But then she feels something different. The privilege of love may have been heavenly, but it was hellish as well. When she was in love, her life was constant tension, fear, agitation. Being here with the children is a long-awaited rest, a reward.

Until now, her sexuality had been occupied by love (I say "occupied" because sex is not love; it is merely the territory love marks out for itself) and therefore had a dramatic, responsible, serious component to it, something Tamina watched over with anguish. Here with the children in the realm of the insignificant it finally reverted to what it had originally been: a toy for the production of sensual pleasure.

Or to put it another way, sexuality freed from its *diabolical* ties with love had become a joy of *angelic* simplicity.

20

If the first time the children raped Tamina the act had all sorts of startling undertones, with repetition it quickly lost whatever message it might have had and turned into a routine that became less and less interesting and more and more dirty.

Soon the children started quarreling among themselves. The ones who were excited by the games of love began to hate the ones who were indifferent to them. And among Tamina's lovers there was definite hostility between the ones who felt they were her favorites and the ones who felt rejected. And all these petty resentments began to turn in on Tamina and weigh on her.

Once, when the children were leaning over her naked body (standing by the bed, kneeling on the bed, straddling her body, squatting at her head and between her legs), she felt a sudden sharp pain: one of the children had given her nipple a hard pinch. She let out a scream and went berserk, throwing all the children off the bed and flailing her arms around her.

She realized the pain had been caused by neither chance nor lust; one of the children hated her and was out to hurt her. She put an end to her amorous encounters with the children.

21

All at once the realm where things are light as a breeze knows no peace.

The children are playing hopscotch, jumping from one square to the next, right leg first, then left, then both. Tamina joins in (I can picture her tall body among the small figures of the children, and as she jumps, her hair flies out around her face and her heart is all boredom), and the canaries start shouting that she's stepped on a line.

The squirrels, of course, protest she hasn't, so both teams stoop down over the lines to look for the imprint of Tamina's foot. But lines drawn in sand lose their shape easily, and so does Tamina's footprint. It is a moot point, and the children have been yelling it out for a quarter of an hour and getting more and more involved in the argument.

At one point Tamina gives a fateful wave of the hand and says, "Oh, all right, so I did step on the line."

The squirrels begin shouting at Tamina that it isn't true, she must be crazy, she's lying, she never touched it. But they have lost the argument—their claim, once exposed by Tamina, has no weight —and the canaries let out a whoop of victory.

The squirrels are furious. They scream "Traitor" at her, and one boy gives her a push that nearly topples her. She tries to grab hold of them, and they take that as a signal to pounce on her. She puts up a good defense. She is a grownup, she is strong (and full of hate, oh yes, she pounds away at those children as if they were everything she ever hated in life), and before long there are quite a few bloody noses in the crowd, but then a stone flies out of nowhere and hits her on the forehead, and she staggers a little, clutching her head. It is bleeding, and the children move away from her. Suddenly everything is quiet, and Tamina makes her way back to the dormitory. She stretches out on her bed, determined never to take part in the games again.

22

I can see Tamina standing in the middle of the dormitory full of children in bed. She is the center of attention. "Tits, tits," calls out a voice from one corner. Others join in, and soon she is engulfed in a rhythmic "Tits, titties, tits . . ."

What not so long ago had been her pride and weapon—her black pubic hair, her beautiful breasts—was now the target of their insults. In the eyes of the children the very fact of her adulthood made her grotesque: her breasts were as absurd as tumors, her pubic area monstrously hairy, beastlike.

They began tracking her down, chasing her all over the island, throwing driftwood and stones at her. She tried to hide, run away, but wherever she went she heard them calling out her name: "Tits, titties, tits . . ."

Nothing is more degrading than the strong running from the weak. But there were so many of them. She ran and was ashamed of running.

Once she set an ambush and caught and beat three of them. One fell down, two started to make a getaway. But she was too fast for them; she grabbed them by the hair.

And then a net slipped down over her, and another and another. That's right, all the volleyball nets which had been stretched out just above the ground in front of the dormitory. They had been waiting for her. The three children she had just beaten were a decoy. And now here she is, imprisoned in a tangle of nets, twisting and turning, thrashing out in all directions, dragged along by the jubilant children.

23

Why are the children so bad?

But they're *not* all that bad. In fact, they're full of good cheer and constantly helping one another. None of them wants Tamina for himself. "Look, look!" they call back and forth. Tamina is imprisoned in a tangle of nets, the ropes tear into her skin, and the children point to her blood, tears, and face contorted with pain. They offer her generously to one another. She has cemented their feelings of brotherhood.

The reason for her misfortune is not that the children are bad, but that she does not belong to their world. No one makes a fuss about calves slaughtered in slaughterhouses. Calves stand outside human law in the same way Tamina stands outside the children's law.

If anyone is full of bitterness and hate, it is Tamina, not the children. Their desire to cause pain is positive, exuberant: it has every right to be called pleasure. Their only motive for causing pain to someone not of their world is to glorify that world and its law.

24

Time takes its toll, and all joys and pleasures lose their luster with repetition. Besides, the children really aren't all that bad. The boy who urinated on her when she lay tangled beneath him in the volleyball nets gave her a beautiful open smile a few days later.

Without a word Tamina began taking part in the games again. Once more she jumps from square to square, right leg first, then left, then both together. She will never try to enter their world again, but is careful not to find herself beyond it either. She tries to keep right on the borderline.

But the calm, the normality of it all, the *modus vivendi* based on compromise, have all the terrifying earmarks of a permanent arrangement. While Tamina was being tracked down, she forgot about the existence of time and its boundlessness, but now that the violence of the attacks has died down, the desert of time has emerged from the shadows—frightening, oppressive, very like eternity.

Make sure you have this image firmly engraved in your memory. She must jump from square to square, right leg first, then left, then both together, and make a show of caring whether or not she steps on a line. She must go on jumping day after day, bearing the burden of time on her shoulders like a cross that grows heavier from day to day.

Does she still look back? Does she think about her husband and Prague?

No. Not anymore.

25

The ghosts of statues long torn down wandered around the podium where the president of forgetting was standing with a red scarf around his neck. The children clapped and called out his name.

Eight years have gone by since then, but I can still hear his words sailing through the blossoming apple trees.

"Children, you are the future," he said, and today I realize he did not mean it the way it sounded. The reason children are the future is not that they will one day be grownups. No, the reason is that mankind is moving more and more in the direction of infancy, and childhood is the image of the future.

"Children, never look back," he cried, and what he meant was that we must never allow the future to collapse under the burden of memory. Children, after all, have no past whatsoever. That alone accounts for the mystery of charmed innocence in their smiles.

History is a succession of ephemeral changes. Eternal values exist outside history. They are immutable and have no need of memory. Husak is president of the eternal, not the ephemeral. He is on the side of children, and children are life, and life is "seeing, hearing, eating, drinking, urinating, defecating, diving into water and observing the firmament, laughing, and crying."

What apparently happened after Husak came to the end of his speech to the children (I had closed the window by then, and Father was about to remount his horse) was that Karel Gott came out onto the podium and sang. Husak was so moved that the tears streamed down his cheeks, and the sunny smiles shining up at him blended with his tears, and a great miracle of a rainbow arched up at that moment over Prague.

The children looked up, saw the rainbow, and began laughing and clapping.

The idiot of music finished his song, and the president of forgetting spread his arms and cried, "Children, life is happiness!"

26

The island resounds with the roar of song and the din of guitars. There is a tape recorder sitting in the open space in front of the dormitory and a boy standing over it. Tamina recognizes him. He is the boy on whose ferry she long ago came to the island. She is very excited. If he is the boy, his ferry can't be far off. She knows she mustn't let this opportunity slip by. Her heart begins to pound, and the only thing she can think of is how to escape.

The boy is staring down at the tape recorder and moving his hips. The children come running to join him. They jerk one shoulder forward, then the other, throw their heads back, wave their arms, point their index fingers as if threatening someone, and shout along with the song coming out of the tape recorder.

Tamina is hiding behind the thick trunk of a plane tree. She does not want them to see her, but cannot tear her eyes from them. They are behaving with the provocative flirtatiousness of the adult world, rolling their hips as if imitating intercourse. The lewdness of the motions superimposed on their children's bodies destroys the dichotomy between obscenity and innocence, purity and corruption. Sensuality loses all its meaning, innocence loses all its meaning, words fall apart, and Tamina feels nauseous, as though her stomach has been hollowed out.

And the idiocy of the guitars keeps booming, the children keep dancing, flirtatiously undulating their little bellies. It is little things of no weight at all that are making Tamina nauseous. In fact, that hollow feeling in her stomach comes from the unbearable absence of weight. And just as one extreme may at any moment turn into its opposite, so this perfect buoyancy has become a terrifying *burden of buoyancy,* and Tamina knows she cannot bear it another instant. She turns and runs.

She runs along the path down to the water.

Now she has reached the water's edge. She looks around. No boat.

She runs all along the shore of the island looking for it, the way she did that first day. She does not see it. Finally she comes back to the spot where the tree-lined path opens onto the beach. The children are running around, all excited.

She stops.

The children notice her and hurl themselves in her direction, shouting.

27

She jumped into the water.

It wasn't because she was frightened. She'd thought it out long before. The ferry to the island hadn't taken that long. Even though she couldn't see the other shore, she wouldn't need superhuman strength to swim across.

Yelling and shouting, the children ran down to the place where she had jumped in, and several stones splashed down near her. But she was a fast swimmer and was soon out of range of their weak arms.

On she swam, feeling well for the first time in ages. She could feel her body, feel its old strength. She had always been an excellent swimmer and enjoyed every stroke. The water was cold, but she welcomed it. She felt it was cleansing her of all the children's dirt, of their saliva and their looks.

She swam for a long time, and the sun began sinking into the water.

And then it got dark, pitch black. There was no moon, no stars, but Tamina tried to keep herself headed in the same direction.

28

Where was she heading, anyway? Prague?

She did not know if it still existed.

The little town in the west of Europe?

No. She simply wanted to get away.

Does that mean she wanted to die?

No, no, not at all. In fact, she had a great desire for life.

But she must have had some idea about the world she wanted to live in.

Well, she didn't. All she had left was her body and a great desire for life. Those two things and nothing more. She wanted to get them away from the island and save them. Her body and her desire for life.

29

Then it began to get light. She strained her eyes to catch a glimpse of the other shore.

But all she could see was water. She turned and looked back. There, a few hundred feet away, was the shore of the green island.

Could she possibly have swum the whole night in place? She was overcome with despair, and the moment she lost hope her arms and legs seemed to lose their strength, and the water felt unbearably cold. She closed her eyes and tried to keep swimming. She no longer hoped to reach the other side; all she could think of now was how she would die, and she wanted to die somewhere in the midst of the waters, removed from all contact, alone with the fish. She must have dozed off for a bit while her eyes were closed, because suddenly there was water in her lungs and she began coughing and choking, and in the middle of it all she heard children's voices.

Splashing and coughing, she looked around. Not far away there was a boat with several children in it. They were shouting. As soon as they noticed she had seen them, they stopped shouting and rowed up to her, staring. She saw how excited they were.

She was afraid they would try to save her and she would have to play with them again. Suddenly she felt a wave of exhaustion come over her. Her arms and legs seemed numb.

The boat was almost upon her, and five children's faces peered eagerly down at her.

She shook her head desperately as if to say, "Let me die. Don't save me."

But she had no reason to be afraid. The children did not budge. No one held out an oar or a hand to her, no one tried to save her. They just kept staring at her, wide-eyed and eager. They were observing her. One of the boys used his oar as a rudder to keep the boat close enough.

Again she inhaled water into her lungs and coughed and thrashed her arms about, feeling she could no longer keep herself afloat. Her legs were getting heavier and heavier. They dragged her down like lead weights.

Her head ducked underwater. By struggling violently, she managed to raise it back up several times, and each time she saw the boat and the children's eyes observing her.

Then she disappeared beneath the surface.

PART SEVEN
The Border

1

The thing he always found most interesting about a woman during intercourse was her face. The motions of her body seemed to set a large reel of film rolling, and her face was the television screen the film was projected onto. It was an exciting film full of turbulence, expectation, excitement, pain, cries, tenderness, and spite. Unfortunately, Edwige's face was a blank screen, and Jan would stare at it, tormented by questions he could find no answers for. Was she bored with him? Was she tired? Did she dislike making love? Was she accustomed to better lovers? Or was she hiding something beneath that motionless surface, experiences Jan could have no idea of?

Of course he might have asked her. But they had fallen into a strange pattern. Though normally talkative and open with each other, they would both lose the power of speech once their bodies intertwined.

He could never quite explain the phenomenon. Maybe it was because in matters other than erotic Edwige was more likely to take the initiative. Even though she was younger, she had spoken at least three times as many words and given ten times as much counsel and advice. He looked on her as a kind, knowing mother who had taken him by the hand and was guiding him through life.

He often thought of breathing obscene words into her ear while making love, but even in his thoughts it ended in disaster. He was certain he would find a gentle smile of protest and condescending indulgence, the smile of a mother looking on while her little boy steals a forbidden cookie from the kitchen cabinet.

Or he thought of whispering something absolutely banal, such as "Is it good?" With other women even that simple query had always sounded improper. By giving the love act a name, if only an innocent little word like "it," he paved the way for other words, words that would reflect physical love as in a set of mirrors. But he could predict how Edwige would respond. Of course it's good, she would tell him patiently. Do you really think I would voluntarily do something I don't like? Not very logical of you, is it, Jan?

As a result, he neither whispered obscene words nor asked if it was good. He held his peace, while their bodies went through the long, frenzied motions of setting an empty reel spinning, a reel with no film on it.

He often blamed himself for putting the damper on their nights together. He had created a caricature of Edwige-as-lover that now stood between them and made it impossible for him to penetrate the real Edwige, her senses and obscene depths. Things were so bad that after each of their tongue-tied nights he made a vow he would not make love to her the next time. He loved her as an intelligent, faithful, irreplaceable friend, not as a mistress. But how do you separate mistress from friend? Whenever they got together, they would sit and talk late into the night, which meant that Edwige would drink and give him her views on everything, and when Jan was dead tired she would suddenly stop and smile a blissfully benign smile, at which point Jan, as if responding to an irresistible suggestion, would touch one of her breasts and she would stand up and start to undress.

Why does she want to make love with me? he asked himself many times. He could never find an answer. All he knew was that their silent copulations were inevitable, as inevitable as a man standing at attention when he hears his national anthem though neither he nor his country derives any benefit from it.

2

Over the last two hundred years the blackbird has abandoned the woods for the city—first in Great Britain at the end of the eighteenth century, then several decades later in Paris and the Ruhr Valley. Throughout the nineteenth century it captured the cities of Europe one after the other. It settled in Vienna and Prague around

1900, and journeyed eastward to Budapest, Belgrade, and Istanbul.

Globally, the blackbird's invasion of the human world is beyond a doubt more important than the Spaniards' invasion of South America or the resettlement of Palestine by the Jews. A change in the relationship of one species to another (fish, birds, people, plants) is a change of a higher order than a change in the relationship of one or another group within the species. The earth does not particularly care whether Celts or Slavs inhabited Bohemia, whether Romanians or Russians occupy Bessarabia. If, however, the blackbird goes against nature and follows man to his artificial, anti-natural world, something has changed in the planetary order of things.

And yet nobody dares to interpret the last two centuries as the history of the blackbird's invasion of the city of man. We are all prisoners of a rigid conception of what is important and what is not. We anxiously follow what we suppose to be important, while what we suppose to be unimportant wages guerrilla warfare behind our backs, transforming the world without our knowledge and eventually mounting a surprise attack on us.

If someone were to write Jan's biography, he might summarize the period I have been talking about in the following terms:

The liaison with Edwige marked a new stage in the life of the forty-five-year-old Jan. Forswearing at long last the empty, unstructured life he had been leading, he resolved to leave the town in the west of Europe where he had been living, and cross the ocean, the better to devote his energies to the important project which later gained him such etc., etc.

But how is Jan's imaginary biographer going to explain to me why Jan's favorite book during this period was the ancient tale of Daphnis and Chloe? The love of two near-children who do not know what physical love is. The bleating of a ram blends with the roaring of the sea, a lamb grazes under the branch of an olive tree, and Daphnis and Chloe lie naked, full of a vague, boundless desire. They embrace, they press, they intertwine. And there they stay for a long, long time, unaware of what to do next. They think that pressing together is the be-all and end-all of love's joys. They are aroused, their hearts are pounding, but they do not know what it means to make love.

Yes, that is the passage that fascinates Jan.

3

_____

Jeanne the actress sat with her legs crossed under her like the legs of Buddha statues sold in antique shops the world over. She talked a blue streak, hardly lifting her eyes from her thumb, which was tracing small circles around the rim of the circular coffee table in front of the couch.

It was no nervous habit, like tapping the foot or scratching the head; it was conscious and deliberate, charming and graceful; it was meant to describe a magic circle around her, making her the center of attention—her own and everyone else's.

She followed the journey of her thumb with great delight, only occasionally looking up at Jan, who sat opposite her. She was telling him she had just been through a nervous breakdown. Her son, who lived in another town with her former husband, had run away from home and stayed away for several days. The father of her son was such a brute he'd phoned her half an hour before she was due to go on. Jeanne the actress had run a fever, come down with a splitting headache, and caught a nasty cold to boot. "I couldn't even blow my nose, my sinuses hurt so!" she said, flashing her big, beautiful eyes at Jan. "My nose was like a cauliflower!"

She smiled the smile of a woman who knows that even a red, congested nose looks good on her. She lived in exemplary harmony with herself. She loved her nose, loved the daring with which she called a cold a cold and a nose a cauliflower. The unconventional beauty of her red nose complemented her courageous spirit, and the circular movement of her thumb combined both charms in its magic arc and transformed them into the insoluble unity of her personality.

"That fever really got me down, you know? And you know

what the doctor told me? He said, 'I have only one piece of advice for you, Jeanne. Stop taking your temperature!' " And after laughing long and loud over her doctor's joke, she added, "Oh, by the way, guess who I just met! Passer!"

Passer was an old friend of Jan's. The last time Jan had seen him, months before, he was going in for an operation. Everybody knew it was cancer, but Passer, bursting with incredible vitality and faith, believed the doctors' lies. In any case, the operation was a very serious one, and Passer had once told Jan when they were alone, "When it's over, I won't be a man anymore, if you know what I mean. My life as a man is over."

"I met him last week at the Clevises' country place," she went on. "What a wonderful man! Younger than any of us. I just adore him!"

Jan should have been glad that the beautiful actress liked his friend, but it did not make much of an impression on him, because everyone loved Passer. On the irrational market of social popularity his stock had risen sharply in the past few years. It had become an almost indispensable ritual to say a few nice things about Passer during dinner-party chit-chat.

"You know those beautiful woods all around the Clevises' place? Well, they're full of mushrooms, and I just adore mushrooming! But when I asked people to go with me, nobody felt like it. And then Passer said he would. Passer! You know how sick he is! Let me tell you, he's younger than any of us."

She looked down at her thumb, still making its circles along the edge of the table, and said, "Anyway, the two of us went out mushrooming. It was terrific! We wandered all over the woods and then found a little café, a dirty little country café. The kind I just adore! The kind where you order cheap red wine, where workingmen drink. Passer was terrific! I just adore him!"

4

During the period when all this took place, the beaches of Western Europe were crowded every summer with women who wore no tops, and the population was divided between partisans of bared breasts and their adversaries. The Clevis family—mother, father, and fourteen-year-old daughter—were sitting in front of their television set watching a debate on the topic with representatives of every possible intellectual current of the day. The psychoanalyst gave a fiery defense of the naked breast, invoking the liberalization of social mores and its role in delivering the individual from the power of erotic illusions. The Marxist never quite took a stand on the topless issue (the membership of the Communist Party included both puritans and libertines, and it was not politically expedient to set one side against the other); instead, he skillfully twisted the debate around to the more basic problem of the two-faced moral standards of bourgeois society, which was on its way to destruction. The representative of the Christian viewpoint felt duty-bound to defend the top, but did so only halfheartedly; even he could not escape the spirit of the time. The only argument he could cite in its favor was the innocence of little children, which everyone was obliged to respect and protect. He was immediately attacked by an energetic woman who declared that childhood was the perfect time to overcome the hypocritical taboo against nudity, and recommended that all parents walk around naked at home.

Jan arrived at the Clevises' just as the moderator was announcing the end of the debate, but the excitement it had generated remained in the air for quite some time. They were all liberals and therefore anti-bra in general. To them the grandiose gesture with which millions of women threw off the infamous article of clothing as if on command symbolized mankind throwing off the chains of slavery. Bare-breasted women paraded around the Clevis apartment like an invisible battalion of Amazons.

As I have pointed out, the Clevises were good progressives with good progressive ideas. There are many varieties of progressive ideas, and the Clevises lent their support to only the best of them. The best of all possible progressive ideas is the one which is provocative enough so its supporters can feel proud of being different, but popular enough so the risk of isolation is precluded by cheering crowds confident of victory. If, for instance, the Clevises were anti-clothes instead of anti-bra, if they claimed people should walk the streets naked, they would also be supporting a progressive idea, but definitely not the best of all possible ones. It would be extremist enough to become difficult, it would take an inordinate amount of energy to defend (the best of all possible progressive ideas practically defended themselves), and its supporters would never have the satisfaction of seeing a completely nonconformist position suddenly become a position everyone accepts.

Listening to them fulminate against tops and bras, Jan thought of the small wooden object called a level that his grandfather, who had been a bricklayer, would routinely set on the surface of a wall as it went up. Under a tiny plate of glass in the middle of the instrument was a drop of water with a bubble in it which, according to its position, would tell whether the bricks were even or not. The Clevis family could serve as a spiritual air bubble. Offer them any idea, and they would provide a perfect indication of whether it was the best of all possible progressive ideas.

After they had gone through their rather jumbled version of the debate for Jan's sake, Papa Clevis leaned over to him and said jokingly, "As long as the breasts are good-looking, the reform's a winner, don't you think?"

Now why did Papa Clevis formulate his opinion in precisely those terms? He was a perfect host, and always tried to find just the right way of putting things for his guests. Since Jan had the reputation of a womanizer, Papa Clevis did not express approval of naked breasts in terms of his deep-felt and valid *ethical* enthusiasm over the end of a millennium of slavery; rather, he compromised and (in deference to his idea of Jan's tastes and contrary to his own convictions) expressed it in terms of *aesthetic* enthusiasm over the charms of a well-formed breast.

He tried to be both precise and diplomatic. He did not dare to say straight out that ugly breasts should remain covered. But though never stated, this admittedly unacceptable idea followed only too clearly from his original statement, and was an easy target for his fourteen-year-old daughter.

"Then what about your beer bellies?" she exploded. "What about those ugly beer bellies you shamelessly parade around the beaches?"

"Bravo!" exclaimed Mama Clevis, laughing and clapping.

Papa Clevis joined in. He saw immediately that his daughter was right and that he was once again the victim of the unfortunate propensity for compromise his wife and daughter often chided him about. He was in fact so deeply peace-loving a man that he was even willing to concede his compromise, make an about-face, and accept his daughter's more radical view. And since the statement she had attacked reflected the position he felt Jan would be likely to take, rather than his own position, he was grateful for the excuse to stand unhesitatingly by his daughter and satisfy his paternal instincts.

Excited by the applause of both her parents, the girl went on. "I suppose you think the reason we don't wear tops is to give you a thrill. No, we do it for ourselves, because we like it, because it feels better, because it brings our bodies closer to the sun! You are incapable of seeing us as anything but sex objects!"

Mama and Papa Clevis gave her another round of applause, though this time their bravos had a slightly different ring to them. Their daughter's statement was true enough, but it was also rather inappropriate considering her age. If an eight-year-old boy says, "Don't worry, Mother. I'll save you if anyone tries to hold you up," the boy's parents will applaud him. After all, his intentions are clearly praiseworthy. But since they also show him to be a bit too sure of himself, his parents temper their praise with an ironic smile. That same ironic smile tempered the Clevises' second bravo, and their daughter, who noticed the irony and took a dim view of it, repeated obstinately, "Those days are gone forever. You won't catch me being anybody's sex object."

This time her parents merely nodded—straight-facedly, so as not to provoke any more proclamations.

Jan, however, could not resist addressing one remark to her. "If you knew how terribly easy it is not to be a sex object."

He said it softly, but with such sincere sorrow in his voice that it seemed to resonate for a long time through the room. It was a remark they could not pass over in silence, but could not react to either. On the one hand, it did not deserve approval, because it was not progressive; on the other hand, it did not deserve refutation, because it was not particularly anti-progressive. It was the worst of all possible statements; it belonged outside the circle of fashionable issues. It was a statement beyond good and evil, a statement absolute in its incongruity.

There was a short period of silence, during which Jan smiled an embarrassed smile, as if apologizing for what he had said. Then Papa Clevis, past master at bridging gaps between his fellow men, changed the subject to Passer, a common acquaintance. Their admiration for Passer brought them back together. Clevis praised Passer's optimism, that tenacious love of life that no doctor's prescriptions had been able to stifle. And now Passer's existence was limited to a narrow strip of life without women, without food, without drink, without mobility—without a future. He'd been to visit them recently at their country place. Jeanne the actress had been there too.

Jan wondered how the Clevis level would react to Jeanne, whose egocentric mannerisms he found close to unbearable. But the bubble indicated that Jan had guessed wrong. Clevis was unconditionally approving of the way she had treated Passer. She'd devoted herself entirely to him. It was so warmhearted of her. Especially with the tragic times she'd been through.

"Tragic times?" asked forgetful Jan in amazement.

Could Jan possibly not have heard? Her son ran away from home and stayed away for several days! She'd had a regular nervous breakdown! But as soon as she set eyes on Passer, who after all is on death row, she forgot all about herself. Just to bring him out of his depression, she squealed cheerfully, "Who wants to come mushroom hunting with me?" Well, Passer said he would, so the rest of us begged off. We could tell she wanted to be alone with him. For three hours they walked around the woods. Then they stopped at a café for some wine. Passer isn't allowed to do any walking or drinking. He came back exhausted, but happy. The next day they had to take him to the hospital. "From what I hear, in pretty bad condition," said Papa Clevis. "You ought to go see him," he added reproachfully.

5

At the beginning of man's erotic life, Jan said to himself, there is arousal without climax; at the end there is climax without arousal.

Arousal without climax is Daphnis; climax without arousal was the girl from the sporting goods rental place.

A year ago, when he first met her and invited her back to his apartment, she came out with an unforgettable statement. "I'm sure it will be good technique-wise; emotion-wise, though, I don't know."

He told her that as far as he was concerned she could be absolutely sure about the emotional side of things. She accepted his word the way she accepted deposits on skis at the store, and never spoke about emotions again. As for technique, she had just about worn him down.

She was an orgasm fanatic. The orgasm was her religion, her only goal, the primary rule of hygiene, a symbol of health; but it was pride as well, because it distinguished her from less fortunate women, like having a yacht or a famous fiancé.

It wasn't easy to give her one, either. "Faster," she'd urge him on, "faster," and then "Take it easy, take it easy," and then again "Harder, harder." She was like a coxswain shouting orders to the crew of a racing shell. Completely caught up in her own erogenous zones, she would guide his hand to the right place at the right time. Whenever he looked at her, he would see her impatient eyes and the feverish thrashings of her body—a portable apparatus for manufacturing the minor explosion that had become the meaning, the goal of her life.

The last time he left her apartment he suddenly thought of Hertz, an opera director in the small Central European town where he had spent his youth. Hertz required his women singers to perform their entire roles for him in private during special nude blocking rehearsals. To ensure that they held their bodies just so, he had them insert pencils into their rectums. Since the direction in which the pencil pointed indicated the position of the spinal column, the meticulous director was able to control every step, every motion of the singer's body, with scientific precision.

Once a young soprano lost her temper and denounced him to the management. Hertz defended himself by saying he had never molested any of the singers, that he had never even touched them, which was true enough, but only made his pencil antics seem more perverse. Hertz was finally run out of town.

His case had become famous, however, and Jan began attending opera performances at a tender age. All the women—with their overblown gestures, twisted heads, and wide-open mouths—he would picture naked. As the orchestra wept and they clasped their left breasts, he would see pencils sticking out of their bare behinds. His heart would pound. He was aroused by Hertz's arousal! (To this day he cannot see an opera in any other light, and to this day whenever he enters an opera house, he feels like a little boy sneaking off to watch a dirty movie.)

Hertz was a sublime alchemist of vice, Jan said to himself. He found the magic formula of arousal in the form of a pencil stuck up the rectum. Jan was ashamed. Hertz would never have let himself be hoodwinked into the exhausting command performance Jan had just played on the body of the girl from the sporting goods rental place.

6

Just as the invasion of the blackbird represents the reverse side of European history, so the story I am telling takes place on the reverse side of Jan's life. I have put it together from bits and pieces of events that Jan probably never paid particular attention to, because the obverse side of his life was taken up with all kinds of other cares and worries: the offer of a job in America, pressing professional commitments, preparation for departure.

Not too long ago he ran across Barbara on the street. She asked him reproachfully why he never accepted invitations to her house. Barbara's house had a reputation for group sex parties. Jan was afraid of scandal and had refused her invitations for years. This time, though, he smiled and said, "I'd be glad to come." He knew he would never set foot in the town again, so there was no need to maintain discretion. He pictured Barbara's house full of gleeful naked bodies, and said to himself it might not make such a bad farewell party.

Yes, Jan was saying goodbye. He had come to grips with the fact that in several months he would be crossing the border. But the word "border" in the common geographical sense of the term conjured up another border as well, an intangible and immaterial border he had been thinking of more and more lately.

What border was that?

The woman he had loved most in the world (he was thirty at the time) used to tell him (it would make him desperate to hear it) that her life was hanging by a thread. Oh yes, she wanted to live, she loved life, but she also knew that her "I want to live" was spun from the threads of a cobweb. It takes so litile, so infinitely little, for a person to cross the border beyond which everything loses meaning: love, convictions, faith, history. Human life—and herein lies its secret—takes place in the immediate proximity of that border, even in direct contact with it; it is not miles away, but a fraction of an inch.

7

Every man has two erotic biographies. Usually people talk only about the first: the list of affairs and of one-night stands.

The other biography is sometimes more interesting: the parade of women we wanted to have, the women who got away. It is a mournful history of opportunities wasted.

But there is also a third, mysterious, unsettling category of women: the women we could never have had. We liked them, they liked us, but it didn't take long for us to see that they were out of reach, that for them we were *on the other side of the border.*

Jan was on a train, reading, when a pretty girl he did not know took a seat in his compartment (the only empty seat was the one just opposite him) and nodded to him. He nodded back, trying to think of where they could have met. He returned to his book, but couldn't get into it. He felt the girl looking at him, wondering about him, expecting something from him.

"Where do I know you from?" he asked, closing the book.

No wonder he had trouble remembering. They had met five years before at the house of some people he hardly knew. But he did remember finally, and asked her a few questions: what exactly had she been doing at the time, who was in her crowd, where did she work now, and did she enjoy it.

He was used to lighting a quick spark between himself and a woman. This time, though, he realized he sounded like a member of the personnel office interviewing an applicant for a job.

He stopped talking. He opened the book and tried to read, but had the feeling he was being observed by an invisible examining committee that maintained a complete file on him and noted his every move. He obstinately stared down at the pages without any idea of what was on them, vaguely aware that the committee was patiently keeping track of the number of minutes he remained silent. It was part of his final grade.

Again he closed the book, again he tried to start up a breezy conversation with the girl, and again he realized it wouldn't work.

He decided that the reason he had not been successful was that they were in a compartment full of people, so he invited her to the dining car, where they could be alone. There the conversation was a bit freer, but he was still a long way from igniting a spark.

They went back to the compartment. Again he opened the book, and again he couldn't make head or tail of it.

For a while she sat quietly across from him. Then she stood up and went into the corridor to look out the window.

He was extremely upset. He liked the girl, but everything about her behavior was silent provocation.

He tried one last time to rescue the situation. He went out into the corridor and stood next to her. He told her that the reason he hadn't recognized her was probably that she had changed her hairdo. He pulled back the hair from her forehead and looked at her suddenly different face.

"Oh yes, now I recognize you," he said. Of course he didn't recognize her. That wasn't the point. All he wanted was to press his hand firmly against her forehead, bend her head slightly, and look into her eyes.

How many times in his life had he put his hands on various women's heads and said, "Let me see how you'd look like this." That imperious touch, that imperious glance, had been known to turn the tide on the spot. It seemed to look forward to (and recall from the future) the all-important scene of total possession.

But this time it had no effect. His own glance was much weaker than the glance he felt weighing on him, the dubious glance of the examining committee, which was perfectly aware he was repeating himself and made it clear that all repetition was mere imitation and all imitation was worthless. Jan suddenly saw himself through her eyes. He saw the pitiful pantomime of his touch and glance, a hackneyed St. Vitus dance robbed of all meaning by years of repetition. Having lost its spontaneity, its obvious, direct impact, it suddenly seemed unbearably onerous, like hundred-pound weights attached to his arm. The girl's glance created an eerie field of increased gravity around him.

He could not continue. He let go of her head and looked out the window at the gardens passing by.

The train reached its destination. As they were leaving the station, she said she lived nearby and invited him over.

He refused.

He thought about it for weeks afterward. How could he have said no to a girl he liked?

He was on the other side of the border from her.

8

The male glance has often been described. It is commonly said to rest coldly on a woman, measuring, weighing, evaluating, selecting her—in other words, turning her into an object.

What is less commonly known is that a woman is not completely defenseless against that glance. If it turns her into an object, then she looks back at the man with the eyes of an object. It is as though a hammer had suddenly grown eyes and stared up at the worker pounding a nail with it. When the worker sees the evil eye of the hammer, he loses his self-assurance and slams it on his thumb.

The worker may be the hammer's master, but the hammer still prevails. A tool knows exactly how it is meant to be handled, while the user of the tool can only have an approximate idea.

The ability to see transforms the hammer into a living being, but a good worker must be able to bear up under its insolent glance and, with a firm hand, turn it back into an object. It would therefore seem that a woman undergoes cosmic transformation in two directions: up from object to being, down from being to object.

More and more often Jan had been losing at the worker/hammer game. Women had been giving him bad looks, spoiling it.

Was it because they had begun to organize and reform their perennial fate? Or was Jan just getting old and taking a different view of women and their glances? Was the world changing, or was he changing?

It was hard to say. One thing was certain, though: the girl in the train had looked him up and down with eyes full of distrust and doubt. The hammer had fallen from his hands before he even raised it.

Not long ago he had run into Ervin, who complained to him about Barbara. She had invited him over. He found two girls there he didn't know. They talked for a while, and suddenly, out of the blue, Barbara brought a beat-up old timer in from the kitchen. Without a word she and the girls began taking their clothes off.

"You know what I mean?" he complained. "They took their clothes off so impassively and lethargically you'd have thought I was a dog or a flower pot."

Then Barbara had ordered him to get undressed too. He didn't want to miss a chance to make love to two new girls, so he did as she asked. When he was naked, Barbara pointed to the timer and said, "Take a good look. If you don't have a hard-on within one minute, you're out on your ear."

"The girls stared down at my crotch, and as the seconds flew past, they broke out into an ugly laugh. Then they threw me out!"

It was a case of the hammer deciding to castrate the construction worker.

"That Ervin's an arrogant bastard, and I secretly sympathized with Barbara's penal commando," Jan told Edwige. "And anyway, Ervin and his friends have done similar things to women. Once a girl went to his place ready to make love, and they undressed her and tied her to the couch. The girl didn't mind being tied up, that was part of it all. The scandalous thing was that they didn't do anything to her, didn't touch her, they just ogled her. The girl felt she'd been raped."

"And rightly so," said Edwige.

"But I can see how his girls might get a real thrill out of being stripped, bound, and ogled. Ervin didn't get any thrill out of his experience, he got his balls cut off."

It was late in the evening. They were sitting in Edwige's apartment with a half-empty bottle of whiskey on the coffee table in front of them. "What do you mean by that?" she asked.

"What I mean," answered Jan, "is that when a man and a woman do the same thing, it isn't the same thing. The man rapes, the woman castrates."

"What you mean is that castrating a man is a foul deed, whereas raping a woman is beautiful."

"What I mean," said Jan in self-defense, "is that rape is an integral part of eroticism, whereas castration is its negation."

Edwige tossed down her drink in one gulp. "If rape is an integral part of eroticism," she said angrily, "then eroticism as a whole is anti-woman and we need a new kind of eroticism."

Jan took a sip of whiskey and thought for a while. Then he went on. "Many years ago in the country I used to live in, some friends and I put together an anthology of things our mistresses said while making love. And you know what word came up most often?"

She didn't.

"The word 'no.' The word 'no' repeated over and over: *no, no, no, no, no, no, no* . . . The girl would come to make love, but when the man put his arms around her, she would push him away and say no, lighting up the act of love with the red light of that most beautiful of all words and transforming it into a miniature facsimile rape. Even when they were on the brink of orgasm, they said *no, no, no, no, no,* and a good number of them cried out *no* right in the middle of it. Since that time 'no' has been the queen of words for me. Did you used to say *no* too?"

Edwige answered that she never said no. Why would she ever say something she didn't mean? " 'When a woman says no, she really means yes.' I've always hated it when men say that. It's as stupid as all human history."

"Yes, but that history is a part of us. We can't escape it," Jan objected. "The woman who runs away to defend her honor. The woman who gives herself, the man who takes. The woman who veils herself, the man who tears off her clothes. Time-honored images, every one of them, and all a part of us!"

"Time-honored and idiotic! More idiotic than holy images! What if women are sick of following old patterns? What if they're tired of doing the same things over and over? What if they want to invent new images, a new set of rules?"

"True, they are idiotic images. True, they do tend to perpetuate themselves. But what if our desire for the female body is dependent on them? If we go ahead and root them out of ourselves, will a man still be able to make love to a woman?"

Edwige burst out laughing. "I wouldn't worry about that if I were you!" Then she gave him a motherly look. "And don't think all men are like you. How can you tell what men are like when they're alone with a woman?"

Jan really didn't know what men were like when they were alone with a woman. During the silence that had set in, Edwige's face began to acquire the blissful look that meant it was getting late, coming close to the time when Jan would set the empty reel spinning on her body.

"Besides," she added after some thought, "making love isn't that important."

"You don't think making love is that important?" he asked, just to be sure he had heard properly.

"No," she said, smiling at him tenderly, "making love is not that important."

In an instant, he completely forgot what they had been discussing. He had made a crucial discovery: Edwige saw physical love as a sign, a symbolic act, a confirmation of friendship.

That was the first night he ever dared to say he was tired. He lay down next to her like a chaste friend and let the reel be. And as he gently stroked her hair, he saw a reassuring rainbow of peace arching over their future together.

9

Ten years earlier Jan had received irregular visits from a married woman. They had known each other for years, but hardly ever saw each other because the woman had a job, and even when she took time off to be with him, they had to be quick about it. First they would sit and talk a while, but only a very short while. Soon Jan would get up, walk over to her, give her a kiss, and take her in his arms.

When he released her, they would separate and begin to undress quickly. He threw his jacket on the chair. She took off her sweater and put it over the back of the chair. She bent down and began sliding off her pantyhose. He undid his trousers and let them drop. They were in a hurry. They stood opposite each other, leaning forward, he lifting first one, then the other leg out of his trousers (he would raise them high in the air like a soldier on parade), she bending to gather up the pantyhose at her ankles and pull her feet out of them, raising her legs as high in the air as he did.

Each time it was the same. And then one day something happened. He would never forget it: she looked up at him and smiled. It was a smile that was almost tender, a smile full of sympathy and understanding, a bashful smile that seemed to apologize for itself, but nonetheless a smile clearly brought on by a sudden insight into the absurdity of the situation as a whole. It was all he could do not to return it. For if the absurdity of the situation emerged from the semi-obscurity of habit—the absurdity of two people standing face to face, kicking their legs in the air in a mad rush—it was bound to have an effect on him as well. In fact, he was only a hair's breadth away from bursting out laughing. But he knew that if he did, they would not be able to make love. Laughter was like an enormous trap waiting patiently in the room with them, but hidden behind a thin wall. There was only a fraction of an inch separating intercourse from laughter, and he was terrified of overstepping it; there was only a fraction of an inch separating him from the border, and across the border things no longer had any meaning.

He controlled himself. He held back the smile. He threw off his trousers, went right up to her, and touched her body, hoping to drive away the demon of laughter.

10

Passer's health, he heard, was getting worse. The only thing keeping him going was morphine, and he wasn't himself for more than a few hours a day. Jan took a train to his out-of-the-way sanatorium, reproaching himself all the way for not having been to see him more often. He was horrified to find him looking so much older. The few strands of gray hair left on his head described the same graceful curve his thick brown hair had once described, but his face was only a memory of that former face.

Passer greeted him with his usual exuberance. He grabbed him by the arm and pulled him energetically into his room, where they sat face to face at a table.

Long ago, the first time Jan met him, Passer had spoken about mankind's great hopes, his fist pounding the table, his eyes flashing endless passion. This time he spoke about the hopes of his body rather than the hopes of mankind. The doctors claimed that if he got through the next two weeks of intensive injections and excruciating pain, he'd be all right. As he told Jan about it, his fist pounded the table and his eyes flashed. His passionate discourse on the hopes of the body nostalgically echoed his discourse on the hopes of mankind. Both passions were equally illusory, but Passer's burning eyes shed a magic light over both.

Then he switched to Jeanne the actress. With a chaste masculine kind of reticence he confessed to Jan that for the last time in his life he had completely lost his head. He had fallen madly in love with Jeanne, knowing full well that in his position it was the silliest madness of all. He spoke with glowing eyes about their jaunt through the woods, about the mushrooms they'd pursued like buried treasure, and about the café where they'd stopped for wine.

"She was fantastic! You know what I mean? She didn't play the worried nurse, she didn't give me any of those sympathetic looks that remind you you're an invalid, a relic. No, she laughed and drank with me. We drank a whole liter of wine! I felt eighteen again! There I sat, at death's door, and I felt like singing!" Passer pounded his fist on the table and looked at Jan with his burning eyes, above which the three strands of gray hair plainly evoked a once-powerful mane.

Jan said we were all at death's door; the whole world, with its propensity for violence, cruelty, barbarism, was at death's door. He said it because he loved Passer and it seemed monstrous to him that this man, so splendidly pounding his fist on the table, would die ahead of a world so undeserving of love. He tried to will the end of the world; it might make Passer's death more bearable. But Passer refused to accept the end of the world. He pounded the table and carried on about the hopes of mankind. He said we were living in a time of great changes.

Jan had never shared Passer's enthusiasm for observing how things change, though he did appreciate his desire for change, considering it the oldest desire in man, mankind's most conservative conservatism. But while appreciating it, he wanted very much to rid Passer of it. Now that Passer was on the border of life and death, Jan wanted to discredit the future in his eyes and give Passer as little reason as possible to be depressed about what he would be missing.

"Everybody thinks we're living in important times," he said. "Clevis talks about the end of the Judeo-Christian era, others about the end of Europe, still others about a world revolution and Communism. But that's all nonsense. If our times represent a turning point in history, it's for an entirely different reason."

Passer stared at him with his burning eyes, above which the three strands of gray hair plainly evoked a once-powerful mane.

"Do you know the joke about the English lord?" Jan continued.

Passer pounded his fist down on the table and said no, he didn't.

"An English lord said to his lady the morning after their wedding night, 'I do hope you're pregnant, my dear. I shouldn't want to go through all those ridiculous motions again.' "

Passer smiled, but without pounding his fist on the table. It was not the kind of story he would get excited about.

"Well, you can forget about world revolution! We are living in the great historical era when physical love will be once and for all transformed into ridiculous motions."

A delicate trace of a smile appeared on Passer's face. Jan knew it well. It was a smile of tolerance, not joy or approbation. They had always had very different views, and whenever their differences were about to make themselves felt too openly, one of them would quickly smile that smile at the other just to make it clear their friendship was in no way endangered.

11

Why does the image of the border keep coming back to him?

He tells himself it's because he's getting old. Every time something is repeated, it loses a part of its meaning. Or rather, it gradually loses its vital force, that vital force which automatically, inherently, presupposes meaning. For Jan, therefore, the border is the greatest possible degree of admissible repetition.

Once he was watching a play, when out of the blue, in the middle of the action, an extremely clever comic actor began counting, very slowly and with great concentration: one, two, three, four . . ., enunciating each of the numbers with the utmost deliberation, as if they had gotten away from him and he was gathering them up again: five, six, seven, eight. . . . When he reached fifteen, the audience began to laugh, and by the time he had slowly and with greater and greater concentration made his way up to a hundred, people were falling off their seats.

At another performance the same actor sat down at a piano and began playing the left-hand accompaniment to a waltz: um pah pah, um pah pah. His right hand hung down at his side—there was no melody at all, just a continuous um pah pah, um pah pah—but he looked out at the audience meaningfully, as if the accompaniment itself were an exquisite musical achievement, worthy of great emotion, applause, delirium. And on he played—twenty, thirty, fifty, a hundred times: um pah pah, um pah pah. The audience began choking with laughter.

Yes, cross the border and you hear that fateful laughter. And if you go on farther, *beyond* laughter?

As Jan sees it, the Greek gods were once passionately involved in the affairs of man. Then they confined themselves to looking down from Olympus and laughing. And for ages now they have been asleep.

But I feel Jan is wrong in thinking that the border is a line dissecting man's life at a given point, that it marks a turning point in time, a definite second on the clock of human existence. No. In fact, I am certain the border is constantly with us, irrespective of time or our age; external circumstances may make it either more or less visible, but it is omnipresent.

The woman Jan loved so dearly was right in saying she was kept alive only by the threads of a cobweb. It takes ridiculously little, an insignificant breeze, to make what a man would have put down his life for one minute seem an absurd void the next.

Some of Jan's friends who, like him, had left the country of their birth were devoting all their time to fighting for its lost freedom. They had all experienced the feeling that the bond tying them to their country was mere illusion, that only a kind of dogged sense of destiny made them willing to die for something completely devoid of meaning for them. They all knew the feeling and at the same time were afraid to know it; they turned their heads aside so as not to see the border, so as not to sail across (tempted by both the dizzying height and the intervening chasm) to the other side, where the language of their tortured nation would sound as meaningless as the twittering of birds.

If Jan defines the border for himself as the line of the greatest admissible repetition, I must correct him. The border is not a product of repetition. Repetition is only a means of making the border visible. The line of the border is covered with dust, and repetition is like the whisk of a hand removing the dust.

I would like to remind Jan of an important experience he had in his childhood. He was about thirteen at the time. There was a lot of talk about life on other planets, and he fantasized that creatures from outer space had more erotic parts on their bodies than their earthbound equivalents. The thirteen-year-old child, who aroused himself in secret by staring at a stolen picture of a naked dancer, had begun to feel that the women of his own planet, endowed with the oversimplified triangle of one set of genitals and two breasts, were erotically underendowed. He dreamed of a creature with a body offering ten or twenty erotic regions instead of that miserable triangle, a body offering inexhaustible sources of arousal to the naked eye.

What I am trying to say is that even when he was still very much a virgin, he knew what it meant to be bored with the female body. Even before experiencing climax, he had made a mental voyage to the farthest reaches of arousal. He had exhausted its possibilities.

Since tender childhood, therefore, he had lived in sight of that secret border beyond which a female breast is nothing more than a soft sphere hanging on the chest. That border was his lot from the very beginning. When at thirteen he yearned for new erotic regions of the female body, he was as aware of the border as he was thirty years later.

12

It was windy and muddy. A straggly semicircle of mourners stood around the open grave. They included Jan and nearly all his friends: Jeanne the actress, the Clevises, Barbara, and, of course, the Passers—Passer's wife and his son and daughter, both in tears.

Two men in shabby clothes were lifting the ropes the coffin rested on when a nervous man with a piece of paper in his hand came up to the grave, turned to the gravediggers, looked back at his paper, and began to read. The gravediggers looked over at him, trying to gauge whether to put the coffin down beside the grave again. Then they began lowering it slowly into the pit, apparently having decided to spare the corpse the torture of a fourth speech.

The sudden disappearance of the coffin caught the speaker off guard. He had written his entire speech in the second person singular, and as he exhorted the corpse, reassured it, agreed with it, comforted it, thanked it, and answered the questions he had put in its mouth, the coffin was making its way down into the grave. Finally it settled on the bottom, and the gravediggers pulled out the ropes and stood there trying to look unobtrusive. When they realized the speaker was addressing his tirade right at them, they lowered their eyes in embarrassment.

The more aware the orator became of the incongruity of the situation, the more the two sad figures attracted his attention. Finally he tore his eyes away from them and turned toward the semicircle of mourners. But that did not help his second-person delivery at all. He seemed to be addressing the dearly departed as if he were hiding somewhere among them.

Where should he have looked? In anguish he stared down at the paper, and even though he knew the text by heart, he kept his eyes riveted on it.

Everyone present felt a certain uneasiness. It was heightened by the neurotic bursts of wind constantly attacking them. Papa

Clevis had pulled his hat down firmly over his temples, but the wind was so strong it lifted it off his head and set it down halfway between the open grave and the Passer family.

His first impulse was to make his way up to them slowly and then dart out for the hat, but that, he realized, might make it look as though he thought his hat was more important than the dignity of the rites honoring his friend. Instead, he decided to stay where he was and pretend nothing had happened. It was the wrong decision. From the minute the hat landed in the no-man's-land before the grave, the assembly of mourners found it impossible to follow the orator's words. Now they were even more uneasy. Though modestly immobile, the hat was clearly disturbing the funeral more than Clevis would by taking a few steps and retrieving it. So he finally said "Excuse me" to the man standing next to him and emerged from the group. He now stood in the empty space (about the size of a small stage) between the grave and the mourners. But just as he bent down for the hat, a gust of wind moved it out of his reach and dropped it at the feet of the orator.

By then no one was thinking of anything but Papa Clevis and his hat. The orator was not aware of the hat, but even he had realized there was something disturbing his audience. When he finally lifted his eyes from the paper, he was amazed to see a stranger standing a foot or two away from him and apparently ready to jump the rest of the way. He quickly looked back down at the paper, hoping perhaps that by the time he looked up again the improbable vision would have vanished. But when he did, there was that man still standing there staring at him.

Papa Clevis could move neither forward nor back. Storming the feet of the orator seemed too daring, retreating without the hat seemed ridiculous. So he stood there, motionless, nailed to the spot by indecisiveness, trying vainly to come up with a viable way out.

Desperate for help, he looked over at the gravediggers standing motionless on the other side of the grave and staring straight at the orator's feet. But once again the wind began coaxing the hat in the direction of the grave. Clevis made up his mind. He took a few energetic steps forward, stretched out his arm, and bent over. Unfortunately, the hat slid farther out of his reach. He had finally just caught up with it when it tipped over the side and fell into the pit.

Clevis's first impulse was to stretch his arms out after it. Then he decided to act as though no hat had ever existed and he just happened to be standing there. He tried his best to be completely natural and relaxed, but with all eyes trained on him it was not easy. He contorted his face to avoid everybody's glance, and walked back to the front row next to Passer's sobbing son.

Once the dangerous specter of the man about to leap had disappeared, the man with the paper calmed down, raised his eyes to the crowd, which by now had no idea of what he was talking about, and pronounced the final sentence of his oration. Then he turned to the gravediggers and said with great pomp, "Victor Passer, those who loved you will never forget you. May the earth not weigh heavily upon you."

He bent down over a pile of dirt at the edge of the grave, picked up the small shovel sticking out of it, shoveled up some dirt, and peered down into the grave. At that moment the entire assembly of mourners was racked by a silent wave of laughter. They all knew that the orator, poised with the shovel of dirt over the grave, was staring at the coffin lying at the bottom of the pit and the hat lying on the coffin. (It was as if in a last vain plea for dignity the dead man had wished to keep his head covered in deference to the solemnity of the occasion.)

The orator managed to control himself, and threw the dirt on the coffin in such a manner as to avoid the hat, afraid, perhaps, that Passer's head actually was hiding underneath it. Then he passed the shovel to Passer's widow. Yes, they all had to drink the cup to the dregs. They all had to join the terrible battle with laughter. They all had to follow Passer's wife, daughter, and sobbing son, shovel up some dirt, and lean over into the pit where there was a coffin with a hat lying on it. It was as though the indomitably vital and optimistic Passer had stuck his head out for one last look.

13

Barbara had about twenty guests. They were sitting all over her large living room—on the couch, in the chairs, on the floor. The center of their somewhat less than undivided attention was a girl doing an amateur bump-and-grind routine. She came from a provincial town, Jan was told.

Barbara was holding court in a large plush armchair. "Aren't you taking a bit too long?" she asked, giving the girl a cold look.

The girl looked back and tried to convey with a roll of the shoulders the disgust she felt at the lack of interest and attention on the part of the audience. But Barbara's cold glance brooked no excuses, even mute ones, and the girl, though not abandoning her vague, inexpressive movements, began to unbutton her blouse.

From that moment Barbara paid no more attention to her. She looked from one guest to the next. Each time her glance lit on one or another couple, they would immediately stop talking and obediently turn back to the girl stripping. Then Barbara lifted her skirt, inserted her hand between her thighs, and again scanned all corners of the room belligerently, making sure that others were following suit, in other words, that the team was doing its warm-ups.

Finally things got off to a sluggish but certain start. The girl from the provinces, now long since naked, was lying in the arms of one of the men. The others were scattered around the various rooms. Barbara, however, was everywhere at once—eternally vigilant and infinitely demanding. It bothered her no end to find her guests dividing up into couples and going off to their own little nooks. When Jan put his arm around a girl, Barbara turned to her and said spitefully, "Get him to invite you home if you want him all to yourself. This is a party." And she grabbed her by the arm and shoved her into the room next door.

Jan caught the eye of a pleasant-looking bald young man who was sitting by himself and had seen Barbara's intervention. They smiled. The bald man went up to Jan, and Jan said, "Major Barbara."

The bald man laughed and said, "She's training us for the Olympics." Together they began observing her.

Kneeling down next to a man and woman making love, she inserted her head between their faces and pressed her lips up against the woman's. The man respectfully moved away from his partner, obviously thinking that Barbara wanted her for herself. Barbara put her arms around the woman and clasped her tightly, while the man stood over them, self-effacing and deferential. Still kissing the woman, Barbara lifted one arm and drew a circle in the air. The man understood that it was meant for him, but could not quite make out whether she was ordering him to stay or go. He watched carefully as the motion grew more and more energetic and impatient. Finally Barbara removed her lips from the woman's and told him what she wanted of him. The man nodded, dropped back down to the floor, and nestled up in back of the other woman, who was now squeezed in between Barbara and him.

"We're all characters in Barbara's dreams," said Jan.

"Yes," answered the bald man. "But there's always something wrong. Barbara is like a clockmaker who has to move the hands of his clocks himself."

As soon as she had put the man in position, she lost interest in the woman she had been kissing so passionately a moment before. She stood up and went over to a couple of very young lovers obviously hanging onto each other for dear life off in a corner of the room. They were both still half dressed, and the boy was doing his best to cover the girl with his body. Like extras on an opera stage who open their mouths without singing and thrash their arms around ridiculously to create the illusion of a lively conversation, they were trying to make it as clear as they could that they were completely absorbed in one another. All they wanted was to be left alone.

Barbara was not fooled. She kneeled down next to them, stroking their hair and talking to them. Then she went off to the next room and came back immediately with three completely naked men.

She kneeled back down next to the lovers, took the boy's head in her hands, and kissed it. The three naked men, following the commands of her glance, bent down over the girl and removed the rest of her clothes.

"After it's over, there will be a meeting," said the bald man. "Barbara will call us all together, seat us in a semicircle around her, rise, put her glasses on, and tell each of us what we did right and what we did wrong, praising the diligent and scolding the shiftless."

When the two shy lovers finally began sharing their bodies, Barbara stood up and headed toward Jan and his new friend. She gave Jan a quick smile, then took the bald man by the hand and led him away. At almost the same moment Jan felt the soft touch of the girl from the provinces who had opened the evening with her striptease. Barbara's clock was in good working order, he said to himself.

The girl took charge of him with enterprising ardor, but his eyes continued to wander to the other side of the room, where the bald man's penis was in Barbara's hands. Both couples were in the same situation. The two women were leaning over the same way doing the same things. They looked liked enterprising gardeners working in a flowerbed, twin gardeners, one the mirror image of the other. The men's eyes met, and Jan saw the bald man's body shaking with laughter. They were united as only an object can be united with its mirror image: if one shook, the other shook as well. Jan turned his head so the girl caressing him would not feel hurt. But the mirror image kept calling him back. When he finally looked over again, the eyes of the bald man were bulging out of his head with suppressed laughter. The men were united by multiple telepathic connections. Not only did each know what the other was thinking, they both knew the other knew. Moreover, all the images they had applied to Barbara were still running through their heads, and they were making up new ones. They looked over at each other and at the same time tried not to let their eyes meet. They knew that laughter in this context was as much a sacrilege as laughter in church when the priest raises the host. But as soon as that image went through their heads, they laughed even more. They were too weak. Laughter was stronger. Their bodies began quaking uncontrollably.

Barbara looked down into her partner's face. The bald man finally capitulated and let all his laughter burst out. Sensing that the source of the problem lay elsewhere, she turned and looked at Jan. "What's wrong?" the girl from the provinces was asking him at that moment. "What are you crying for?"

In a flash Barbara was at his side, hissing, "Don't think you can pull another Passer's funeral on me!"

"Sorry," laughed Jan, the tears running down his cheeks. She asked him to leave.

14

Before leaving for America, he took Edwige to an abandoned island with a few miniature villages, some lazy sheep in the meadows, and one lone hotel on a private beach. They each took a single room.

He knocked at her door. "Come on in," her voice called from the far end of the room. At first he didn't see anyone. "I'm in here peeing," she shouted from the bathroom. The door was open.

There was nothing new about that. She could have a whole crowd over and think nothing of announcing she was going to have a pee and carrying on a conversation through the half-open bathroom door. And it wasn't flirtatiousness or indecency on her part; on the contrary, it was the obliteration of both.

Edwige refused to acknowledge a number of burdensome traditions. She would not accept the idea that a naked face is decent, but a naked behind indecent. She could not understand why the salty liquid that flows from our eyes is exalted and poetic, and the liquid we excrete from our bladders repellent. It all seemed silly, artificial, and senseless to her, and she treated it the way a child in revolt treats the rules of a Catholic boarding school.

She came out of the bathroom beaming, and let Jan kiss her on both cheeks. "Shall we go to the beach?" she asked.

He agreed.

"You can leave your clothes here," she said, throwing off her robe. She was naked underneath.

Jan always felt a little strange undressing in front of others, and he envied the way Edwige moved in her nudity. She might just as well have been wearing comfortable house clothes. In fact, she moved much more naturally naked than dressed. By throwing off her clothes, she seemed to throw off the hard lot of womanhood and become a person pure and simple, without sexual characteristics. She made it seem that sex resided in clothes and nakedness was a state of sexual neutrality.

They went naked down the steps to the beach, where other naked people were sitting in groups, taking walks, and swimming— naked mothers and naked children, naked grandmothers and naked grandchildren, the naked young and the naked elderly. There were naked breasts galore, in all shapes and sizes—beautiful, less beautiful, ugly, gigantic, shriveled. Jan came to the melancholy conclusion that not only did old breasts look no younger next to young ones but that the opposite was true, and all of them together were equally bizarre and meaningless.

And once again he was overwhelmed by the vague and mysterious idea of the border. Suddenly he felt he was at the line, crossing it. He was overwhelmed by a strange feeling of affliction, and from the haze of that affliction came an even stranger thought: that the Jews had filed into Hitler's gas chambers naked and en masse. He couldn't quite understand why that image kept coming back to him or what it was trying to tell him. Perhaps that the Jews had also been *on the other side of the border* and that nudity is the uniform of the other side. That nudity is a shroud.

The feeling of affliction Jan felt at the sight of all those naked bodies on the beach became more and more unbearable. "It's so strange to see naked bodies everywhere," he said.

"I know," she said. "And the strangest thing of all is that every one of them is beautiful. Look hard, and you'll see that even old bodies, even sick bodies, are beautiful if they're bodies pure and simple, bodies without clothes. They're as beautiful as nature. An old tree is no less beautiful than a young one; a diseased lion is still king of the beasts. Human ugliness is the ugliness of clothes."

Jan and Edwige never understood each other, yet they always agreed. Each interpreted the other's words in his own way, and they lived in perfect harmony, the perfect solidarity of perfect mutual misunderstanding. He was well aware of it and almost took pleasure in it.

They walked slowly along the beach, the sand burning beneath their feet, the bleating of a ram blending into the roaring of the sea, a dirty lamb browsing on the island's withered grass under the branch of an olive tree. Jan thought of Daphnis. There he lies, spellbound by Chloe's nakedness. Though aroused, he does not know what to do, and the feeling goes on—unlimited, unabated, endless, boundless. He felt an overpowering desire to go back to that boy, back to his own beginnings, to the beginnings of mankind, to the beginnings of love. He yearned for yearning. He yearned to hear his heart pound. He yearned to lie beside Chloe, completely innocent of physical love, completely innocent of climax. He yearned to transform himself into pure arousal, the long, mysterious, inscrutable, wonder-working arousal of a man over the body of a woman. "Daphnis!" he said out loud.

The lamb was still browsing on the withered grass, and Jan sighed "Daphnis" again. "Daphnis, Daphnis . . ."

"Is that Daphnis you're saying?"

"Yes," he said. "Daphnis."

"Glad to hear it," said Edwige. "It's time we got back to him. Back to the times before Christianity crippled mankind. That's what you meant, wasn't it?"

"Yes," said Jan, even though he had meant something completely different.

"Think of the natural paradise he must have lived in," she went on. "Sheep and shepherds. People at one with nature. Freedom of the senses. That's what Daphnis means to you, isn't it?"

Again he assured her that was just what he had in mind.

"You're right," said Edwige. "And this is Daphnis Island!"

And because he enjoyed developing their agreements based on mutual misunderstanding, he added, "And the hotel we're staying at is *On the Other Side.*"

"Yes," cried Edwige, all excited. "On the other side of the inhuman world our civilization imprisons us in!"

A group of naked people was coming toward them. When Edwige introduced Jan to them, they shook hands, said their nice-to-meet-yous, and reeled off their names and titles. Then they spoke of many things: the temperature of the water, the hypocrisy of a society that cripples body and soul, the beauties of the island.

"Jan has just pointed out we should call it Daphnis Island," said Edwige, apropos of the last topic. "I think he has something there."

Everyone was delighted with the idea, and a man with an extraordinary paunch began developing the theory that Western civilization was on its way out and we would soon be freed once and for all from the bonds of Judeo-Christian thought—statements Jan had heard ten, twenty, thirty, a hundred, five hundred, a thousand times before—and for the time being those few feet of beach felt like a university auditorium. On and on the man talked. The others listened with interest, their naked genitals staring dully, sadly, listlessly at the yellow sand.

AFTERWORD:
A Talk with the Author
by Philip Roth

*This interview is condensed from two conversations I had
with Milan Kundera after reading a translated manuscript of his*
Book of Laughter and Forgetting—*one conversation while he was
visiting London for the first time, the other when he was on his first
visit to the United States. He took these trips from France; since
1975 he and his wife have been living there as émigrés, in Rennes,
where he taught at the University, and now in Paris. During our
conversations, Kundera spoke sporadically in French, but mostly in
Czech, and his wife, Vera, served as his translator and mine. A final
Czech text was translated into English by Peter Kussi.*

PR: Do you think the destruction of the world is coming
soon?

MK: That depends on what you mean by the word "soon."

PR: Tomorrow or the day after.

MK: The feeling that the world is rushing to ruin is an
ancient one.

PR: So then we have nothing to worry about.

MK: On the contrary. If a fear has been present in the
human mind for ages, there must be something to it.

PR: In any event, it seems to me that this concern is the
background against which all the stories in your latest book take
place, even those that are of a decidedly humorous nature.

MK: If someone had told me as a boy: One day you will
see your nation vanish from the world, I would have considered
it nonsense, something I couldn't possibly imagine. A man knows
he is mortal, but he takes it for granted that his nation possesses
a kind of eternal life. But after the Russian invasion of 1968, every
Czech was confronted with the thought that his nation could be
quietly erased from Europe, just as over the past five decades forty
million Ukrainians have been quietly vanishing from the world

without the world paying any heed. Or Lithuanians. Do you know that in the seventeenth century Lithuania was a powerful European nation? Today the Russians keep Lithuanians on their reservation like a half-extinct tribe; they are sealed off from visitors to prevent knowledge about their existence from reaching the outside. I don't know what the future holds for my own nation. It is certain that the Russians will do everything they can to dissolve it gradually into their own civilization. Nobody knows whether they will succeed. But the *possibility* is here. And the sudden realization that such a possibility exists is enough to change one's whole sense of life. Nowadays I even see Europe as fragile, mortal.

PR: And yet, are not the fates of Eastern Europe and Western Europe radically different matters?

MK: As a concept of cultural history, Eastern Europe is Russia, with its quite specific history anchored in the Byzantine world. Bohemia, Poland, Hungary, just like Austria, have never been part of Eastern Europe. From the very beginning they have taken part in the great adventure of Western civilization, with its Gothic, its Renaissance, its Reformation—a movement which has its cradle precisely in this region. It was here, in Central Europe, that modern culture found its greatest impulses: psychoanalysis, structuralism, dodecaphony, Bartók's music, Kafka's and Musil's new esthetics of the novel. The postwar annexation of Central Europe (or at least its major part) by Russian civilization caused Western culture to lose its vital center of gravity. It is the most significant event in the history of the West in our century, and we cannot dismiss the possibility that the end of Central Europe marked the beginning of the end for Europe as a whole.

PR: During the Prague Spring, your novel *The Joke* and your stories *Laughable Loves* were published in editions of 150,-000. After the Russian invasion you were dismissed from your teaching post at the film academy and all your books were removed from the shelves of public libraries. Seven years later you and your wife tossed a few books and some clothes in the back of your car and drove off to France, where you've become one of the most widely read of foreign authors. How do you feel as an émigré?

MK: For a writer, the experience of living in a number of countries is an enormous boon. You can only understand the world if you see it from several sides. My latest book, which came into being in France, unfolds in a special geographic space: Those events which take place in Prague are seen through West European eyes, while what happens in France is seen through the eyes of Prague. It is an encounter of two worlds. On one side, my native country: In the course of a mere half-century, it experienced democracy, fascism, revolution, Stalinist terror, as well as the disintegration of Stalinism, German and Russian occupation, mass deportations, the death of the West in its own land. It is thus sinking under the weight of history, and looks at the world with immense skepticism. On the other side, France: For centuries it was the center of the world and nowadays it is suffering from the lack of great historic events. This is why it revels in radical ideologic postures. It is the lyrical, neurotic expectation of some great deed of its own which however is not coming, and will never come.

PR: Are you living in France as a stranger or do you feel culturally at home?

MK: I am enormously fond of French culture and I am greatly indebted to it. Especially to the older literature. Rabelais is dearest to me of all writers. And Diderot. I love his *Jacques le fataliste* as much as I do Laurence Sterne. Those were the greatest experimenters of all time in the form of the novel. And their experiments were, so to say, amusing, full of happiness and joy, which have by now vanished from French literature and without which everything in art loses its significance. Sterne and Diderot understood the novel as a *great game.* They discovered the *humor* of the novelistic form. When I hear learned arguments that the novel has exhausted its possibilities, I have precisely the opposite feeling: In the course of its history the novel *missed* many of its possibilities. For example, impulses for the development of the novel hidden in Sterne and Diderot have not been picked up by any successors.

PR: Your latest book is not called a novel, and yet in the text you declare: This book is a novel in the form of variations. So then—is it a novel or not?

MK: As far as my own quite personal esthetic judgment goes, it really is a novel, but I have no wish to force this opinion on anyone. There is enormous freedom latent within the novelistic form. It is a mistake to regard a certain stereotyped structure as the inviolable essence of the novel.

PR: Yet surely there is something which makes a novel a novel, and which limits this freedom.

MK: A novel is a long piece of synthetic prose based on play with invented characters. These are the only limits. By the term synthetic I have in mind the novelist's desire to grasp his subject from all sides and in the fullest possible completeness. Ironic essay, novelistic narrative, autobiographical fragment, historic fact, flight of fantasy: The synthetic power of the novel is capable of combining everything into a unified whole like the voices of polyphonic music. The unity of a book need not stem from the plot, but can be provided by the theme. In my latest book, there are two such themes: laughter and forgetting.

PR: Laughter has always been close to you. Your books provoke laughter through humor or irony. When your characters come to grief it is because they bump against a world that has lost its sense of humor.

MK: I learned the value of humor during the time of Stalinist terror. I was twenty then. I could always recognize a person who was not a Stalinist, a person whom I needn't fear, by the way he smiled. A sense of humor was a trustworthy sign of recognition. Ever since, I have been terrified by a world that is losing its sense of humor.

PR: In your last book, though, something else is involved. In a little parable you compare the laughter of angels with the laughter of the devil. The devil laughs because God's world seems senseless to him; the angel laughs with joy because everything in God's world has its meaning.

MK: Yes, man uses the same physiologic manifestation—laughter—to express two different metaphysical attitudes. Someone's hat drops on the coffin in a freshly dug grave, the funeral loses its meaning and laughter is born. Two lovers race through the meadow, holding hands, laughing. Their laughter has nothing to do with jokes or humor, it is the *serious* laughter of angels expressing their joy of being. Both kinds of laughter belong among life's pleasures, but when it is carried to extremes it also denotes a dual apocalypse: the enthusiastic laughter of angel-fanatics, who are so convinced of their world's significance that they are ready to hang anyone not sharing their joy. And the other laughter, sounding from the opposite side, which proclaims that everything has become meaningless, that even funerals are ridiculous and group sex a mere comical pantomime. Human life is bounded by two chasms: fanaticism on one side, absolute skepticism on the other.

PR: What you now call the laughter of angels is a new term for the "lyrical attitude to life" of your previous novels. In one of your books you characterize the era of Stalinist terror as the reign of the hangman and the poet.

MK: Totalitarianism is not only hell, but also the dream of paradise—the age-old dream of a world where everybody would live in harmony, united by a single common will and faith, without secrets from one another. André Breton, too, dreamed of this paradise when he talked about the glass house in which he longed to live. If totalitarianism did not exploit these archetypes, which are deep inside us all and rooted deep in all religions, it could never attract so many people, especially during the early phases of its existence. Once the dream of paradise starts to turn into reality, however, here and there people begin to crop up who stand in its way, and so the rulers of paradise must build a little gulag on the side of Eden. In the course of time this gulag grows ever bigger and more perfect, while the adjoining paradise gets ever smaller and poorer.

PR: In your book, the great French poet Eluard soars over paradise and gulag, singing. Is this bit of history which you mention in the book authentic?

MK: After the war, Paul Eluard abandoned surrealism and became the greatest exponent of what I might call the "poesy of totalitarianism." He sang for brotherhood, peace, justice, better tomorrows; he sang for comradeship and against isolation, for joy and against gloom, for innocence and against cynicism. When in 1950 the rulers of paradise sentenced Eluard's Prague friend, the surrealist Závis Kalandra, to death by hanging, Eluard suppressed his personal feelings of friendship for the sake of supra-personal ideals, and publicly declared his approval of his comrade's execution. The hangman killed while the poet sang.

And not just the poet. The whole period of Stalinist terror was a period of collective lyrical delirium. This has by now been completely forgotten but it is the crux of the matter. People like to say: Revolution is beautiful, it is only the terror arising from it which is evil. But this is not true. The evil is already present in the beautiful, hell is already contained in the dream of paradise and if we wish to understand the essence of hell we must examine the essence of the paradise from which it originated. It is extremely easy to condemn gulags, but to reject the totalitarian poesy which leads to the gulag by way of paradise is as difficult as ever. Nowadays, people all over the world unequivocally reject the idea of gulags, yet they are still willing to let themselves be hypnotized by totalitarian poesy and to march to new gulags to the tune of the same lyrical song piped by Eluard when he soared over Prague like the great archangel of the lyre, while the smoke of Kalandra's body rose to the sky from the crematory chimney.

PR: What is so characteristic of your prose is the constant confrontation of the private and the public. But not in the sense that private stories take place against a political backdrop, nor that political events encroach on private lives. Rather, you continually show that political events are governed by the same laws as private happenings, so that your prose is a kind of psychoanalysis of politics.

MK: The metaphysics of man is the same in the private sphere as in the public one. Take the other theme of the book, forgetting. This is the great private problem of man: death as the loss of the self. But what is this self? It is the sum of everything we remember. Thus, what terrifies us about death is not the loss of the future but the loss of the past. Forgetting is a form of death ever present within life. This is the problem of my heroine, in desperately trying to preserve the vanishing memories of her beloved dead husband. But forgetting is also the great problem of politics. When a big power wants to deprive a small country of its national consciousness it uses the method of *organized forgetting*. This is what is currently happening in Bohemia. Contemporary Czech literature, insofar as it has any value at all, has not been printed for twelve years; 200 Czech writers have been proscribed, including the dead Franz Kafka; 145 Czech historians have been dismissed from their posts, history has been rewritten, monuments demolished. A nation which loses awareness of its past gradually loses its self. And so the political situation has brutally illuminated the ordinary metaphysical problem of forgetting that we face all the time, every day, without paying any attention. Politics unmasks the metaphysics of private life, private life unmasks the metaphysics of politics.

PR: In the sixth part of your book of variations the main heroine, Tamina, reaches an island where there are only children. In the end they hound her to death. Is this a dream, a fairy tale, an allegory?

MK: Nothing is more foreign to me than allegory, a story invented by the author in order to illustrate some thesis. Events, whether realistic or imaginary, must be significant in themselves, and the reader is meant to be naïvely seduced by their power and poetry. I have always been haunted by this image, and during one period of my life it kept recurring in my dreams: A person finds himself in a world of children, from which he cannot escape. And suddenly childhood, which we all lyricize and adore, reveals itself as pure horror. As a trap. This story is not allegory. But my book is a polyphony in which various stories mutually explain, illumine, complement each other. The basic event of the book is the story of totalitarianism, which deprives people of memory and thus retools them into a nation of children. All totalitarianisms do this. And perhaps our entire technical age does this, with its cult of the future, its cult of youth and childhood, its indifference to the past and mistrust of thought. In the midst of a relentlessly juvenile society, an adult equipped with memory and irony feels like Tamina on the isle of children.

PR: Almost all your novels, in fact all the individual parts of your latest book, find their denouement in great scenes of coitus. Even that part which goes by the innocent name of "Mother" is but one long scene of three-way sex, with a prologue and epilogue. What does sex mean to you as a novelist?

MK: These days, when sexuality is no longer taboo, mere description, mere sexual confession, has become noticeably boring. How dated Lawrence seems, or even Henry Miller with his lyricism of obscenity! And yet certain erotic passages of George Bataille have made a lasting impression on me. Perhaps it is because they are not lyrical but philosophic. You are right that with me everything ends in great erotic scenes. I have the feeling that a scene of physical love generates an extremely sharp light which suddenly reveals the essence of characters and sums up their life situation. Hugo makes love to Tamina while she is desperately trying to think about lost vacations with her dead husband. The erotic scene is the focus where all the themes of the story converge and where its deepest secrets are located.

PR: The last part, the seventh, actually deals with nothing but sexuality. Why does this part close the book rather than another, such as the much more dramatic sixth part in which the heroine dies?

MK: Tamina dies, metaphorically speaking, amid the laughter of angels. Through the last section of the book, on the other hand, resounds the contrary kind of laugh, the kind heard when things lose their meaning. There is a certain imaginary dividing line beyond which things appear senseless and ridiculous. A person asks himself: Isn't it nonsensical for me to get up in the morning? to go to work? to strive for anything? to belong to a nation just because I was born that way? Man lives in close proximity to this boundary, and can easily find himself on the other side. That boundary exists everywhere, in all areas of human life and even in the deepest, most biological of all: sexuality. And precisely because it is the deepest region of life the question posed to sexuality is the deepest question. This is why my book of variations can end with no variation but this.

PR: Is this, then, the furthest point you have reached in your pessimism?

MK: I am wary of the words pessimism and optimism. A novel does not assert anything; a novel searches and poses questions. I don't know whether my nation will perish and I don't know which of my characters is right. I invent stories, confront one with another, and by this means I ask questions. The stupidity of people comes from having an answer for everything. The wisdom of the novel comes from having a question for everything. When Don Quixote went out into the world, that world turned into a mystery before his eyes. That is the legacy of the first European novel to the entire subsequent history of the novel. The novelist teaches the reader to comprehend the world as a question. There is wisdom and tolerance in that attitude. In a world built on sacrosanct certainties the novel is dead. The totalitarian world, whether founded on Marx, Islam, or anything else, is a world of answers rather than questions. There, the novel has no place. In any case, it seems to me that all over the world people nowadays prefer to judge rather than to understand, to answer rather than ask, so that the voice of the novel can hardly be heard over the noisy foolishness of human certainties.

A NOTE ABOUT THE TRANSLATOR

Michael Henry Heim teaches Czech and Russian literature at the University of California, Los Angeles. He has translated a volume of stories *(The Death of Mr. Baltisberger)* by Bohumil Hrabal, another major contemporary Czech writer, and, in cooperation with Simon Karlinsky, has published a collection of Anton Chekhov's letters *(Anton Chekhov's Life and Thought)*. Mr. Heim's recent translations of Chekhov's plays have been produced throughout the United States and Canada.